PROZAC HIGHWAY

To Lahl
keep on

Persimmon
Blackbridge

# PROZAC
# Highway

a novel by

# PERSIMMON
# BLACKBRIDGE

PRESS GANG PUBLISHERS

VANCOUVER

The Publisher acknowledges financial assistance from the Book Publishing Industry
Development Program of the Department of Canadian Heritage, the Cultural Services
Branch, Province of British Columbia, and the Canada Council for the Arts.

CANADIAN CATALOGUING IN PUBLICATION DATA

Blackbridge, Persimmon, 1951–
    Prozac highway
    ISBN 0-88974-078-X
    1. Title.
PS8553.L3187P76 1997        C813'.54 C97-910698-2
PR9199.3.B46P76 1997

Edited by Jennifer Glossop
Copy edited by Nancy Pollak
Design by Val Speidel
Cover photograph by Susan Stewart, © 1997
Typeset in Sabon and OcrB
Printed by Best Book Manufacturers
Printed on acid-free paper
Printed and bound in Canada


Press Gang Publishers
225 East 17th Avenue, Suite 101
Vancouver, B.C.  V5V 1A6   Canada
Tel: 604 876-7787   Fax: 604 876-7892

*To my family on Madness.*

----------

## < ACKNOWLEDGEMENTS >

*In the Meatworld:*

I'd like to thank Lizard Jones (AKA my writers' group) for starting me on this thing and holding my hand all the way to the end. Also Megan Greenberg for improvising Cynthia, Lycrecia Behn and Lenny Gagnon for Prozac stories, Bonnie Ausman for outpatient commitment info, Joan Robillard for medical procedures, Mary Bryson for net advice, Jean and Jack for support and encouragement, and Irit Shimrat for lending me her handle and listening to me moan. Also, always, Lorna Boschman for calming me down, making me laugh, and doing the dishes when it wasn't even her turn.

Big thanks to Jennifer Glossop, Barbara Kuhne and Nancy Pollak (the world's most amazing editorial team), and to Della McCreary, publisher plus. And to Val Speidel for her fresh and always brilliant book design, to Susan Stewart for rearranging her life to take the cover photo and Margaret Dragu for being the model.

I got encouragement and crits at various stages of the manuscript from Lorna Boschman, Penny Goldsmith, Barbara Pulling, Sheila Gilhooly, barbara findlay, Sarah Davidson, Silva Tenenbein, Larissa Lai, Irit Shimrat and Della McCreary.

*In the Networld:*

Thanks to Dennis Budd for 700 pages of Kassebaum Amendment downloads, the folks at Support Coalition and Quinn Rossander for outpatient commitment help, Lynn Worden for lithium stories, Patrick Burton for grammar and usage, CybrWay'n for bipolar tact, Graeme Bacque for support and hanging in, Pat Risser, Jerry Edmon Fordyce, Art Lee and Vicki Fox Wieselthier for general inspiration, and Sylvia Caras, David Oaks, Joe Rogers, Ria Strong, Rodney Salvage and Kevin Childs for permission to para-phrase.

Thanks also to Jeff Vogel and Spiderweb Software, Inc. (www.spidweb.com) for the names of various monsters and spells, plus hours of excellent procrastination.

And finally, back in the Meatworld, more thanks to Della McCreary, the person without whom this book would not.

# PROZAC HIGHWAY

WHEN YOUR CAR is spinning out of control heading for the guardrail, you have all the time in the world. The empty night beyond the railing floats slowly toward you and there's nothing to do but wait and see if you end up alive or dead.

It was different for Roz. She was driving. I could feel her beside me, focused tight on the road, playing into the skid, looking for her chance to grab control. She would save us or not. If she saved us, we'd have to deal with injuries, wrecked car, how to get to Seattle. We'd still have to show up at the bookstore and chat with the owners before the gig. Maybe they hadn't known how to pull in an audience for a couple of queers, and we'd be performing to an empty room. Or to an audience of curious hets who wouldn't understand the sex or know when it was okay to laugh. Or to a room full of anti-porn dykes ready to hate us.

On the other hand, if we went through the rail and into the river it would be cold. Our bodies panicking for air. Survival is an instinct, programmed into our cells, I told myself as the railing drifted nearer. I didn't really feel like performing anyway.

"Come on, it's just Seattle," Roz had said, a month earlier, leaning over the back of my chair while I reformatted her résumé. "A three-hour drive down the coast. Let's do it."

"Why do *I* always have to fix your résumé?" I had asked. I changed the typeface: New York. Ugly. I changed it back to Palatino. Still ugly.

"My résumé's fine. Let's go to Seattle."

The railing was much larger now, filling my vision. Grey metal screwed to the occasional post, bright in the headlights, wet from the rain. "Light rain after a long dry spell produces hazardous driving conditions." Driver's ed, 1968. Apparently it was true.

"We don't have any new material," I had said.

"So we'll do old stuff. It'll be fun."

"We're supposed to be writing new stuff. We're supposed to have a whole new show for the Performance Festival."

"Yeah, but you're not writing, you're sitting on your butt."

"I'm doing research."

"Research. That's a good one."

Roz was pulling hard into the spin. If we hit sideways instead of head on, the rail had a better chance of holding. It was hard to tell how strong it would be. I had never really examined a guardrail closely before.

"The doctor says you're supposed to be avoiding stress," I had said.

Roz gave my chair a shove. "Oh gee, Mom, I forgot."

Almost there. Roz was swearing softly under her breath. I couldn't really get worked up. Live, die. Live, die. On the whole, living seemed more complicated.

I had changed the typeface again, to Times. I wasn't her mother, but I was old, old. Forty-two.

"Fine, I'll go by myself then," Roz said.

The black sky beyond the guardrail rose and filled the windshield. Another half inch. Another. Another. Okay, here we go.

Maybe I blacked out. The next thing I knew Roz was leaning forward to turn off the engine. Then it was very quiet.

"Nice driving," I said.

Roz looked at me, her mouth working as though she was trying not to puke. Then she threw her head back and howled, pounding the steering wheel.

"Nice driving! Fucking-A right it was!" She kicked open the car door and yelled at the sky, "Fuck you! I whipped your ass tonight."

Shock, I thought. She fumbled at her seat belt with shaking fingers, pulled herself out of the car. I followed. Across the highway, the guy who had sideswiped us was standing by his car looking scared. I waved at him. He waved back uncertainly and started walking toward us. We were down the road a ways, spun right around facing back toward Vancouver. Fine by me.

"My neck hurts," Roz said. "Jesus. Are you all right?"

"I think so," I said. "I was quite relaxed when we hit. That's supposed to be good."

"Relaxed. Yeah, that's good." Her whole body was shaking. "Fuck it's cold."

Thanks to a little reckless driving on Roz's part—dodging through Seattle's maze of freeways at seventy mph, with one headlight and a leaking rad—we were only forty-five minutes late. One of the most delightful things about being depressed is that near-death experiences have little impact. Life, however, was another story. Life was standing in a room full of strangers, trying not to bolt. Life was the bookstore boys trying to engage me in a little friendly chitchat while I ran around setting up projectors.

"How's your car?" one asked.

"It's ... fine," I said, looking around at the crowd that may have been cheerily expectant forty-five minutes earlier, but was now definitely on the grumpy side.

"Are you nervous?" asked the other. Why did people always ask this right before a performance?

"No," I said.

"Break a leg," said the first one, as Roz grabbed me on her way to the stage. Maybe I would. Maybe I would fall on the steps and they'd have to take me to the hospital. But I hated hospitals. Maybe even more than performing. Or maybe not.

Then someone handed me a mike and I was on. Autopilot was supposed to take over and get me through the next twenty minutes. We had done this piece half a million times on tour last fall. I had practised every gesture, every nuance of expression. Roz says "I think she's shy," and I say, "I don't know how to talk to her," and

Roz says, "She never talks to me." The video projected behind us is kind of a day-in-the-life-of-a-nerd, with me playing the nerd and Roz playing the cool co-worker who has an inexplicable crush on her: no sound track, no plot, just real-time office life at its most boring. Occasionally a slide flashes on the screen, a black-and-white rectangle floating still and ghostlike over the bright video colours. Nice effect. The slides are old, recycled from a photo installation we did three years ago. Me naked. Roz naked. Me naked with plastic flowers. Roz naked with a sledge hammer. Then, as nerd and cool circle each other on stage telling the audience about their mutual crush (nerd's shy hopes, cool's graphic fantasies), the slides come faster: Roz's tongue on my lips, my hands on her breasts, her face between my legs. Old slides, before-the-operation slides. Our live dialogue needs to keep coming at just the right pace so we're in synch with the slides. There's no turning around and peeking.

"I follow her into the Xerox room just to watch her touch the machine."

"She probably doesn't even notice me."

But I hadn't performed since the tour nine months ago. Before everything. Our only rehearsal after Roz hounded me into this gig had gone fine, but what was I doing here in this room of staring strangers? Let me go home. Shut up you can do it you have to. The audience was supposed to be staring, that was their job. Roz's job was to pour out her energy, my job was to be her straight man. Woman. Not to look at the people sitting in the chairs—the man glancing away, the woman with her lips pursed. I didn't belong here anymore.

I should go home.

Roz elbowed me in the ribs as she swished past, telling the

audience what she thought I was wearing under my secretary clothes. Had I missed my line? Damn, where were we?

"I don't know what to say to her," I said. No, that was my first line. Damn. I turned and walked upstage as Roz spoke, not my usual move but it gave me a chance to check the slide: Roz on her knees, me behind her with my hands in her hair. Right. But the next line didn't come and my unchoreographed move had wrapped my mike cord around Roz's, and she almost tripped.

"I don't know what to say to her," I said. The audience laughed.

"I want her naked in the strobe of the Xerox," Roz said walking toward me, angry panic in her eyes.

"I don't know what to say to her," I said, backing away. My mike cord caught on Roz's boot and she pivoted into it on her next line, letting it twist around her ankle. The audience laughed. I tangled myself in Roz's cord as I crossed the stage repeating my one pitiful sentence, and Roz came after me turning her anger into sexual heat, pursuing me into an ever deeper tangle. God, she was good. We played it out until the last slide clicked by and we were wound tightly body to body. The audience clapped.

"That was a novel interpretation," said Roz through clenched teeth.

"I just lost it," I said. "Sorry. It was the accident." But it wasn't.

- - - - - - - - - -

Roz thinks I'm a computer whiz because I format her résumé and get a hundred pieces of email every day. But no one else would ever mistake me for anything but a cyber-cadet. I just sit there watching while mysterious words flash on the screen, informing me of my progress:

```
Config PPP: open
Establishment
Authentication
Network
```

Then I'm connected. The world at my fingertips and I don't even have to leave my apartment. If only my corner store was online. Please send over a case of Nalley's Chili, a six-pack of Coke and a week's worth of toilet paper. But I can still do the corner store in the Real World. I'm okay.

```
Check mail
Transferring messages
1 of 47: Junior
2 of 47: Coalition/Terry
3 of 47: Coalition/Gina
```

It's easy to get forty-seven messages overnight when you're on an active Listserv, and ThisIsCrazy is very active. Someone from alt.support.depression told me about it. "I think you'll fit in better there," she said. I've never understood exactly what she meant. It's true that, to the best of my knowledge, I was the only middle-aged lesbian sex artist posting to alt.support.depression, but I seem to be the only one on ThisIsCrazy too. But she was right. Crazy is better.

The moment I go offline, the phone rings.
　　"I've been trying to reach you all morning." Roz.
　　"I was ... out."
　　"Did you see your doctor yet?"

"Damn! I forgot."

"How did I guess? Listen. Call your doctor. We can't do an insurance claim until you get that whiplash checked out."

"It's not that bad. I'm already feeling better."

"That's not what you said last week when you skipped three cleaning jobs because your neck hurt. That's missed work, pain and suffering, massage bills ... have you seen that massage therapist yet?"

"I need a referral."

"So call your doctor already. Get a referral. And get those forms. You *like* filling out forms."

This is the problem: Roz thinks seeing my doctor will mean raking in the dough. I think seeing my doctor will mean explaining the fresh cut on my arm that has nothing to do with any car accident. Course I could wear long sleeves and hope she doesn't decide I should take off my shirt when she pokes my spine for sore spots. If I were smart I'd never cut myself except in the dead of winter when long-sleeved shirts are *de rigueur*. But when you're in a cutting mood, you don't think about practical details.

"Call her as soon as we hang up."

"Okay."

"Promise?"

"I'm looking up her number now."

I have a phone list on my computer. It doesn't dial for me though. And I have forty-seven downloaded messages waiting.

Email is like time travel. Or sleep walking. In my emailbox, it's still last night: midnight my time, 3:00 A.M. in Toronto where Junior has the insomniac blues. Again.

from: Junior
to: ThisIsCrazy
subject: argghhhhh
I am so sick of this room these four walls stupid little
window looking out onto the building next door this
city. Is anyone awake out there?

from: Coalition/Terry
to: ThisIsCrazy
re: argghhhhh
Hey Junior, of course I'm awake. Do you think if we
stood at our opposite ends of the earth and screamed
anyone would hear? Probably not. How's your court case
going? Me, I'm ready to shuck this hellhole and run.
The new executive director at the Coalition is on my
case like a wannabe ward attendant. "The Coalition has
to project a more responsible image," he says. Meaning
I look like a mental patient. Well guess what? I *am* a
mental patient. Give me one good reason not to punch
this guy's face in.

from: Coalition/Gina
to: ThisIsCrazy
re: argghhhhh
I want to second everything Terry said. IMHO the board
has fucked up big time hiring this guy. He's not even a
c/s/x!

The Coalition is a mental patients' drop-in centre in Sydney, Australia. Terry and Gina work there doing advocacy for people in the bin, support for people trying to stay out of the bin, and International Liaison, which means hanging out on ThisIsCrazy.

D'isMay is their almost next-door neighbour, posting from the University of Tokyo.

> from: D'isMay
> to: ThisIsCrazy
> subject: done!!
> Well, gang, I handed in that goddamn psych paper today
> *on time* and I think it's all right. No, that's a lie,
> I think it's brilliant (manic modesty). Thanks for all
> your support and listening to me freak. And thanks to
> Parnell for the cites on the Illinois abuse case. Where
> do you find these things? And speaking of finding, does
> anyone have the full text of the Kassebaum Amendment?

Then Junior is back with an offer to do the executive-punching himself plus an update on his court case. He was arrested last fall at a demo against welfare cuts and charged with "intimidating the legislature" for yelling too loud. We get regular reports on the slow grinding of the wheels of just-us, as postponement follows postponement and Junior's nerves get progressively more frayed. Nights are the worst. Better write something—a personal post to Junior, not to the whole list.

> from: Jam
> to: Junior
> re: argghhhhh

Hey kid, what's happening? Here I am, answering your
call of distress a mere ten hours late. Why are we never
online at the same time? I think you should move to a
different time zone. Considering your disgusting
provincial government, that's probably not a bad idea.

What next? Charlie (1:00 A.M. California) writes an angry reply to
Parnell's angry reply to George's defense of psych drugs. Then there's
a few quiet hours until the east coast Americans wake up.

from: Fruitbat
to: ThisIsCrazy
Intro
Hello ThisIsCrazy. I'm new here, been lurking a few days
just to get the feel of it. Never done an email list
before. Supposedly this will go to some computer in
Minneapolis and then end up in hundreds of emailboxes
around the world. I hope it works. I'm broadcasting to
you from the fabulous downtown Baltimore Public Library,
which has 4 computers, a Freenet hook-up, an hour time
limit, and a whole line-up of homeless folks who hang
out on the net. Me, I'm a cut above (not), living in a
psychiatric boarding home with my bag of pills.
    Has anyone here ever come off of Thorazine? How slow
do you have to do it? What are the withdrawals like?
Anything to watch out for (like you know, your heart
stopping if you go off too fast)? Thanks.

Thorazine. Nope, never done that one. Sorry.

from: Lucy
to: ThisIsCrazy
re: still down — six months and counting
Dear Jam — you really should see a doctor. There are all
kinds of nutritional imbalances and allergies that can
contribute to feeling depressed. Why do nothing when a
simple supplement might help?

Lucy is a sixty-eight-year-old het who lives by herself on a disability
pension in rural Virginia. Who takes a million different herbs and
has endless lists of what she must and mustn't eat. Who goes to town
for church on Sundays and shopping on Wednesdays and other than
that stays in her cabin and cruises the net. Parnell is something different, living on the dirty side of Newark, keeping himself out of the
psych ward by working as a patients' rights advocate.

from: Parnell
to: ThisIsCrazy
re: argghhhhh
Ok, Terry — I'll give you three good reasons not to slug
the son of a bitch. One: He might call the cops and
you'd end up in jail. Two, he might call the Emergency
Response Team and you'd end up in the nuthouse. Three:
you might hurt your hand. Keep your eyes on the prize,
my friend. You started that place, it's not going to
slip away that easily.

from: Fruitbat
to: ThisIsCrazy

huh?

Can someone please tell me what c/s/x means? And what's
the IMHO that Gina was talking about? The International
Mental Health Organization? Or???

That one I do know.

from: Jam
to: ThisIsCrazy
re: huh?
Hey Fruitbat, welcome to the Crazy family. We should
send out a glossary — every newbie always asks the same
questions. I speak of course as a venerable veteran of
five months <grin>. Your lesson for today: IMHO is not
an organization, it's net-speak for In My Humble
Opinion. Could also be IMNSHO (Not-So-Humble), etc.
C/S/X is a mad movement abbreviation for Consumer (someone who's on the receiving end of psychiatric services)/
Survivor (an uppity consumer: someone who's been there
and thinks it sucks)/ eX-inmate (someone who really
really really thinks it sucks). Very awkward, I know, but
it's fairly inclusive, which is the point. Used to be if
you were a C and I was an X, we wouldn't speak to each
other except to yell, but there's been a lot of blood
under the bridge since those days.

Open. Send. Close. The phone rings. My doctor's office. "We'd like
to confirm your appointment for next Thursday at ten."
    "Did I make an appointment?"

"Your friend phoned it in. She said we should confirm with you."

Telling the receptionist that Roz is a fucking bitchface nosy-ass busybody seems more complicated than taking the appointment, so I unearth my daybook and write it down. June 11, 10:00 A.M. The one blemish on an otherwise unmarked day.

Why did I buy this daybook? I never even look at it. It lives at the bottom of the pile of paper that used to be my desk. Last year's book was thick with have-tos and should-bes, scrawled over notes about tour details, deadlines, dates. Gradually thinning out over the winter. A slow change, nothing you'd really notice. The weeks still cluttered with meetings, parties, art openings. I was planning to go. Sometimes I even got dressed up. Even got as far as my front door. This year's book is like a southerner's fantasy of the True North: white and empty. With a single set of footprints trudging toward the horizon: my cleaning jobs.

Full-time cleaning is a dreary and difficult business, but part-time is not bad. It's the perfect work for the busy-artist-between-grants. The pay's okay if you clean for guilty liberals, the hours are flexible, and you don't tend to fret about work in the middle of the night. I've scrubbed part-time for twenty-three years. I'm good at it. I was raised to be a housewife, it's in my blood. Of course, after twenty-three years I have a bad back, allergies to most major cleaning products and nothing on my résumé except "housework" and "lesbian sex art." Cleaning the same toilet I've cleaned every week for the past twenty years seems harder now that I'm old. It takes me ten minutes to do a really good job, which means over sixty hours of my life gone down that one toilet. And I do nine toilets a week. Will I be doing this in my fifties? My sixties?

Neither artists nor cleaning ladies get old age pensions. And grants are drying up.

I really should think about my future. Make plans, read the want ads, go to college and become a different person. But I still have enough money to buy canned chili and pay my net bill. And I have thirty-six downloaded messages waiting.

----------

Crazy is silent. 4:00 A.M. Where are you when I need you? Junior's insomnia shift (subject: jail) is long over. It's noon in Manchester, but Rory works nights, sleeps late. In Japan it's 9:00 P.M., but there's nothing from D'isMay except an old post from my afternoon.

```
D'isMay
re: intro
Hi Fruitbat, welcome aboard. Don't know anything about
Baltimore cept for what Nina Simone tells me, which is
grim. And she wasn't even on Thorazine. As far as I
know. So what's your story? How'd you end up in a psych
home? How'd you find ThisIsCrazy? Tell all. It's always
good to have another US whiteboy online. Just kidding.
It's that old bipolar tact. You'll get used to it.
```

Then a fast comeback from CloudTen, sent early evening from Denver.

```
CloudTen
re: intro
Come off it May. You have no idea what Fruitbat is.
He/she could be purple for all you know. On the net we
```

shed our identities and become whatever we want. Who's
to know? Divisions like race, gender, and nationality
have no meaning in a global electronic reality.

Next there's a short flurry of embarrassment when Cyber Joe mis-
posts a personal email to the whole list (love letter to JJ at the
Paradise, very sweet though I should have deleted it as soon as I realized it was private, bad girl). Then D'isMay is back.

D'isMay
re: intro
Sorry, Ten. But if I say someone on the net is a US
whiteboy, I have an 80 percent chance of being right.
Not bad odds. It's easy to say divisions have no meaning
when ya'll are all the same.

You'd think that would bring them out of the woodwork. But no, all
the U.S. whiteboys must be fast asleep. Okay, who should I write to?

from: Jam
to: Junior
re: jail
Kid. Worrying about going to jail isn't going to help
and it's wearing you to a frazzle. And you know what?
It probably won't happen. You don't have a criminal
record — that counts big. Your psych record is
irrelevant in this situation — it was a demo with a lot
of other people. Normal people. Protective camouflage.
Safety in numbers. Maybe they'll just torture you with

```
postponements for awhile and then drop the whole thing.
Or give everyone a whopping big fine and you can spend
your summer organizing fundraising events. And maybe
you'll meet some cute number on the planning committee.
Fret about that, boy!
```

I've read all of yesterday's messages twice. And I'm sick of computer solitaire. I could wash my dishes. I could vacuum. I could read a good book except I don't have one. I could return my phone messages, except it's 5:00 A.M. *Roz:* "We gotta have a meeting about the new show, soon, call me." *Cynthia:* "Hi, Jam, it's me. I looked for you at Sexpertise but no luck. How're you doing? Let's do coffee soon." Cynthia. She and Roz are the only two who haven't given up leaving messages. Slow learners.

I could cruise the Web, look for shareware games. Okay. Http://www.spidweb.com. What's new? BATTLESTAR. Nah. WORLD WAR TWO TANK COMMANDER. Nah. SWORDQUEST. A 4500k file. Twenty minutes to download, maybe twenty-five. Fine, I can afford it. If you read and write offline, avoid the chat rooms and use a cheap local server, it's possible to live on the net and still eat gourmet canned chili.

I make tea while the computer downloads, decodes and unstuffs. When I return there's a little SWORDQUEST folder on the desktop. Close out of the Web and click open the crossed-swords icon. The usual momentous music and fancy graphics display. Yeah yeah I know I know.

More momentous music, and then I'm supposed to choose between creating my own party or using prefab characters. Hey, I'm an artist. It's complicated, though, worse than filling out a census form. Rows of boxes to click and blanks to fill in: name/sex/age/

race—as in elf, orc, human—profession—as in fighter, mage, thief—and then there's twenty-five skill points to parcel out among different attributes: strength/dexterity/wisdom click click click. Finally I have a mage chick named RiverRat with a fair amount of intelligence, dexterity, defensiveness and not much else. There's five more slots for characters but I'm sick of census forms. A quick check through the pre-fab file. Els the Amazon. Sounds good. I add her to RiverRat's party and start the game.

There's an introductory text telling me I'm a party of adventurers who find themselves in the war-torn land of Grimalda. Then it's all pictures, green grass with a little house graphic and little pointy mountain graphics at the edge of the screen and tiny icons for my characters in the middle. Click the mouse to move. Easy. Click click and we walk across grass toward mountains. The landscape scrolls with us. Look, here comes a little figure running across the plains. Kind of like a red bear with a sword. Oh no, it's attacking us. Orc hits Els: 5 points damage says the text box at the bottom of the screen. Els has 25 points before she's dead. Click click. Nothing. Orc hits RiverRat: 10 points damage. Danger. Danger. Oh no. Shift click. Option click. Left arrow click. Nothing. What's the fight command here? Orc hits RiverRat: 10 points damage. There's a realistic little death-scream and River-Rat's icon turns into a skull-and-crossbones. RiverRat is dust. Els just stands there. Command click. Tab click. Orc hits Els: 5 points damage. Orc hits Els: 10 points damage. Danger. Danger. Orc hits Els: 10 points damage. Eeeeaah. Els is dust.

That was exciting. Maybe I should read the instructions. Back to desktop open SWORDQUEST, open Docs. Mail in your shareware fee and we'll snail you a manual. Thanks. Close Docs. Start new game? No, I can't face the census forms. Revert to previously saved game file.

And here we are, back in the meadow, un-killed. Click click walk toward the house graphic. Oh no, here comes another red bear. Run toward the house graphic. Now what? Click on the front door. Nothing. Option click. Nothing. Click click, walk RiverRat onto the front door and the screen changes from green for grass to lots of little houses. `You have entered the city of Taro.` Whew. Here comes a little townsperson to greet us. `Thief stabs RiverRat: 10 points damage. Danger. Danger.`

----------

"This wasn't from the accident," Dr. Lewis said.

"No," I said. There were two cuts, the first shiny pink, the second still scabbed over. Underneath were the silver lines of older scars.

"When did you start doing this ... again?" she asked with the deep caring look doctors produce at times like this. It wasn't like we were life-long pals. I had seen her once or twice a year for the last few years. She seemed nice enough, short and practical with curly blonde hair and a tired face.

"A month ago."

"What's been going on?"

Where does it come from, this sudden urge to lie to your doctor? Oh Dr. Lewis, it was just an accident. I was eating dinner and the knife slipped. Or I was abducted by aliens who experimented on my arm. Or I got hit in the head and couldn't remember who I was, and I came to with these cuts on my arm and a card with your name and address in my pocket. I didn't even recognize the street name. I asked someone where it was, and they told me it was on the other side of town. When I got across town, someone else told me it was back here. People are strange.

No. Behave yourself.

I gave her the more or less real story: feeling down, blah blah blah, no energy, blah blah, staying home, blah, isolation.

"Are you feeling suicidal?" she asked. They always ask that if you slash, even if the cuts are somewhere safe like on your upper arms. I think they all get the same checklist in doctor school: *Are you feeling suicidal, have you planned how to do it, do you have the pills/gun/ ten-storey building required?*

"No." They get really worried if you say yes. And besides, I wasn't feeling suicidal. Suicide requires some kind of active drive.

"Sounds like depression," she said. "I have a couple of pamphlets you might like to read. Make an appointment for next week and we'll talk about options. In the meantime, I'd like you to get some tests. There are a number of straightforward physical factors that can cause depression." She scribbled me four different forms for the local lab.

Oh goody, I thought. Lucy will like this.

----------

Roz had her own unaccidental scars. Surgery scars.

"Do you want to see?" she had asked.

Seven months ago. But first there was the diagnosis.

We were just back from touring, three long weeks of one-night stands in dyke bars and Women's Studies departments. Lesbian story-telling with enough improbable sex to make it fly in the bars and enough multilayered techno-imagery on the screen behind us to pass for post-modern in the universities.

I don't remember when she first told me, where we were, what she said. I just remember me saying, "Oh christ no," and then her saying something else, probably cracking a joke, and then me realizing I wasn't supposed to say *oh christ no*. If you tell all your friends and they all say *oh christ no*, where does that leave you?

We were supposed to be thinking up a new project so we could apply for a grant and have a new show ready for next year's big Performance Festival. I wasn't having much luck coming up with ideas. Neither was Roz. I ended up writing the grant by myself because Roz was in the hospital, then out again, recovering. Three months later we got our rejection notice with a nice letter attached suggesting we apply again with a more detailed project description. I guess it wasn't the best proposal I ever wrote. Maybe our new application would fare better, a more detailed version of "we don't really know what we're doing."

"Do you want to see?" Roz had asked, back in her own place by then, sitting up in bed.

"Yeah, sure."

She pulled up her T-shirt. The black stitches like barbs of wire against hot skin were familiar, expected—I know what sewn flesh looks like. But I had thought the cut would be a tidy line across her chest like the one on the poster at the Women's Bookstore. Instead it was lumpy and puckered like a sixth-grade sewing project. There was a tube with yellowish liquid coming out of the wound and seeping down to a flat, white plastic thing taped to her ribs.

"It's that transgendered look," Roz said. "Do you like it?"

I didn't think it was funny. But I didn't say anything. Roz was the one who got to say what was and wasn't funny about breast cancer.

Jam first met Roz in the change room at the Britannia community centre swimming pool in the early eighties. It was the Thursday night women's swim, known to many as dyke night at the pool, though straight women were there too. But dykes ruled.

What do you hide in the change room? What do you lay bare, defying shame? Your thick thighs, stretch marks, shabby underwear? Jam dressed quickly, the long-sleeved shirt first. She had no new wounds in those days, just faint marks of old razor blades that no one would have noticed anyway. She was stable. She was never going to flip out again. She had it all figured out. But she still kept her left side casually turned toward her locker until the shirt was on. Then she dried her hair.

She was the only lesbian in the locker room with long hair. Sometimes she had painted fingernails. Sometimes she put on lipstick in the change room mirror. God knows how she got away with it. Maybe other dyke-feminists talked about her behind her back, called her a fem-bot or male identified. But no one said it to her face. If she showed up at the Women's Bookstore benefit dance in a dress, people would still talk to her, dance with her even. In the seventies, that wasn't something you could count on. Maybe it was because she was an artist and artists are supposed to be weird. But Jam knew what she could and couldn't get away with. She was good at watching her back. She pulled on the long-sleeved shirt as fast as she could.

Roz was new to Vancouver. She was a Yank from Chicago and didn't quite have the hang of Canadian ways. She walked up to Jam who was standing under the hair dryer.

"Hi," she said. "I like your paintings." She stood there grinning, her towel slung casually over her shoulder, drops of water still clinging to her pink skin. Telling an artist you like her work is a very good opening line. "Thanks." Jam smiled back.

"If you ever need a model, I'd be glad to," Roz said. The way she said it, her sly glance and slow drawl, it was not quite a direct come-on, but close. It probably wouldn't work on 90 percent of Canadian girls. But Jam wasn't going to let the new girl in town out-bold her. She let a long moment pass, running her eyes over big shoulders, small breasts, bony knees.

"Sure," she said. "Tomorrow?"

Jam teased Roz for the next week.

"Don't move," she'd say and walk close, check some detail on Roz's sprawled, naked body and then return to her painting. Jam was painting dreamland lesbians in those days, floating in the sky touching each other with exquisite gentleness. Just to see a picture of a woman who seemed to be a lesbian was still a big deal in those days. To paint like that in art school had been an act of courage. Now it meant women who used to ignore her at parties were eager to chat. Jam didn't mistake this for friendship, but she enjoyed it in a cynical kind of way. She was a medium-sized fish in a small pond, which was better than being plankton any day.

Roz made her move late in the afternoon of the sixth day. She was getting tired of sitting in the same position till her butt went numb, waiting for the right moment.

"You know what I'd like to do?" she asked, shaking her legs out.

Jam was in the bathroom, washing her brushes. She could barely hear Roz over the running water.

"Pardon?" she yelled over her shoulder.

Roz tried to stand up, but her legs weren't working. She pulled on the old pink terrycloth robe that Jam kept for frozen art models.

"You know what I'd like to do?" Roz yelled.

"No, what?" Jam yelled.

"I'd like to go to bed with you," Roz yelled.

"What?"

Roz contemplated a number of different answers. "Oh fuck you," she finally muttered.

Jam turned off the water and stuck her head around the corner. "Thought you'd never ask."

Roz stood up, dropped the bathrobe and walked across the floor toward Jam. Either her legs had recovered or she was trying very hard to keep her knees from buckling. If she was trying it didn't show. Eyes locked on Jam's, she put all the smooth danger she had into that walk. Jam had never seen anyone except experienced art models show such casual disregard for being the only naked person in a room. She stood by the bathroom door and watched. Oh my. Those big hands, long thighs, riot of pubic hair. No bikini wax here. Sweet little breasts. Nothing she hadn't been staring at for days, but now, walking to her with no shame. Standing in front of her. Those big hands touching her. They lurched into each other, mouth into mouth, tongue on tongue. Their nipples shooting electric messages back and forth. Jam dropped her brushes. Later. First taste the million textures of skin. Hands wild, cunts desperate, on the floor now, Roz's skin smeared with paint from Jam's clothes. Roz's hands up under the shirt, struggling with brassiere hooks. Jam let her work for it. Oh yes you act so Chicago cool but you're not very experienced in the lingerie department. Was it politics or shyness that made all those rules for the just-come-out feminist lesbians back then? You were supposed to get naked as fast as possible and lie side by side. Roz eventually succeeded with the bra, grabbed the prize, but left shirt and jeans buttoned, lay under Jam saying, "Yes yes oh god take me more please harder," as Jam slid one cautious finger into her slit. Penetration was still questionable, could earn you a lecture afterwards. But Roz had no shame, begged for it. Three fingers, four, harder, deeper. Jam hadn't known you could fuck like that, was scared, entranced. Roz writhed on her hand screaming and came, came, came.

Jam was too wound up to orgasm that day, but she did the next day and the next.

Roz never said anything about the scars. Maybe she didn't see them.

When they weren't fucking they were fighting.

"Why do you always have to drive?" Jam complained on their way to the Lesbian Crisis Line benefit dance.

Roz shrugged. "It's my car."

"Well, you use my toaster."

"That's different."

"How is it different?"

By the time they got to the Oddfellows' Hall, where most of the benefits were held, they weren't speaking. But the band was hot and it only took one song before they were making a spectacle of themselves on the dance floor, circling closer and closer, eyes locked, bumping into other dancers in their single-minded fierceness. Closer, closer, only inches between them, half inches, swimming in the electric air until Roz reached out and grabbed her, or was it Jam who threw herself into Roz's arms. There was a long line-up in the women's can, no one in the men's. Jam pulled Roz into a cubicle, locked it. Roz pushed Jam against the door, her hands up under Jam's dress, fumbling with her cotton briefs. Jam laughing as Roz pulled them down, off, threw them into the next stall. "You won't be needing those, sugar." Roz's fingers deeper, deeper, Jam wet and reckless, hands hard on Roz's breasts. They froze at the sound of the door, footsteps, someone entering the cubicle beside them. Pause. Unbuttoning her jeans, maybe, or staring at the discarded panties. Then the long, full sound of beer piss. Pause. Silence. Roz unfroze, pushed hard body to body against the stall door. Her hand slow and relentless. "She knows we're here," she whispered in Jam's ear. "She can hear your breathing, you just can't keep it quiet enough, she knows what I'm doing to you. Do you care? Do you care who knows? Do you want me to stop?"

"No, I don't care don't stop don't stop." She didn't say please, even though it was in all the songs—*please please I'll do anything*—but it was loud in her mind.

"The people in your paintings never look like us," Roz complained. "They don't fuck like us. Is that how you fuck in your fantasies?"

"You know how I fuck in my fantasies," Jam said. Which wasn't entirely true, Jam never told anyone everything. "I don't know. It's political, I guess. Positive images of lesbians."

"Yeah, and you and I are so negative and evil. Why doesn't anyone ever have long hair? Why don't they fuck on the kitchen table?"

She thought about it. She went back to her studio and tried to paint differently, to paint what sex really felt like, but she didn't know how. Then Roz pulled out an old camera from a box under her bed, and they started taking photos of each other. They pooled their money, bought a pawn-shop camera with a self-timer and made pictures of themselves sexing each other. They stopped writing each other poems and wrote sex stories.

"Tell the truth," they said. "Scare yourself." It was frightening. First they didn't show anyone else and then they did. They took their pictures to the women's gallery that had shown Jam's paintings, and scared the curator. Jam explained why it was all right, why it was feminist, why it was good. She wrote a careful artists' statement. When women viewers wrote in the gallery comments book, some said, "You learned this from the boys, it's nothing but porn." But most said, "You've given me a lot to think about." Jam filled out grant applications and they bought a Nikon.

In between they fought. "Why do I always do all the cooking?" Roz complained.

"You want grilled-cheese sandwiches? I'll cook," Jam said.

"I'll lend you my cookbooks."

"I don't do cookbooks."

Eventually they broke up, screaming on the telephone, on street corners, at art openings. But they couldn't give up the work. They took pictures of each other naked furious hurt, rented a video camera, fought and fucked. Because they were broken up, they didn't fuck in real life anymore, but they continued to do it in front of the camera. At first it was confusing. They yelled, cried, hurtled accusations at every break, going grimly back to sex when the break was over. But they were in love with the pictures. They poured over contact sheets, video footage, hot anguished images that gripped them more deeply than accusations. They made a video that toured the gay and lesbian festivals, put up another photo show. They turned each other's stories into scripts and performed in bars and then in galleries.

Performance was sweet and terrifying as sex itself. The audience said I love you, I love you. Sometimes they lit up with laughter. And there was always that moment, the line that made half the audience freeze in their seats, then three or four of them unfreeze and walk out. Jam knew when the line was coming. She didn't want them to get mad, didn't want to lose their love, but she still kept the line.

Tell the truth. Scare yourself.

Eventually Roz and Jam acquired some polish, learned how to get a laugh whenever they wanted one, developed a following, performed in distant cities, had their own modest fame.

Eventually people stopped walking out.

----------

According to the pamphlets Dr. Lewis gave me, depression is sometimes called the common cold of mental illness. I'd never heard anyone call it that, even on alt.support.depression. Maybe it was what shrinks say when they meet for lunch: "Ah yes, depression, the common cold of mental illness."

The "Twelve Signs of Depression" pamphlet said 6 percent of the gen. pop. have it. "Depression: What You Need to Know" said 15 percent. They both had a checklist to tell if you're clinically depressed or not. On one I scored nine out of twelve, on the other I scored eleven out of sixteen. Either way, it was a solid pass.

All of a sudden, depression had acquired a capital D. I wasn't just a fucked-up person. I was a person with a Depressive Disorder, walking to my doctor's office. Save me, doctor, save me!

Dr. Lewis's office was in a big medical building on Tenth Avenue, a carefree walk on a summer day. East Vancouver was far from the beaches and glittering skyline of Chamber of Commerce brochures, my neighbourhood for twenty years. Rows of fifties-modern houses with the occasional Victorian, looking awkward and self-conscious like the tall girl in grade school. I didn't have a problem leaving my house, I really didn't. I was fine as long as I stuck to the side streets where I wouldn't have to say hi to friends, jostle with strangers. Take the stairs to the fifth floor, I'm not scared of elevator crowds, I just like the exercise.

My blood tests were in. Negative, negative, negative. I had flunked them all except for anemia. Iron pills. Okay. Maybe iron pills would save me.

"You've had psychiatric problems before," my doctor said, flipping through my file.

Ah yes. The file.

Where does it come from, this unfortunate urge to tell the truth to your doctor? I'd told the truth twenty-odd years ago on an intake form at a medical clinic, and it had followed me like a stray dog for the rest of my life. One of those dogs that bites out of the blue and pisses on your foot.

"Some people seem to have a biochemical predisposition toward depression," my doctor said. "I see your father was hospitalized for bipolar disorder—what used to be called manic depression. It has a strong genetic link."

Another stray dog from that same careless moment of truth. My father's ancient diagnosis seemed to touch off an automatic reflex in doctors, like the test where they hit your knee with a hammer. Wham—"You're bipolar!"

"I don't think I'm very manic," I said.

"Manic episodes can present in very different ways. It's not something a layperson can diagnose. And quite a few artists seem to be bipolar. It's nothing to be ashamed of."

Why do I immediately start to feel ashamed when my doctor tells me I don't have to? She was trying to be nice and reassuring. She had that concerned look again. She asked if I'd thought about some sort of treatment for my condition.

"Not really." Actually, I had. You'd have to be really out of touch not to know what the treatment for my condition was supposed to be.

"Anti-depressants are very effective," said my doctor.

"I took them at Mountainview Day Therapy," I told her. "It was awful. If I wasn't depressed before, I sure was after."

"Mountainview," Dr. Lewis said, leafing back through my file. "Oh, Elavil. I would never prescribe Elavil anymore—too many side effects. But Prozac is very clean."

"I try to avoid drugs," I said, "since, you know, my teenage addict years." It's a great line. I was just a run-of-the-mill acidhead, but now they jump to respect my clean-and-sober.

"Think about it for awhile. Come back next week, and we'll talk some more. In the meanwhile you might be interested in this pamphlet," said my doctor. "Prozac and You."

----------

According to "Prozac and You," waking early and not being able to get back to sleep is a Symptom of Depression. It's so good to know what's a Symptom and what's just my regular Fucked-Up Behaviour. Especially at 4:00 A.M. Luckily I have a backlog of email to entertain me which I ignored all day 'cause I was going to seriously work on new writing for the Performance Festival show. I ended up with a list of possible plot options, four pages of garbage and two reasonable first sentences. Somehow I don't think Roz will be impressed. I spent most of the day playing SWORDQUEST. My party was killed by thieves four times while I learned the fight commands. They starved to death twice before I figured out that I had to buy food in the town. I need to mail in that registration cheque. Maybe tomorrow.

Why did they have to put the mailbox on the busiest corner of Commercial Drive—heart of the dyke ghetto—right in front of the store where Roz works, where everyone hangs out, where I'd have to say hi and answer questions? Prozac is supposed to give you a chattier personality. Shy girls find dates and job opportunities. Bullies stop kicking sand in your face. Maybe next week.

```
PPP open
Network
check mail
```

Terry and Gina are getting together with other Coalition members to talk about the executive director situation. D'isMay got an A on her psych paper. There's a job for a consumer-advocate in Atlanta. Parnell says George is a sell-out and George says he's not. Sarah posts all twelve pages of U.S. Senate Bill 1180, including the Kassebaum Amendment. It's thick with legalese, but the basics are clear: take funding from homeless-outreach programs and put it into homeless-psych-drug programs.

Next are a few comments on my visit with Dr. Lewis.

```
Charlie
re: Jam's appointment
I too spent many years denying being bipolar. It's hard
to deal with the social stigma that comes from having a
```

mental illness, but healing can't begin until you accept
who you are.

D'isMay
re: Jam's appointment
What the fucknhell is wrong with being bipolar? Fix that
attitude!

Junior
re: Jam's appointment
Buzz off Charlie. If you find it useful to have a
psychiatric label, that's your business. But telling Jam
to take whatever her doctor dishes out is consumer
behaviour at its worst. Dump the doctor Jam. You're
having a hard enough time without this shit.

Paradise Clubhouse/Howard
re: Jam's appointment
Why should you be mad that your doctor called you
bipolar? Bipolars are the queens of the fucking world
(ITheirTotallyArrogantO). The main thing diagnoses are
good for is sussing out what your shrink thinks of you —
Bipolar Affective Disorder means they like you, Unipolar
means you're boring, Borderline Personality Disorder
means they hate you, and Schizophrenic means you scare
the shit out of them because they can't keep up with
your thinking (IMSchizophrenicO). Anyway there's already
too many bipolars on this list so I think you should go
for something really exotic: Asperger's Autism anyone?

Howard is an old hacker who did criminally insane time for being nuts while committing some computer misdemeanor. When he got out, he started hanging around at the Paradise Clubhouse, in Kansas City, Kansas. "Clubhouse" is a code word for mental patients' drop-in centre, the kind run by an equal (uh-huh) partnership of paid mental-health professionals and unpaid consumers. The Paradise staff like Howard despite his cranky nature because he fixes all their computer problems in return for client net-access, which is how the Paradise became the only clubhouse in the world that subscribes to ThisIsCrazy.

Sarah is less cranky, lives just across the state line in Missouri where she's a serious disability rights gal.

```
Sarah
re: Jam's appointment
Your doctor's opinion is an opinion. It's not science
and I wouldn't exactly call it art either. If the shoe
doesn't fit, don't wear it.


Fruitbat
re: Jam's appointment
Like Sarah says. Go barefoot. Believing in your
diagnosis is big-time trouble. IMHO of course (see, I'm
learning). Shrinks rewrite the story of your life to fit
your DSM category. Then your friends watch for symptoms:
"Oh no, too many mixed metaphors, she's schizing out!" I
guess some folks find it a useful road map to their
inner landscape or something, but I just get lost. It
turns a situation (I hear voices) into an identity (I'm
a schizophrenic).
```

You can always count on getting a clear directive from ThisIsCrazy. I like the Fruitbat one. Send off a reply, nothing too deep. I don't do deep at 4:00 A.M.

> Jam
> schizing out (was Jam's appointment)
> I'm worried about you, Fruitbat. I counted four and a
> half metaphors in a one-paragraph post. I think you need
> help. Time to up your meds? <gd&r> (That's grin, duck
> and run to you, newbie.)

Meanwhile the whiteboy identity question is getting settled.

> Fruitbat
> re: Intro
> Not bad, D'isMay. Got me on two out of three. US
> whitegirl here, fresh out of Baltimore State, and I
> don't mean university. Do you really want the whole
> pitiful story of my incarceration? How about the Classic
> Comic version? Wrong time, wrong place, talking back to
> my voices (downtown no one looks twice, but wander into
> a "nice" neighborhood and you're in shit deep). Someone
> got scared and called the police. I was off guard,
> couldn't dance fast enough and that was that. They're
> not supposed to commit you these days unless you're a
> "danger to self or others." That can cover a lot of
> territory. But I'm dangerous all right. Watch out. I hit
> the cop. Yeah, it was stupid, but I have this thing

about strange men grabbing me on the street. And like I said, I was a little ... disoriented. Got me six months as a guest of the state.

I was in once before, when I was twenty. I thought I was so good at passing nowadays that I'd never get caught again, but apparently not. If anyone has experience with staying focused in the Real World while hearing voices, I could use some tips. I'm not hearing voices now — Thorazine has made me normal, if normal includes not being able to think, walk or see straight. All in all, I'd rather learn to live with the voices.

So, Ms. or Mr. D'isMay: should I go with the odds and guess that you're a US whiteboy? Or do I make an assumption based on the Tokyo address you seem to be posting from?

D'isMay
re: Intro
Assume I'm a US blackgirl living in Tokyo hoping her manic cycle will last long enough to finish grad school before I hit the pit again. Studying (can you believe it?) psychology. Get some big letters after my name and raise hell. Infiltrate the system. And you'd best believe I will.

Don't know anything about hearing voices, but other folks on the list do and some are med-free too. Go for it, gal! That Thorazine is evil.

```
Junior
re: Intro
How can you still buy that change-from-within crap,
D'isMay? I've seen it a million times — some bright
young thing thinks they're going to humanize the system
and then the next thing you know they're either selling
their soul for $90,000 a year, or they're out on their
asses. Which will you be?
    P.S. Fruitbat — Congratulations on the cop. I hope
you hit him hard.
```

Who says Canadians are polite? Of course Junior has probably never actually hit anyone in his life.

```
Fruitbat
re: Intro
Sorry Junior. It was the most embarrassing of girlie
punches. I don't exactly work out at the gym or
anything. I'm a scrawny little thing at the best of
times, which this wasn't. But apparently it's the
thought that counts.
```

At this point Joe Bones wades in with Everything You Always Wanted to Know about Thorazine But Were Afraid to Ask. Joe knows all these drug things—he was studying to be a doctor before he got carted off to the bin. When he got out, they wouldn't let him back in med school. Sometimes he gives D'isMay advice about how to pass in the system, for which she is typically grateful (~Yeah, Joe, I \*know\* I should never stand on my desk in the middle of

a History of Behaviourism lecture and yell 'Skinner is the
devil.' I KNOW.")

    Joe Bones
    re: Intro
    Fruitbat: Thorazine is a brand name for chlorpromazine,
    the mother of all neuroleptics. Most of what you
    describe are typical Thorazine side effects. Withdrawal
    is not easy. You should be sure to do it with a doctor.
    If your brain has gotten used to operating through a
    chemical haze then stopping the drug can make you really
    flip out. You need to go slow and be prepared for a hard
    time. You've got to educate your doctor and your family
    to give you time and support to come out the other side.
    Maybe you'll have better luck than I did.
        But believe me, there are plenty *more* problems with
    staying on. The stuff you describe is the least of it.
    You should read the Physician's Desk Reference: "death"
    is a possible "side effect" of Thorazine. Then there's
    tardive dyskinesia: uncontrollable muscle tics — hits 20
    to 40 percent of neuroleptic users. So by all means, if
    you're ready to function without it, go for it.

Naturally, Charlie won't let Bones go unchallenged.

    Charlie
    re: Intro
    Trying to scare newbies with your horror stories, Joe?
    Many people do just fine on Thorazine and find its side

```
effects a reasonable trade off for being able to
function in the community and have decent lives.
Neuroleptics have been around a long time because they
*work*.
```

Then JJ at the Paradise comes on with a rather different point of view.

```
Paradise Clubhouse/ JJ
re: Intro
You make some good points, Charlie, but side effects
like TD are not such a good trade off. I still take my
Haldol because otherwise I get real crazy. But when
you're chewing your cheeks and blinking your eyes non-
stop, it's a real big problem. People cross the street
to avoid you. Thank God for the Paradise where people
will talk to you no matter how you look.
```

I have to stop reading for awhile. I could try to write but it's five in the morning. You can't work at five in the morning. I could mail my registration cheque now while it's dark, sure why not? It isn't that I can't leave the house, it's just that I don't feel like it most of the time.

My kitchen door opens right on the tiny front garden (spacious 1 bdrm apt, grnd lvl, prvt entrnce). It's starting to get light at the edge of the sky, but there are no people. The occasional car, off to work in the burbs on some strange morning shift, or heading for the Trans-Canada and out of here. The air is summer-warm, smells of mock orange blossoms. Everyone grows flowers in this city. Some in precise rows, pansies in the military, some in a riot of brambles. Then you look up and see big, blue mountains. Vancouver is the second prettiest city in the world. I forget which the first prettiest is.

Walk down to the gate, stand there a few minutes. Open the gate. Go on, what's your problem? Walk the dark blocks to the Drive. When I first moved here it was all Portuguese coffee bars and dusty five-and-dimes. Now we have Starbucks and trendy cafés, last year's street dreams sulking on chain-store mannequins. Roz says artists are the shock troops of gentrification—people should pay us *not* to move into their neighbourhoods.

I turn the corner, walk down the block. It has that early dawn ghost-town look, all the bustle and charge put away for the night. Traffic light directs non-existent cars. Wait for walk and cross to Kropotkin's Papers, the anarchist stationery store where Roz works. Someone is asleep in the doorway—a teenage girl in a long, flower-print dress. You see more and more of that, the long dresses and the sleeping in doorways both.

I imagine Roz at the counter, making jokes with the customers, showing them how to use the Xerox, taking money and putting pencils in bags. Or Roz in rehearsal, giddy with ideas, phoning galleries while I sort slides. Roz driving to the beach in a winter storm to play tag with the ocean, coming back with wet shoes and wind in her eyes. She does that every year. But years are uncertain, and winter a long road from here. A random wave could drag her under long before the storms come.

I'm all the way home before I realize I didn't mail the registration cheque.

Blam! Els hits thief: 12 points damage. Blam! Thief hits Els: 3 points. Els has Leather Armour, it says on her inventory sheet, which you can call up by clicking on the stats bar at the side of the screen. It doesn't show on her little icon, but I imagine it as old and scuffed and very tough looking. It keeps her from being hit too hard. I imagine her as scuffed and tough looking too, grey-streaked hair, whipcord muscles. RiverRat has no armour, just a cloak she stole off a dead orc. Blam! `Thief hits RiverRat: 20 points.` Eaaaaah. `RiverRat is dust.` I'm getting tired of RiverRat being dust. `Revert to last saved game.` Els is tired of it too. "When are you going to learn to fight?" she asks. Or she would if SwordQuest had a `Talk` button.

"I'm not a fighter, I'm a mage," RiverRat would reply. I keep trying to imagine her as a tall and mysterious femme, mistress of arcane powers, but she just doesn't have the stuff.

"So when are you going to learn to cast vicious killing spells?" Els asks.

"I can cast Feisty Slap of Pain," RiverRat objects.

"Slap is a wimp spell. We're spending all our time just trying to survive from one fight to the next. We're not stealing treasure or going on quests. It's boring. It's beneath my dignity as an Amazon."

"Okay, okay," says RiverRat. "So what do we do?"

"We go to town, buy some food and get the shit beat out of us. Then we go looking for a Wizard who's willing to teach you."

"That sounds good," RiverRat says.

----------

Thursday was Trudi-and-Allison-Day, my most boring job. Probably they didn't tidy up before I came over; probably they just led very clean lives. I told myself my work had meaning: if you dust a shelf that has no dust, you are not wasting your time, you are ensuring it will never *get* dusty. Preventive cleaning, the latest thing.

I preferred Sam-and-Tina-Day because their house was always really dirty without being gross. Gross is cat puke on the carpets and pots left soaking till the mold is an inch tall with bizarre creatures lurking in the bottom, farting noxious fumes. Sam and Tina's was just sticky floors, bathtub rings, clothes on the floor—the stuff of exciting cleaning. They left me alone to get on with my work, unlike Trudi. Trudi felt she had to hang out to prove what a groovy boss she was, which is fine if you're friends, but we weren't friends and she was always following me around and standing where I needed to vacuum. If Sam was home, she was on the phone being a consultant. I never quite got what she consulted about, but she was always leaving important faxes under the bed, or going off to exotic locales like Carrot River, Saskatchewan. Tina, on the other hand, was never home. She was the only dyke on Vancouver City Council, and she was always at some meeting. I liked to think of her voting against developers while I cleaned her bathroom. They also serve who only kneel and scrub. Jam Johnston, Cleaning Lady to the Stars.

Trudi was on her way out when I arrived.

"Hi, Jam, I'm late for class, see you!" she said, kissing the air by my cheek. Only Women's Studies professors air-kiss their cleaning ladies. That's a lie. Only Trudi. She was also the one who had introduced me to a friend of hers by saying, "Jam cleans for me sometimes, but her *real* work is as an artist." The friend had nodded to me, on my knees rubbing at scuff marks on the white tile floor, and said, "I don't know, that looks like real work to me."

Good line.

That was Alex, who later became my ex-whatever-she-was.

Trudi and Allison's house was two floors, a four-hour job. I was moving slowly, my brain like a fogged-in airport, planes circling. Did I vacuum the living room rug already or was that last week (month, year)? Some houses I could tell by the dirt but not here. Vacuum it again, just in case. Wipe the table. Scrub the sink. I told myself this was what a Broadway actor in a hit show feels like, repeating the same lines night after night. Dust the baseboards. Make the bed. Two more hours. Trudi and Allison both had their own work rooms with their own computers. Trudi's was an IBM, Allison's was a Mac. DOS-crossed lovers. In the old days I used to write stuff in my head while I was working, type it on the Mac between tasks. Print it out and trash the file before I left. Can't trust these cleaners. They steal and write poetry.

One hour.

I thought about the two first sentences and the list of possible plot options I had written the week before. Maybe I'd come up with something while I scrubbed the bathroom. Their tub was long and beautiful with old-fashioned feet and a new enamel job. It gleamed with preventive scrubbing. Dirt wouldn't dare. One time when Trudi and Allison were on vacation, Roz and I had done sex pictures in it. They were good pictures, but we never showed them because I might have lost my job. I could write about the bathtub, climbing in with all my clothes on, Roz on top of me, nipples hard under her thin, wet shirt, water overflowing onto the floor.

But the next line didn't come. The tub gleamed. The planes were still circling in the fog, flying blind, hoping the air traffic controllers would keep them from midair collisions.

----------

Knock. On the kitchen door. Damn. Answer? Nah. I'm looking up Bipolar Affective Disorder—affectionately known as BAD, the whooping cough of mental illness—on the Web.

> When someone is in a manic "high," he may be overactive
> or overtalkative. His attention span is often short and
> he can easily be distracted.

Distracted. Yeah, I'm distracted. Some goddamn idiot is still pounding on my goddamn door. Can't you see I'm not home? My attention span is short. I'm out pacing the streets, talking rapidly.

> Sometimes, the "high" person may be irritable or have
> inflated ideas about his importance in the world. He may
> be full of grand schemes, ranging from business deals to
> romantic sprees. He often shows poor judgement in these
> ventures.

Okay, let's face it, I *have* been irritable a time or two and shown bad judgement in my romantic sprees. Distracted, irritable, bad judgement. Three out of eight: D+, fuck you, Doctor.

More knocking. Then footsteps on the path to the back. Jesus. I hit the floor just before the intruder taps on the window over my computer. If I lie very still they probably won't see me. The window hasn't been washed in awhile.

"Jam, I know you're in there."

Roz. Great. Everyone else in this entire city knows you're supposed to call in advance and make an appointment for two weeks down the road. Dilemma: should I stand up and reveal myself or risk being caught hiding on the floor? Oh hi, just dropped my pencil down here. Can't seem to find it.

Then the thought that, for the last seven months, has instantly followed behind the usual mix of love and irritation. Roz: cancer.

"Christ what a pit," Roz said, putting the kettle on for tea. "Don't you ever wash your dishes?"

"If you had called before dropping by, I would have had time to prepare for the white glove test," I answered.

Roz started running water in the sink. Was she really going to wash my dishes? She added soap. Yes. It wasn't that she was a social worker type, it was just that she was restless, nosy and had no manners. If I was a feminist therapist I would tell her she didn't have proper boundaries, but my dishes were getting done so I didn't care.

"How are you feeling?" I asked. I tried to say it casually, not as though what I really wanted to know was had she seen her doctor recently and was she still cancer-free.

Roz dropped a plate into the dishwater with a deliberate splash. "Why does everyone keep asking how I'm *feel*ing?" she said. She dropped a cup, another splash. "Why do they all ask with those same wide eyes and hushed voices?" She dropped a frying pan, dishwater sloshing over the counter and onto the floor. "I'm *feel*ing just peachy. How are you *feel*ing?"

Fuck you, I was just asking, aren't I allowed to ask anymore?

"I'm okay," I said. Didn't ask: Are you getting lots of rest, taking your vitamins? I already knew what she'd say. "Cancer isn't caused by staying up late, you know. It's from corporate pollution, chlorine in the water supply, I see you're still buying bleached toilet paper." Sorry Roz.

There was an awkward pause while I tried to think of something non-controversial to say and Roz scrubbed on my frying pan as though the elimination of grease was her life's passion. The kettle whistled and I made tea. Passed her a cup, she said thanks, we both sipped. Tea is very effective in these situations.

"Guess we haven't heard from the Canada Council yet," Roz said, finishing the frying pan and moving on to a petrified chili pot.

"It's only been a month. Probably the jury hasn't even met yet."

"Can we call and find out?"

"We can call and irritate the grants officer but she's not going to tell us anything before the official letters go out. August probably. You know all that."

"Yeah and it bugs me. The festival is in October. We can't just sit on our butts. How're you doing for money?"

"Let's just say I'll be real glad if we get this grant."

"That bad, eh?"

"I phoned an ad into the *Gay Blade:* reliable cleaning lady, reasonable rates, excellent references. Rich fags will be calling me in droves. How's your financial empire?"

"Not bad. I'm doing thirty hours a week at Pot's." Kropotkin's Papers paid a lot worse than cleaning but Roz liked the atmosphere. It was a good place for meeting girls, she said.

"We need a plan," said Roz.

"Right."

"How's this: We keep writing for the rest of June and do rewrites in July. We'll leave the video stuff till we know about the grant, and then we'll either do fancy techno-glam with our pots of loot or something simple but gorgeous with nothing."

"Right."

"And we'll rehearse like demons in September. No more forgetting your lines."

"It was the accident."

"No more accidents then. So how's the new story going? The science fiction butt-fucking one."

"Still working on it," I said. I had the first line. It was a good first line.

"Want to show me?"

"Not yet. It's got a ways to go."

"Do you think it'll work for performance?"

"It'll be great. You can be the alien."

"Gee thanks."

"Typecasting."

Roz splashed dishwater at me. Missed. Maybe she'd wash my floor before leaving.

"You should write something about internet-sex," Roz said. "It's so of-the-moment. You might as well get something useful out of all that bullshit."

"So what are you working on?" I asked, heading off yet another Roz-rant on the evils of info-capitalism and how I waste my time.

Roz turned her back on the dishes, drew air pictures with her wet hands to describe a whole complex sexual scenario featuring the gender confusion of a naive dyke (played by me of course) who careens through encounters with four or five varied partners (played by her) while walking down Davie Street late one night. Why don't these things ever happen in real life? Maybe they would if I left my house.

"Sounds good," I said. In fact it sounded a lot like last year's show, but I didn't have any revolutionary ideas either.

Roz didn't suggest making slides. Maybe dropping the slides was our revolutionary idea. I didn't ask. I knew people would love it if we made sex pictures featuring Roz's scarred chest and single breast. Brave, they'd say. Moving. And it would be. But maybe Roz didn't want to serve up her breast cancer as a performance piece. Maybe she wasn't interested in becoming The One with Cancer and collecting earnest applause.

I didn't ask. I didn't want *my* picture projected on the wall. I knew what people would say: *She's too old. Who wants to see an old broad fucking? We want pert young femmes like in the glossies.*

Anyway, I wasn't fucking these days. I was just cutting my arms and trying to write clever stories about lesbian sex. I had two first sentences already written.

----------

Mrs. Cathcart's house was not bad as cleaning jobs go. Not as dull as Trudi-and-Allison's, not as compelling as Sam-and-Tina's. The main drawback was that Mrs. Cathcart was always home, except when she was out playing bridge. She was a champion bridge player with a table of trophies that I dusted with due reverence.

Mr. Cathcart sold real estate and was never home. I had cleaned their house for fourteen years and never met him. That was usual for straight couples, in my experience. Cleaning ladies were for the wife to deal with, a feminine and slightly embarrassing item like Kotex under the bathroom sink. I had cleaned for many straight people before I started specializing in upwardly mobile lesbian professionals. It was simpler in some ways. In a lesbian house, everyone knows how things should be cleaned and they're willing to impart their conflicting wisdom at the drop of a dust-rag.

Mrs. Cathcart's was an easy walk from my house, seven blocks. It was on the other side of the Drive, but I could handle that. I was cool, sauntering across on the walk light. No one saw me. The Cathcarts lived on a quiet street with skinny cherry trees and competitive gardeners all down the block. Hers was right up there in the top five. I unlocked the front door and called out, "Hi, Mrs. Cathcart! It's me!"

"Hi, Jam," she answered from the kitchen. She was sitting at the counter, writing. I glanced over her shoulder—shopping list, she'd be gone for a few hours, good.

"How're you doing?" I asked. After fourteen years, a bit of friendly chitchat was required.

"Fine, and you?" But not too friendly.

"Fine."

"Could you make sure to vacuum the closet floors?" she asked.

I always vacuumed the closet floors, I didn't know why she felt she had to remind me. Maybe it was social etiquette, taking an interest in my work. Or maybe I hadn't vacuumed well enough last time. One of the good things about working for upwardly mobile lesbians was that I usually understood what things meant. We had been to the same demonstrations, danced to the same tunes at the same bars, before our lives diverged. With Mrs. Cathcart I was often in the dark. She was only a few years older than me, but she was a grown-up in a way I hadn't managed yet. She knew who she was, where she fit. She seemed to know where I fit too.

"Sure, the closet floors, anything else?" I said.

"You might wash the living room windows. If you have time."

"Sure," I said gathering my implements and trudging upstairs. I wanted to ask her how Cynthia was, but that was not in the category of appropriate chitchat. The fact that, as a teenager, Mrs. Cathcart's daughter had adopted the cleaning lady as her confidante still rankled. Although I wasn't exactly blamed for Cynthia's many subsequent misdemeanors, it was better not to refer to her.

I considered Cynthia as I vacuumed the upstairs hall. She was no longer suffering the slings and arrows of adolescence, but she still seemed to feel she owed me something, which meant I owed her something too, like returning her phone calls. It wasn't a big deal. I liked Cynthia. I could tell her all the dirt about her mother, or her mother's house at least, it would be easy. But she was so ... energetic. She would want to know if I had seen this movie or that band, and who I had a crush on, and then she'd want to meet at some groovy new coffee bar (just opened this week, catch it before it's passé) so she could help me plan the seduction. I can't do that stuff anymore, Cynthia. I just can't.

----------

Four in the morning again again again. But today I'm ready for it. I've got a plan a schedule a deadline—I'm on a roll, with the program, doing the right thing. I'm not Clinically Depressed, I'm a writer with a Unique, Erratic Lifestyle. Stumble to the kitchen make some serious coffee. Stumble back open Word. Save As Net-Sex Story. Plot: girl meets girl and fucks her virtually senseless. First sentence: ...

Maybe the plot needs a little more work. Where do they meet? Somewhere cool. Somewhere like ... I'm not sure. I've never actually done net-sex. But I can find out. Close Word, open Netscape. Skip to WebSearch. Sit and wait while several thousand bits of advertising

coalesce on my screen. Buy new stuff. Finally we reach the meat.
Enter key words here: lesbian + sex. Wait. Matches: lesbian:
289,064; sex: 5,174,850. Wow.

> 1) ADULT XXX PICS! NUDE CELEBRITIES PORNO SHAVED
> PUSSIES LESBIAN BOOBS CUM FIST FUCK GANG BANG GROUP ...

This is going to take some weeding through.

> 2) Blonde Babes Swallow It All On JPG Images and Movie
> Clips!!! Plus top glamour models, lesbians, LIVE NUDE
> TELECONFERENCING. Under $1 pm!

Nah.

> 3) Lesbian Safer Sex: Are Lesbians at Risk for
> Contracting HIV from Each Other? Yes!! There have been
> cases reported since the mid 1980s which

I guess my characters could meet at an online AIDS forum.

> 4) All the facts about Gay People — Gays are more
> focused on sex than heterosexuals ...

Well okay. What about XXX Big Tits, why not? Go back and look.

> You are entering a site that contains adult material.
> Press OK if you are 21 or over. Press CANCEL if you are
> under 21.

Okay.

> This site contains 1,000++ pics of sexy dwarfs, genital
> piercings, super fatties, world record gangbangs,
> world's biggest breast, world's smallest pussy, lesbian
> lovers, alligators and beautiful nude women from most
> countries. Click here for FREE pix!

I don't understand sex. I really don't. Click.

> FREE! Babe of the Hour! click here    OR!!! Ultimate
> Hardcore! click here WARNING! EXTREME Sexual Content!

Babe of the Hour is a tall blonde in a bikini, appearing on my screen pixel by labourious pixel. The woman in my story will need a better computer than my old clunker or she'll spend all her time waiting to fuck at fourteen-four bps. It was state of the art once, but then again so was I. Skip to EXTREME Sexual Content. Click, wait. I'm not scared. At first I can't tell what it is, but halfway through the download I recognize a woman's hands, spreading open her labia and giving us all a peek. For this I need a warning? There's got to be more in the next half. Wait. There *is* more. She has a lot of interesting cunt-rings. Kind of Tee-Corrine-does-the-hardware-store except the photography is not as good. Wow. Extreme.

> 5) XXX-pix Big Tits Anal Leather Lesbian Asian Penis
> Bondage Bizarre Teenagersex 18 years Extreme Voted Adult
> Site of the Day December 10, 1993. Please do not
> continue if you are under legal ...

You're going about this all wrong, dodo. Lesbian + sex = wrong. Kewl queers don't use the word lesbian anymore. It's old and stodgy, it's like Womyn-loving-Womyn. Get modern. But I always liked the word lesbian, the tang of danger and desire. Fourteen years old in the girls' locker room after gym, she cornered me. I didn't even know her name. "I hear you're a lezzbian is that right are you a lezzzbian?" Drawling it out soft and menacing. I didn't know if she was the answer to my prayers or the start of four years of high school queer-baiting hell. Lezzzzbian.

But words change their meanings. Try again: homo + grrrl + sex. Nothing.

Dyke + sex. Dyke is still a groovin' word. Word count: dyke: 28,622; sex: 5,174,850.

> 1) Cyberdyke Personals Your Online Route to Romance.
> Meet the Woman of Your Dreams, Soul Mate, or Just
> Someone to Talk to

That'll work. Click.

> Suzi
> I'm 24, tanned, fit, waiting to hear from You!!!

Somehow I'm less than eager. I keep picturing Suzi as Babe of the Hour with her bland smile and scary fingernails. A melle, Howard would call her, short for nor-melle. What could I possibly say to her?

```
Jam
I'm 42, basement-white, mentally unfit, and not really
Interested!!!
```

Trash. Come on, it's research, bozo. Make up a character who *would* be interested. Suzi is probably entirely groovy, her ad dripping with retro-irony, which I would understand if I were young and with-it. I could pretend to understand, and write a post-apocalyptic-neo-online-bonk-a-thon, but I'd probably get it wrong in some subtle but crucial way and people would laugh.

The next posting is more my speed.

```
Peter
Let me eat your pussy
```

Has a certain directness to it. Peter: could be a butch butch, could be a het boy. So? If you're having virtual sex, does it matter what your virtual girlfriend wears between her legs in the Meatworld? Go on, do it, time's running out.

```
Hey Peter,
You want my pussy? Come and get it.
```

Send. That was less than thrilling. But maybe I'll get a great answer in a day or two, then I'll write back and he/she will write back and I'll have material for a real kewl story by next year. There's 28,617 more dyke sites on my search, but the free half-hour-per-day from my server is up. Close Netscape. Open SwordQuest.

Up in the mountains are giant white cave bears with big claws and many teeth. I develop a new fighting strategy: at the first sign of trouble, RiverRat runs in the opposite direction so as to avoid getting in Els's way and being dusted every other second. There are many bears and also snow ghasts and evil mountain trolls. RiverRat gets good at running. Els's short sword works better on orcs. Swish! `Bear claws Els: 12 points damage. Danger, danger.` They need to find a wizard soon.

----------

```
from: Junior
to: ThisIsCrazy
subject: hello
Is anyone there? Please please please be there.
```

```
from: Junior
to: ThisIsCrazy
re: hello
Damn.
```

```
from: Junior
to: ThisIsCrazy
re: hello
Here I am screaming in the night one more time. AND NO
ONE'S THERE.
```

```
from: Jam
to: Junior
```

re: hello
Wait, I'm here. What's happening?


Junior
Hi Jam. Nothing really. Same old.


Jam
Yeah sure. You're screaming in the night but nothing
much is happening? What is wrong with this picture?


Junior
It *is* nothing. Just my stupid trivial life that I'm
too stupid to handle. Take me out and shoot me.


Jam
Junior! *Tell* me in words I can understand what the
hell is going on.


Junior
The usual. Can't sleep. Kicking myself around for every
dumb thing I did/said/thought today. You know.


Jam
Unfortunately I do. I'll tell you my fuck-ups if you
tell me yours.


Junior
I had an immense and boring day of fuck-ups. You really
don't want to know.

Jam

Bet mine was more boring.


Junior

Bet mine was more fucked-up.


Jam

Bet it wasn't.


Junior

Ok, what's the prize for the worst?


Jam

Hmm, I'm not sure. Better be something real good.


Junior

A tinfoil crown — you can snail it to me.


Jam

I don't snail. And what makes you think you'll win?


Junior

Well, to put it bluntly, what can someone who never
leaves her house do that's all that horrifying? As
compared to someone who roams the streets by day and
night looking for trouble.


Jam

Doing nothing has its own discreet horror. You don't

think I can get a lot of self-abuse out of the fact
that I played computer games for 12 hours today while
I was supposed to be writing gems of lesbian literature?
You wouldn't believe how many trolls I killed. They
make this gross sound when they die — eaaughh,
blat!

Junior
Eaaughh, blat for 12 hours? That *is* bad.

Jam
So what did you do?

Junior
I had a beer for breakfast. A warm beer. It kind of
wrecked my whole day.

Jam
Eaaughh, blat. What else?

Junior
After my beer I was feeling sorry for myself and I
called up Jonathan but he's working nights now and so I
woke him up and he was really grumpy.

Jam
So? If the worst thing that happens in his life
is someone calls and disturbs his sleep, he's doing
fine.

Junior

Spoken like a woman who's never worked night-shift. But
the next one's bad. I went down to the drop-in centre
and got in a fight about shock treatment with this old
guy. He was saying how great it was and how it had
really helped him. He had this voice, this voice you get
to recognize. I told him, "Man, they have fucked up your
brain. I can hear the damage when you talk." And he just
looked at me and said, "I've had a hundred shock
treatments. I have to believe it was for something." I
felt so fucking bad. What am I doing, rubbing this guy's
face in it just to make my point.

Jam

Yeah. But listening to someone say shock is good is not
the easiest thing. It's what your parents said when they
signed the consent forms.

Junior

But he's not my parents, so I should smarten up already.
And there's more. After I trashed that old guy I had an
appointment with my legal aid lawyer. I ended up yelling
at him and he threw me out of his office.

Jam

Junior Junior Junior you need that lawyer.

Junior

Yeah, I'm an asshole. So do I get the crown?

**Jam**
You can wear it to court.
So what are you going to do now?

**Junior**
I dunno. Get a new lawyer? Or maybe a personality
transplant. Maybe Chris will give me one of her spares.
So how's your friend Roz? Is she still ok?

**Jam**
Yeah. Look Junior, I hate to do this to you but I'm
falling asleep at the keyboard, and I have to be fresh
for my 4:30 wake-up call.

**Junior**
Ah you traitorous bitch, how can you do this to me. It's
not even 1:00 in Vancouver.

**Jam**
Don't call me a bitch you cocksucking faggot.

**Junior**
<grin> Cocksucking. Now there's an idea.

----------

June becomes July, hot days and bright evenings, sunset at eight-
thirty. I keep the curtains drawn because the long daylight glares on
my computer screen.

D'isMay is working on her thesis, no time for anything but a few random grumbles. Terry and Gina are going to present their concerns at the next Coalition board meeting. Sarah is in Kansas City meeting with local consumer groups about the Kassebaum Amendment. She's got all the Paradise folks working on letters to their senator, Kassebaum herself it turns out. George says he has to agree with Sarah on this one and posts the e-addresses of the entire U.S. Senate. Parnell says hallelujah it's a miracle and George says shut up Parnell you're not the only one with principles. Junior says Jonathan *was* mad about being woken up, thinks Junior is too demanding, wants to cool it. I should write back to him but I don't have the energy. Lucy thinks I need more tests: gluten intolerance, zinc deficiency.

        from: Jam
        to: Lucy
        re: ask your doctor
        I know I should and I know I won't. My doctor doesn't
        believe in food allergies and trace minerals. To get
        those tests I'd have to argue with her, and she'd keep
        telling me what current scientific research shows — why
        bother? It would just make me feel stupid, which I can
        do in the comfort of my own home. Thanks though.

        from: Lucy
        to: Jam
        re: ask your doctor
        How is your doctor ever going to learn anything if you
        aren't willing to educate her? Even without tests, there

are basic supplements that you should be taking. *I'll*
look them up and send you the info. You won't have to do
anything but go to a health food store. Or you could get
a friend to pick them up for you.

   Did you put your iron pills next to your toothbrush
like I told you? Do it now.


What does she think, I'm going to phone Cynthia and say, "Hey, I
know I haven't returned your last three calls, but could you drop by
Le Soleil and pick up some St. John's Wort for me?
   Fruitbat is in the library, or was this morning.


from: Fruitbat
to: ThisIsCrazy
subject: involuntary outpatient
Thanks for all the drug info, Joe. One little problem
though: my doctor is not going to help me withdraw from
Thorazine. I'm on involuntary outpatient commitment — it
was a condition for getting out of the State Hospital. I
have to live in the psych home, take my pills and see a
shrink once a week. For the next six months. Or I'm back
in the bin.

   Six months is not very long if you're living on the
beach in California, but here the days drag along with
nothing to do except smoke cigarettes and get into stupid
arguments. I'm broke and surly. The boarding home gets
our welfare cheques and doles out a little spending money
once a week. If I'm careful, there's just about enough to

```
keep me in tobacco and bus fare downtown. I like the
library, I like talking to you guys, but I miss my life.
P.S. Good luck with Kassebaum.
```

Even I know what "involuntary outpatient commitment" is. It's what the Kassebaum Amendment is all about: forcing people to take drugs even when they're not in the nuthouse. It's not that big here—it's a U.S. thing, but like alot of U.S. things, it tends to trickle up. Most states have outpatient commitment, though not all of them use it much. But if the Kassebaum Amendment goes through, they'll all be on the band wagon. The Kassebaum will take money away from community outreach programs and give it to states that use outpatient commitment on homeless people.

Charlie says the Kassebaum is bad because involuntary treatment should be a last resort and if states get *paid* for forced drugging, it will become a first resort. George says most homeless folks are already suspicious of the system and the threat of forced drugs will drive people away from needed services. Parnell says it turns poverty into a mental illness.

I scroll forward a few hours. Sure enough Parnell is in there, along with the rest of the gang.

```
Parnell
re: involuntary outpatient
Fruitbat — You're on involuntary outpatient commitment
and they're giving you *pills*? You're lucky
(relatively) — most people get a needle in the ass once
a week, something long lasting like Prolixin, to insure
"compliance."
```

Cyber Joe is on an IOC order too — you two should
talk. Of course if the Kassebaum Amendment passes,
you'll have *lots* of company. This whole thing makes me
furious.


Joe Bones
re: involuntary outpatient
Fruitbat — On the one hand, you're under a legal order
to take your meds, and on the other hand you're asking
about withdrawal. What gives? No, don't tell me, I don't
want to know. I'm just going to assume that you (clearly
a law abiding little mental patient) are asking out of
mere curiosity.
   ****Whatever you do, don't cold turkey*****
   If I knew a little more about your current dosage,
etc., I could dig up a great deal of very specific
information about how someone might safely withdraw from
a drug regime very much like yours. Just to satisfy your
curiosity. Of course.


Charlie
re: involuntary outpatient
What are you doing, Bones? YOU ARE NOT A DOCTOR. You
have never even met Fruitbat and know nothing about her
situation. And yet you're advising her to go off her
meds which for all you know are the only thing that keep
her from psychosis. They were right to throw you out of
med school. If Mei Lin had any ethics she'd throw you
off Crazy. But that's probably too much to hope for.

Mei Lin is what's called our list owner, the person who originally set up ThisIsCrazy and makes sure the mail keeps flowing. She's a long-time activist in California with three children, four grandchildren and a history of civil disobedience arrests. I was on Crazy for a month before I realized she had any special kind of position. She never pulls rank except when there's a violation of some agreed-on policy, like not re-posting someone's private mail to the list. We don't have a specific policy against violating outpatient commitment orders, so I'm sure she won't interfere on this one. But she won't let Charlie's dig go without comment either.

> Mei Lin
> re: involuntary outpatient
> Charlie — I don't literally "own" Crazy. We've agreed to
> have an unmoderated list. That means my job is to keep
> the account for the net address, delete subscribers
> whose mail is bounced, and handle any issues that arise
> with the software — not to dictate what can or can't be
> discussed. If list members decide on a different
> structure, I will facilitate that happening.

Parnell won't let it go either.

> Parnell
> re: involuntary outpatient
> Charlie — I didn't hear anyone suggest Fruitbat go off
> her meds. She asked for information, Bones gave it.
> Fruitbat will do what Fruitbat decides to do. And better
> she should know how do it safely.

    Bones — I'd suggest you two continue this discussion
off list.
    P.S. Good luck.

Probably just as well. Though I really want to know what happens.

----------

Click click, down from the mountains. I'm really sick of those bears. Out on the plains, another little house-graphic, maybe a village. Good, we need food. Closer up I can see little orcs running in and out, busy with orcish things. Damn. I'm sick of orcs too.

"It's an adventure," says Els. "There'll be some kind of hidden treasure or important clue."

Click click click. Els and RiverRat sneak up to the back entrance. Yowl yowl: the orcish guards spot them. Blam blam. Blam blam. It takes me three dustings to figure out that Els can stand outside the back door and fight them one at a time, with RiverRat behind her, lobbing Feisty Slaps of Pain. Orc hits Els ten points. Danger. Gulp: Els swallows healing potion blam blam. RiverRat slaps an already wounded orc who falls over eauughh blat, dead orc, then a little choir of computer-voice-angels sings, "Cool!" and RiverRat is Level Two.

Level Two. Wow. Stronger, smarter, way to go RiverRat. "It's about time," says Els, sticking her sword into a large pink orc. Eau-ughh blat. Eventually there are no more orcs and we check the encampment for loot. Food in the kitchen, good. Gold on the corpses. In the middle of the camp is a room with a locked door that Els can't bash her way through. Interesting. Finally finds the key under the orc chief's bed. In the room is a woman wearing a tall pointed cap. It could be a dunce's cap but I'm betting on a Wizard.

"Finally," she says. "Do you have any idea how boring it is to sit around captured by orcs waiting for very slow adventurers to rescue you?"

Summer sun turning the dark curtains in my bedroom to neon fire. What time is it? Morning, 11:30. Guess I fell back to sleep. Which is better, the thick head of sleeping late or the thick head of getting up at 4:00 A.M.? Okay, get up. Kick the sheet onto the floor, lie there. Get up. Swing my feet onto the floor and I'm no longer lying in bed, I'm sitting on the couch. Unpulled-out pull-out beds are good like that. And if you sleep in your clothes you don't have to get dressed in the morning. "Time Saving Strategies" by Janice Johnston. My name once. Changed when I was a teenage hippie, not to Starlight or Windy but to something thank god innocuous enough to live with later. Can you imagine being a middle-aged Sunshine? Though "Jam" is also a bit strange for forty-two. Sounds more like sixteen— rock 'n' roll 1969 *Kick Out the Jams* album of the week, The Motor City Five with John Sinclair later in jail for politics or dope I forget which, right on. A long time ago. You're not supposed to act like sixteen when you're middle aged. It's pitiful. Mutton dressed like lamb. But if you sleep in your clothes you don't have to worry if they're age-appropriate. Slept-in clothes are inappropriate for every age. "Fashion Tips" by What's-Her-Name.

Coffee. Did you know that coffee drinkers are less likely to commit suicide? Yes. Put on the kettle, turn on the computer. Measure out coffee spoons, download mail. Junior had another bad night. There were cops in the hallway of his building. Someone told him they had an open warrant, whatever that is, to search the place at any time on suspicion of whatever. He lives in subsidized housing in Toronto's mental patients' ghetto where things have been tense since the welfare cuts, so it's probably true. I should write to him, something perky about the simple joys of life that persist even through police raids. Later. Open the curtains, stare out the window. Grass. Flowers. Close the curtains. There's nothing to eat in the house. Have another cup.

I've been trying to write a personal post to Fruitbat. I've gotten as far as

```
Hey Fruitbat,
```

After that it falls apart.

```
Can you still go barefoot when even your brain chemistry
is under someone else's control? How do you do it? I
need to know.
```

No. You can't talk like that to people you've just met, even on the crazy-people's list.

```
Hey Fruitbat, sorry to hear about your outpatient
commitment order.
```

Great. Now you sound like one of those drugstore sympathy cards.

```
With Deepest Sympathy
on the Loss of Your Self-Determination:
Words aren't enough to express all that I mean
```

```
When I say I'm so sorry you get force-fed Thorazine.
But it may help at this time,
and bring some ease to you
To know if you were sixty-five
you'd get shock treatment too.
```

Do I need to footnote that or does Fruitbat already know the over-sixty-five shock stats? Stop it, you're getting delirious, eat something. Back to the kitchen, still no food. Put on shoes. I don't sleep in my shoes, I'm okay. Check the mirror. Yes, you're fully clothed, hair unbrushed but good enough for the corner store.

Outside is white and painful till my basement eyes adjust. The mock orange are over, hollyhocks now boldly exposing their sex to the local bees. I like this neighbourhood. The store is half a block away. Mr. and Mrs. Lam. They have a reputation for being unfriendly, but I worked on them for weeks when they first moved here, smiling and asking after the baby (in kindergarten now). They weren't that hard. I used to do stuff like that. We still say hi how are you. They carry my favourite rice crackers, very techno-punk, like eating Styrofoam, and cheap too. I get six packages, stocking up. Bye, they say.

Walk back open the gate unlock the door. Home, cool and black and safe.

----------

```
from: Jam
to: Fruitbat
re: various posts
Hey Fruitbat. Been trying to follow your words of wisdom
```

about situations becoming identities. It's not easy.
That calm certain voice of authority jerks my leash
every time. And I'm still out here in the freeworld. How
on earth do you do it as a guest of the state?

I wish I could send you volumes of hallucination
advice. But I've only had two hallucinations in my
entire life so I don't have much practical experience.
My one tip: Try not to get lost while chasing
hallucinations in the woods. But probably you don't have
major forests in Baltimore. Do you?

It's passable. Humorous yet sincere. Cool yet warm. Dumb yet stupid. Send it already. There, it's gone. Crossing the continent in a few crackling seconds, and then sitting around at Baltimore Freenet for hours until Fruitbat shows up at the library. Course she might decide to spend her bus fare on cigarettes. Life is so uncertain.

Check mail. Junior had another sleepless night. D'isMay suggested he try melatonin and they got into a fight. Junior said she was pushing drugs on him and D'isMay said it's not a drug. When Lucy came on in the eastern standard morning, she said D'isMay was right, melatonin is a natural, non-addictive substance that can help with insomnia. By then Junior was gone. Asleep, hopefully.

Meanwhile, Lucy wants to know if I've noticed any difference from taking all those new supplements. Whoops. I take an iron pill, consider a trip to the health food store. Ten blocks of weekend shoppers. Maybe tomorrow. Then there's Howard being Howard.

from: Paradise/Howard
to: ThisIsCrazy

re: hallucination control

Shut up by a little Thorazine? Wimp voices, Fruitbat.
You can tell them I said so. I've taken enough Haldol to
paralyze an elephant, and my voices never stopped
chatting. So I dropped the drugs and reached a tenuous
truce with the loudmouths within.

    \*\*Voices are not a problem.\*\* The only problem is
people's reaction to them, especially your own. Never
jump out a window because some voice says you can fly.
Just because it's a hallucination doesn't mean it's
smart. When a voice tells me to do something, I just
say, "Buzz off, I'm not your errand boy." Works for me.

    When you have five or six voices talking at once, it
can be very hard to maintain a normal lifestyle. My
solution is to forget the normal lifestyle. Sorry, but
that's how it is. Melles become hysterical when faced
with anything outside their (very limited) experience.
But who cares if people won't sit next to you on the
bus? Who cares if security guards follow you around
whenever you dare set foot in their department stores?
Who cares if the old ones don't want you in their
subsidized housing and the young ones throw stones at
your windows and call you names?

    And that's my advice for today. That'll be 70 bucks.

There's a whole series of hallucination advice posts from the
Paradise. I guess it was the afternoon's entertainment. JJ has a few
words and Sarah a few pages. I never even knew she did hallucinations, she usually writes about cross-disability activism.

Paradise/JJ
re: hallucination control
One of the things I like about the Internet is it's all
in print and I don't get confused by voices. But for
people with visual hallucinations, this would not help.

Paradise/Sarah
re: hallucination control
Hallucinations can be socially difficult. You answer a
question no one asked or you yell at someone who's not
there who just insulted your dog, etc. There are ways to
tell the difference between hallucinations and real
world phenomena, but most of them are also socially
difficult. I have a friend who says, "Kick it. If it
moves it's real, if it doesn't, it's a hallucination."
Good strategy, but you can see the potential for
awkwardness.
    I look for visual cues. If you hear a voice coming
out of nowhere, it probably isn't real (avoid airports).
If someone *is* there, but their lips aren't moving,
they're probably not talking (avoid ventriloquists).
It's not surefire. You're going to make mistakes
sometimes and reveal yourself as a crazyperson. But
despite what Mr. Howard-the-Cynic says, there *are*
people in the world who aren't too obsessively attached
to normality and have a sense of humour about life.

Other threads are unravelling at the same time. Last night's try
melatonin has turned into an argument about whether Prozac is

"natural" because it's made of natural chemicals by natural chemists. The Kassebaum Amendment thread has been renamed Squeegee Amendment in honour of a cabby in Pittsburgh (dead steel town, home of the homeless) who nearly ran down a street corner squeegee kid, yelling "People like you should be locked up!" while Flip cowered in the back of the cab. Hallucination control eventually drifts from its original subject.

> Doug
> re: hallucination control
> Hi Fruitbat! Welcome to ThisIsCrazy. I live in D.C. Want to get together sometime? What's your real name?

If Fruitbat's looking for a boyfriend, she's in luck. But two hours later (evening in the library), it turns out she's not.

> Fruitbat
> Hi Doug
>   Glad to meet you. I'm a lesbian. Do you still want to know my real name?

Interesting.

Jam was nineteen, living on a commune in rural British Columbia, when she heard the piano player in the woods. She was alone in the cabin. Her friends were in town, running errands. She was supposed to be with them, helping, but she had been crying or something so they went without her. She was a very difficult person to live with at this point in her life. She was often crying or screaming or hitting her head against the wall or falling on the floor in a fit. At first Jam's friends had suggestions for how she might improve her behaviour.

"Pull yourself together," they told her. "Don't be self-indulgent. Act like a grown-up. We do." They did. They had bad times too, but they didn't have falling down fits. And if they cried, it was because something really bad happened, not five times a day for no reason, not in the car on the way to town, not when there were guests.

When she first heard the piano player in the woods, Jam thought it was a radio. But it didn't have a radio sound. It had a live sound like someone was practising. Some kind of jazz. Jam was more of a rock 'n' roll gal, but she liked the dissonant crash under the high, sweet melody, and she went outside to see where it was coming from. She walked down the little dirt driveway to the road, but there was no one, no cars even. Usually if there was a car it was someone coming to visit the commune. There was nowhere else to go on that road. There were no other houses where someone might be practising piano, nothing but woods. The music was coming from the woods. Jam followed it.

It was spring, with soft ground and tiny leaves, skinny paths criss-crossing in a network of tunnels through thick salal, with cedar, Douglas fir and maple knitted overhead, on and on, to the Arctic Circle maybe. Jam looked around, but there was no piano. It seemed close though, maybe down that path, over the next rise, past that ridge.

Jam realized it was a hallucination around the same time she realized she was lost. "Damn," she said, waiting for the panic wave. But there was no panic, just a matter-of-fact calm, as if one problem cancelled out the other. Why worry about hallucinating when you're lost in the woods? Why worry about being lost when you're going crazy?

She kept following the piano. It was a direction, the most interesting direction because it had chaotic and lovely music in it. She walked through the spring, young ferns unfolding, last year's leaves turning to earth underfoot, aspens like ghosts in the fading light. Before it was full dark, she reached a road, a paved road, a road to somewhere, and the music stopped. The piano player led me to this road and then left, Jam told herself. I need to be on this road. She started walking, toward wherever the road went, away from her life. I'll just go, she told herself. I'll walk into a new life somewhere, with $7.32 in my pocket and nothing else. Where will I sleep? How will I find a job? Everything will be strange and difficult, but I'll be where I'm supposed to be and I won't be crazy anymore.

Jam walked down the road in the gathering dark, and when she saw headlights she stuck out her thumb. It was an old pickup truck, red, familiar. Her friends coming back from town.

"Hey, Jam! Hop in," they said.

The next morning she looked in the yellow pages under Psychiatry, under Counselling, under Mental Illness.

----------

Cross the Drive down the block up the front steps. I could still do it.

"Hi, Mrs. Cathcart! It's me."

"Jam! Hi!" came a voice from the kitchen. Cynthia. Damn.

Cynthia was never at her mom's house, I could count on it. But there she was, bouncing down the hall with hair a shade of fluorescent orange that I'd never seen before. It *had* been awhile.

"Jam you jerk you never answered my messages how are you?" she said in one breath, grinning and hugging me.

"The windows really need washing," said Mrs. Cathcart, not deigning to leave the kitchen. Oh no. Whatever had been going on, I was in the middle of it now.

"Sorry," I said, hugging Cynthia back, "I think there's something wrong with my answering machine." I disentangled myself and made it to the kitchen, Cynthia on my heels. "Hi, Mrs. Cathcart, how're you doing? The windows, sure, anything else?"

"Oh, the usual," she said, gesturing vaguely toward the universe in general. "It needs a good dusting."

"Okay, sure," I said kneeling at the cupboard below the kitchen sink to gather my tools: bucket, rags, three brands of cleaning chemicals.

"*She* thinks I should go to the real estate awards banquet for my dad being the king of yuppification and driving poor people out of the East End," remarked Cynthia.

"It's an honour," said Mrs. Cathcart between clenched teeth.

"It's a disgrace," said Cynthia.

Cynthia considered me a member of the family and didn't mind airing their dirty laundry in front of me. I had worked there since she was ten and was quite familiar with their dirt. Mrs. Cathcart, however, considered me the cleaning lady.

"Jam isn't interested in your problems. Let her get on with her work."

I shot Cynthia a please-forgive-me look and bolted for the safety of the vacuum cleaner. I could hear their argument continuing above the suction moan. It was the same fight they always had, only the words changed.

I was upstairs scrubbing the bathroom when Cynthia came up and leaned in the doorway. "Why does she expect me to go to the banquet? She knows I don't like his job."

"She's not too crazy about yours either," I pointed out. Cynthia had been working at a phone sex line for the last year—a big improvement from McDonald's, but not in her mother's eyes.

"Why do I let her get to me?"

"Parents always get to you, it's part of the deal." Words of wisdom from the bottom of the toilet bowl.

"Shit," said Cynthia. She picked up a spare rag and wiped the toothpaste splatters off the mirror, examined her face for a second and then started on the sink. "So how are you really?"

"I'm fine."

"You weren't at Sexpertise."

"Yeah, well … I'm working hard on our new show. Plus I still have, umm, whiplash. From the accident." The lies came automatically. What else could I say—I don't know what's wrong with me, I don't know why? Then she'd say, is there anything I can do? and I'd say no, and there we'd be. It was exhausting just thinking about it. There was something shameful, too, about not running around town to all the groovy events. I didn't want Cynthia to think I was—whatever I was.

"How's Roz?"

"Still fine. As far as I know."

"She'd tell you though, wouldn't she? If it was back?"

"Yeah, of course. She'd tell me." I was almost certain she would. Almost. But Roz was hard to figure. She had a reputation as a forthright individual, not to say a crass loudmouth, but like most loudmouths she was full of silences. She was good at cancer jokes, but bad at letting people help her. And I was—whatever I was.

Back from cleaning, download my mail: George, Parnell, Sarah, Mad-Max, Junior. Fruitbat. Ah. An off-list post to me personally, even.

from: Fruitbat
to: Jam
re: various posts
Jam — They jerk my leash too, better believe it. I don't know how I keep my senses about me as a guest of the state. I guess the truth is I don't. That's why I'm kind of desperate to kick the Thorazine. But Bones says I shouldn't start withdrawing till I'm settled in at the psych home, which according to him will be in two or three weeks and according to me will be never.

Parnell has been great. He keeps sending anti-psychiatry book lists, and since the library is my major hangout, it's perfect. And now you ask me for words of wisdom — makes me feel like a grown-up instead of a nutcase. Yeah, I know, delusions of grandeur.

P.S. Yer right. No forests, except for the chewed-up one on these library shelves.

Email is like Nina Simone singing "Baltimore" with that double rhythm lagging by one beat. Or is it jumping ahead? Fruitbat had already come out to ThisIsCrazy by the time she got my note, which I wrote before I knew she was a lez. So when she wrote this new one (an hour and a half ago, according to the time-stamp), she was out and I wasn't, which was backwards as far as I'm concerned.

It's hard to figure out how to reply to something written in an out-of-synch information stream. I ponder my options while reading the rest of my mail. Junior's post was written at the same time as Fruitbat's, but from a different stream, one where all three of us are out. A stream where Fruitbat will no doubt also be swimming by the time she next checks her email, whenever that may be.

```
from: Junior
to: Jam
"Fruit" bat
I shoulda known. The cop-hitting thing was a dead
giveaway.
```

I consider lecturing Junior on his stereotyped assumptions—straight women hit cops too—but first I want to out myself.

```
from: Jam
to: Fruitbat
happy coming-out day
So you're a friend of Dorothy's, as they say. Welcome to
the *very* exclusive Crazy Queer Auxiliary (you just
increased our membership by a whopping 16 percent). I
shouldn't come out for anyone else, but there's two
other dykes, a queer identified bi-boy and a fag.
Probably more of course, but those are the out-on-the-
list ones.
    P.S. I thought Fruitbat *was* your real name. I
pictured your mother in the delivery room: "What a cute
little dyke. I think I'll name her Fruitbat."
```

Ten minutes later I'm still composing my Junior-lecture. If I put half as much energy into writing lezzie-porn as I do into Crazy, we'd have a new show already. Okay okay, just let me check my mail one more time.

from: Fruitbat
to: Jam
re: happy coming-out day
A lesbian. A real lesbian. I haven't talked to a dyke
in, jesus what's it been, five months. Not since Barbara
Anne was released from Baltimore State. Yup, five
months. You think the club at Crazy is exclusive? The
club at my psych home consists of one Bat, alone in a
sea of uncloseted heterosexuals (well, 19 of them, a
small lake at least). Damn. I miss my life.

I abandon my Junior-lecture altogether.

from: Jam
to: Fruitbat
re: happy coming-out day
State-enforced cohabitation with 19 hets? Nasty.
Statistically there should be one more of you. Complain
to your Congressman. Unless you buy the new right-wing
statistics that say we're less than 2 percent. In which
case they should let you go immediately.

I send it and then fret. Maybe I shouldn't make jokes about her situation, which is pretty grim no matter how you look at it. I start an apology.

Sorry if I sounded

But maybe she wasn't offended. Or maybe apologizing will just make it worse. Check mail.

> from: Fruitbat
> to: Jam
> re: happy coming-out day
> So are you like a *lesbian* lesbian, with dyke bars and
> gay pride marches and vicious infighting and all those
> beautiful things I remember so well? Please say you are!
> Talk lesbian to me!

Dump the apology. Talk lesbian.

> from: Jam
> to: Fruitbat
> re: happy coming-out day
> Let's see … "Rainbow flag, Martina Navritolova, k.d.
> lang, Birkenstocks. Are you butch or femme, did you hear
> Betty and June broke up, what do you expect going out
> with a bi, is Whitney really gay?"

Birkenstocks? That's *so* seventies. This whole post is seventies, what if she's twenty-two or something? Start again. What are the groovin' new lesbian clichés?

It's not a good time for someone to be knocking on my door.

Fruitbat has an hour limit on the library computer, and I don't know how long she's already been there. If there's no line-up she can come right back, but if there is, she'll have to wait through everyone else's hour.

But ignoring Roz does not work, this I know.

"Hi, you're looking very sharp, don't you ever change your clothes?" she said, sprawling at my kitchen table looking a bit on the grunge side herself. It was probably a carefully chosen up-to-the-moment outfit from Value Village, high fashion centre of the East End. Her eyes flicked over the new cuts, both shiny pink now, but she didn't say anything. She'd never said anything about my scars, even when I came to a photo shoot with tiny slices all over my legs. Those pictures caused a stir, you'd better believe. The leather girls treated me with new respect.

"I was cleaning. I didn't know you were dropping by or I would have dressed for the occasion. A hat with a little veil, matching heels, what do you think?"

"Natty. So whatcha up to? Did you go to the Avengers' action?"

"Perfect," I said. " 'Did you go to the Avengers' action?' Let me write that down."

Roz followed me into the bedroom where my email to Fruitbat was still open on the screen. I sat down and typed:

    "Did you go to the Avengers' action?"

"What are you doing?" Roz asked reading over my shoulder.

"There's a new woman on this email-thing I do, and I just found out she's a dyke," I said. "It's great."

Roz looked at the message on the screen, looked at me, shook her head.

"She's living in a psychiatric boarding home," I explained. "She misses lesbians. So I'm writing lesbian things." It sounded pretty dumb put like that. You had to have been there, Roz.

"You've become a cyber-social worker. Great."

I didn't know there was a line till she crossed it and I was ready to sock her. "Fuck off," I said with admirable self-restraint. "She's really interesting. She lives in Baltimore."

"Fascinating," Roz said. "A lesbian in Baltimore. I think there's several in Kamloops too."

"Look, I like her. We're getting to be friends, okay? It's fun."

"I just don't understand why people think it's so groovy to sit alone in a little room staring at a little screen *typing* to each other. When you could go to Sappho's and hang out with real live people."

"Okay it's weird. Fine."

"It's stupid. It's like living through your TV set. Another way to be passive and isolated consumers. Post-modern capitalism at its finest."

I told myself Roz was just making another anti-computer speech. It was an interesting political analysis. It was not about me forgetting how to pass as normal. It was not about Fruitbat being the kind of person only social workers are willing to talk to. I still wanted to sock her.

"Guess I'm a victim of post-modern capitalism then. So sad," I said instead.

"I hear there's a new twelve-step group for Internet addicts."

"Do they have a Web page?"

"You're sick," Roz said. It's a joke, I told myself. She doesn't mean it.

"So?" I said. It was a direct quote from a post Lucy had written when

Howard was being nasty and told her to get a life. I had saved it in a special file for stuff I might need to read again, like three times a day.

> So? I tried to have what people call a "life" and I
> couldn't do it unless I was drugged to the gills, and
> even then I landed in the hospital every six months. Now
> I live by myself and talk to my chickens. So? I'm bored
> and irritable and goddamned lonely — but I haven't been
> locked up in seven years. This is all the life I can
> cope with. It's not so bad — with people like you online
> it's really quite lively.

I had never heard anyone talk like that before, shamelessly admit to such social failure. It was back when I first joined Crazy, when I was still trying, when I still dragged my ass to various hip happenings and forced myself to stay the requisite two hours while my skin screamed. After Lucy's post I stopped. *So?*

But explaining all this to Roz seemed impossibly complicated. I went back to the kitchen, put the kettle on.

"Can you tell our studio audience why it is you find words on a screen more attractive than human beings?" Roz said, following me with an imaginary microphone. It's a joke, ha-ha-ha, where's your sense of humour? I eyed the knife in the dish rack. Maybe I'd have a new career as a psycho killer. Ha-ha.

"You're the one that told me to write about net-sex," I said. "That makes you my co-dependant."

"I might as well get something out of it."

"Drop it." The words came out louder than I'd expected.

Roz looked startled. "Sorry," she said, sounding less than

apologetic. I was supposed to say that's okay, smooth things over, but I turned my back and searched the cupboards for tea. Roz settled back at the table, examining the inner workings of my salt shaker.

The kettle whistled. I poured water, gathered mugs, hesitated a second and then sat down across from her.

"Have we finished our fight?" Roz asked.

"Yes." Maybe.

"Do I get to know what it was about?"

"Post-modern capitalism."

"Ah," she said, sipping her tea, "how deep of us."

"Drop it."

"Okay, okay. So how *is* that story?"

"It's coming along." Peter had not yet returned my message. Maybe she/he had some hacker way of figuring out that I was a wash-out. Maybe I had the wrong kind of software.

"Can I see it?" Roz asked.

"It's only a first draft," I said, backtracking fast. "I want to pull it together a bit more." It wasn't exactly a draft yet, more like a collection of unrelated downloads. `Press OK if you are 21 or over. Alligators and beautiful nude women.`

"What about science fiction butt-fucking, can I see that?"

"It's still pretty rough."

Roz didn't like that. I could tell she wanted to yell at me about our deadline, our timetable, our plans, but she restrained herself. She was going to "give me some space" to "work it out." I knew the strategy: it was favoured by butches across the nation when dealing with cranky femmes, despite its low success rate.

"Did you mail that insurance form?" Roz asked as she got up to leave.

"Yeah," I said. "Almost. I put it in an envelope."

"I'll take it," she said. "I'm going right past the mailbox."

Oh yes please thank you thank you. "Sure. Would you mind taking a few others?"

"No problem."

Excellent. My phone bill, my electricity, my SWORDQUEST registration. I hesitated for a second, thinking about the health food store and Lucy's supplements. Nah. Can't do it.

"See ya," Roz said, loitering at the door.

"Bye," I said.

She kept loitering. She doesn't do those obligatory goodbye hugs, one of the many things I've always admired about her. What is it, Roz? My guilty conscience said it was my non-existent story.

"Don't worry, I'll have something finished by next week. I promise."

"Yeah, that's what you said last week. Try it on someone else."

I walked her out to the gate, said goodbye again, she said see ya again, stood there.

"Nice hollyhocks," she said. Was she going to apologize for insulting my computer? What is it, Roz, spit it out.

"I saw my doctor yesterday."

"Oh yeah," I said casually as if my heart wasn't suddenly pounding, as if she hadn't seen the suppressed flinch. Oh christ no.

"I have to get some tests. My regular check-up. Does she or doesn't she—only her oncologist knows for sure."

"Tests? But there's nothing … is there?"

"It's a check-up," Roz said irritably. "Check. Up. As in look-and-see, get it?"

I knew Roz hadn't told me this in hopes that she could spill her innermost fears to me. But she was leaning on the gatepost, still waiting for something. I took a guess: "You want me to come with?"

"If you want to. It's bound to be boring."

You're welcome. "Boring is my specialty."

"Okay. It's in two weeks: Thursday, ten o'clock."

"Two weeks?"

"Sure, waiting around is an important part of the cancer experience, doncha know? Next I wait for the results and then I wait for the next check-up. Or the next mastectomy, chemo, funeral, whatever."

"Naturally," I said. Trying for that light bantering tone she hit so well when referring to her possible death. Wanting to say, *shut up don't talk like that.*

I said bye again. She said see ya. Watched her stroll off, turn, wave the letters at me, turn. Nice hollyhocks. Went back inside determined to write her that stupid story. Nothing. Went back to my Fruitbat note. Nothing.

Swish: cave bear claws Els. Blam blam Els hits cave bear. Els is always getting hit 'cause she's the warrior, plus her short sword means she has to get right up close. 20 points damage. Danger, danger. Wizard casts Major Heal, Els is healed. RiverRat watches in awed silence. The Wizard isn't a very good fighter but she has big spells. She just waves her hands around and things happen. Divine Thud: kapow! Death Arrows: thunk thunk. Major Heal: ahhhhhh. RiverRat is in luck. Click here to transfer Level Two spell knowledge. Click. The Wizard teaches RiverRat Flame Cloud, Minor Heal and Ice Bolt, which are all that a Level Two mage can handle. There isn't much you can do to mess up Minor Heal except to accidentally heal your enemy, which is nothing compared to how Divine Thud can go wrong.

RiverRat is secretly in love with the Wizard despite the goofy hat. They practise spells while Els goes hunting. The only stuff to eat in the mountains is stuff that fights back, so hunting is tough. But Els is a really good fighter despite her puny sword. Maybe the Wizard has a crush on Els because she's so mighty. Or maybe she likes RiverRat. Or maybe her mind is on higher things. "Pay attention, or you'll never make a proper Bolt!"

----------

Lie in bed thinking I might sleep, but watching the dawn instead. Basement dawn, a slow greying of the window over my desk. Little grey square like the square of the computer screen. Finally I give it up. Kitchen, coffee. Card pinned to the wall tells me to see my doctor today at four. A long day away. A whole different landscape. Must be eight o'clock already in Baltimore. Dear Fruitbat, I hate morning. It's a symptom, I know, I read it in a pamphlet.

```
from: Fruitbat
to: Jam
re: happy coming-out day
Day after coming-out day and all four people you
mentioned (or four different ones, what do I know?)
wrote to say hi. Virtual Heaven. I floated back to the
house and bumped smack into stone cold reality: one of
my roommates listening to a call-in Christian radio show
about hellfire and teen pregnancy. There's three of us
```

in one little room and we try to give each other a lot
of slack, so I go out to the living room where ten guys
are hanging out watching ER. Most of them are nice
enough but they just sit there pretending nothing's
happening while Jerkface Lou follows me around the room
telling me how much he likes my tits and what he wants
to do with them. Back to my room where the radio is now
discussing whether Democrats go to heaven. Probably not
is the consensus. I lie on my bed repeating to myself,
"Martina Navritolova, k.d. lang, did you go to the
Avengers' action … "

I should work. Abandon yesterday's eighty-six downloaded messages
and concentrate on science fiction butt-fucking.

Betty woke slowly, the glow of the flying saucer mimicking dawn
outside her window.

And? And? I can't write this. Yes you can. No I can't. In those cre-
ative writing classes I've never taken, they tell you to write what you
know. And I have no experience with alien lesbian abduction.
    Okay, what *do* you know?

Sometimes I was still cleaning when Mrs. Stella got home from
work.
    "Christ what a day," Mrs. Stella would say, flinging herself
into the big armchair and unstrapping her wooden leg. It really
was made of wood, with plastic and metal bits, a padded leather
top and Velcro straps that went around her knee. "Fix me a

drink, would you sweetie?" I'd bring a glass with whiskey and ice and Mrs. Stella would sip, sigh. "Ahh that's beautiful."

Mrs. Stella was a secretary at the fire department, thirty years now, good union job. She had a string of retired fireman boyfriends, greying and pot-bellied, shyly polite to the cleaning lady. I couldn't remember their names or which was which, but I knew a lot about them in the way that cleaners do. One of them was a four-condoms-a-night guy. Wow, I'd think, emptying the trash, straightening the tangle of sheets. Sometimes the house had the frantic signs of a late-for-work departure with no time for propriety. I would find the half-finished drinks on the coffee table, a skirt abandoned on the kitchen floor and blouse, shoes, pantyhose (one leg knotted off short) scattered around the big armchair. I'd check: yup, four condoms, what a guy. Mrs. Stella wore black lacy underwear (discarded in the doorway or dangling from the desk light), very similar to the underwear I wore.

Then what? Then I clean the fridge. Somehow I don't think they'll accept that for the next dyke sex show. Try again. Think wet cunts, heavy breathing. My tongue caressed her open flower. Explicit sex is hard to write because the physical act itself is so repetitive. You can get pretty silly trying to come up with a brand new way to say, "I moved my hand in and out of her hole for about fifteen minutes and then she came." You *can* just say it like that, unornamented, it's beautifully detached. But even cynicism can degenerate into cliché after awhile. And as for trying to describe rapturous ecstasy, forget it.

Check the time. Eleven. How can it be only eleven? Am I really going to sit here not writing for another five hours and then go see my doctor? No.

```
from: Jam
to: Fruitbat
re: happy coming-out day
It occurs to me that a seething metropolis like Baltimore
must have bars and various other sites of dykedom where
you could talk fluent lesbian, even on an outpatient
commitment order. But what do I know — maybe you have a
rare form of agoraphobia that only lets you go to the
library. Me, I live in the low-rent end of one of
Vancouver's main dykesites. Just walking down the Drive,
a dozen friendly faces say hi. No wonder I never go out.
    You know there's something wrong with you when the
excellent things of life seem like too much work. I talk
to my computer more than I talk to anyone in the
Meatworld (as Howard calls it). My friend thinks it's
trendoidism, my doctor thinks it's genetic, I think I'm
sick of it.
```

As soon as I send it, I wish I hadn't. It's better to keep these golden moments of self-pity to yourself. My break is over. Okay, think sex story.

Mrs. Stella wore black lacy underwear

Go to the kitchen. What was I looking for? I forget. Go back to the bedroom. Oh yeah, tea. I wanted tea. Go back to the kitchen put on the kettle. Back to the bedroom.

Betty woke slowly

I can't stand it. Water boiling. Teapot, tea. Only three bags left, another trip to the corner store. Later.

The glow of the flying saucer

Check mail.

from: Fruitbat
to: Jam
exile on State Street
Sure, I know the dykesites. But that life threw me out.
Or rather she threw me out. The girlfriend. Do you
really want to hear this?

Judy. We lived together for a year, very swoony. And
then I started hearing voices again. She knew about the
last time and was very understanding and lib. But hey,
that was the deep past way before I even met her, and
this was right now in her life. I was telling myself,
"Ok you've been through this before, you can handle it,
be calm and careful," my mantra from before, "calm and
careful," say it over and over, breathe deep, because
panicking is the worst thing.

But Judy panicked. She tried to hang in there for a
couple of months, but you could see the lunatic mass
murderer movie re-runs playing behind her eyes. I ended
up going to the outpatient clinic at State and taking
their drugs (Haldol that time) just to try and keep the
girl. The shrinks thought I was doing real well since I
was slowed down to a crawl, but Judy thought I was going

down fast, not being used to that neuroleptic look. My
boss was not too impressed either; he dumped me. Then
Judy dumped me. Then it turned out all our friends were
actually her friends. Then it turned out our apartment
was her apartment and I was sleeping in the park. After
my backpack got ripped off, I simplified my wardrobe to
boy-drag and girl-drag — girls being slightly better at
panhandling and boys being slightly better at not
getting raped. I was real messed up about Judy and life
in general, taking the Haldol in an erratic kind of way
that Bones tells me was bad bad bad, and I got careless
and you know the rest of it.

    I guess the moral of the story is, don't tell your
girlfriend. But I can't live like that. And you? Is the
"friend" in "my friend thinks it's trendoidism" a
euphemistic lover and do you tell her ... what do you
tell her?

What is she asking? If we were here in the same room, the subtle
shifts and pauses would tell me if she was politely offering me my
share of airtime or deeply interested in my thoughts on the subject—
or checking out the possibilities. "I'm single, are you?" Email has the
most inexpressive typeface. Flattened affect, as they say in shrink-
world. Schizo-affective type.

    Jam
    re exile on State Street
    The friend is an ex-lover from prehistory. I sometimes
    call her my partner just to confuse people. We work

together. Ah god, the story of me and Roz, the story of
my art career, the story of my life and my last
girlfriend. She wasn't really a girlfriend. I don't know
what she was, but she's gone now.

"I don't know, that looks like real work to me." That was Alex, who
later became Jam's ex-whatever-she-was.

Good line.

Jam kept her head down, hid her smile. Trudi laughed, ha-ha-ha
you're such a card, Alex. There was something in that laugh, something in Alex's remark that smelled of old resentments papered over
with politeness. Jam risked a glance. Alex was watching her, ready to
share a smirk. Trudi was fussing with her briefcase, anxious to leave.
Ex-lovers. She gave Alex the smirk. Trudi finished fussing and off
they went, lunch at the new Italian place. Run by Anglos from
Toronto. Jam kept scrubbing—those black scuff marks a certain kind
of boot heel leaves. They do come off eventually.

Jam was upstairs making Trudi and Allison's big double bed when
she heard the front door open, then close. Then silence. Trudi would
have called out, "Hi Jam, it's me!" Allison wouldn't be home in the
middle of the day. Footsteps on the stairs. Jam had often wondered
what she'd do if a daring daylight burglar broke in while she was
working. "Hi, I'm the cleaner. Go ahead and help yourself, just don't
make a mess, okay?" But it was probably Trudi. She went out into
the hall to check.

Alex.

She stood at the top of the stairs. No "Hi there, I forgot my

jacket," no nothing. Just looking at Jam. Jam was wearing her
Miami Beach T-shirt and dirty jeans with a dustrag tucked into the
back pocket. She felt momentarily awkward, then toughened up.
Alex was wearing something tweedy with subtle leather, looking like
a butch university professor, which she was.

Alex let the silence stretch out a bit longer, then said, "You're still
here."

Jam checked her watch. "Two more hours."

"Good."

Silence again. Jam let a slow smile build. Alex came a step closer,
another step. Her hand on Jam's cheek, Jam waiting, letting it build
then Alex's mouth on hers, soft lips for a long second then hard
tongue. They stood in the doorway, bodies pressed close, hands everywhere. When the moaning started, Alex led them into the bedroom.

In general, Jam preferred the ambiguity of hallways. But this time it
was *supposed* to be in the bedroom, on the half-made bed. Trudi's
bed. It was all about Trudi. Alex wanted to fuck Trudi's cleaning lady.

Jam had never been fucked as someone's cleaning lady before.
Mostly she got fucked as a semi-famous artist. After two decades of
cleaning houses it was about time.

There are many reasons to fuck a cleaning lady: her skill, her
strength, her beauty. From Alex it was an insult. But the insult was
aimed at Trudi. Jam was incidental, nothing, a servant. It was kind of
a turn-on to be so invisible. Besides, Jam had her own story. I fucked
your ex-lover in your bed. Your university professor ex-lover. She
tangled her hands in Alex's sixty-dollar haircut, pulled her head
down, bit her mouth. Unbuttoned the tweed thing, the soft leather.
Pushed into Alex's cunt slow and sweet, pulled out fast and insolent.
Alex liked that. Grabbed Jam's breasts with mean hands, bit her

nipples to the edge of pain. Nasty. Someone scratched marks down someone's back. Someone said give it to me bitch come on. They struggled on Trudi's bed, did things to each other's bodies until first one and then the other came in great sobbing waves. Then Alex got dressed and left.

All in all, it was a pleasant change from being fucked as a semi-famous lesbian sex-artist by people who didn't even know how invisible she was. Jam hurried through the rest of her cleaning. Downstairs again, getting her cheque from the kitchen table, Jam noticed new heel marks on the floor.

Alex's boots.

----------

I pack it in at 3:00 P.M. Wrote nothing but the non-story about Mrs. Stella and a whole lot of email. It's early for the doctor even if I walk slow, but I can stop at the health food store with my print-out of Lucy's supplements and then at least I will have accomplished something. Check my look in the bathroom mirror. Not good. Hair getting matted at the back. Which is worse, to look like a crazy person or to look like a white girl trying to do dreads? I run my fingers through it, trash the hairball. Braid it. That'll do for another week. What next? My Miami Beach T-shirt, hmm, not good. Short sleeves, plus I've worn it day and night for two weeks and it's probably getting grotty. Sniff. Yes. But it's my favourite shirt. Keep the shirt you're fine, go.

The health food store was dark and cool, smelled like wilted vegetables. There were too many people; I wished I'd worn something more protective. I found most of Lucy's list in bottles near the front, cruised around looking for the last few. The cooler had fresh wheatgrass juice, good for cancer according to Lucy. I picked one up, read the ingredients: 100 percent pure. Roz would never. I put it in my basket anyway. Then there was a strange cosmetics counter with no Maybelline but plenty of crumbly brown lumps wrapped in tissue paper. Organic Deodorant, one label said. The very thing. I added a lump to my bottles and took it to the counter. Health food stores hadn't changed much since the days of my youth. Many of the customers looked like eerie replicas of me and my friends at nineteen, but the check-out girl wore a tattered undershirt with Fuck Authority written across the chest in ball-point pen, a shaved head showing off her scalp tattoos and assorted piercings. She lingered putting my bottles in a bag and then said all in a rush, "I really like your scars, where did you get them done?"

"I did them myself," I said, startled.

"Wow. How do you get some red and some silver?"

Oh child. "The red ones are just newer. They'll go silver after awhile."

"So like this one will go silver too?" she asked, showing a tiny snake-shaped burn on the soft skin of her forearm.

"Sure. Four months. Six. Depends on how fast you heal."

"So did yours hurt?" she asked.

"Yeah a lot," I lied. Don't try this at home. Besides, they *would* have hurt if I wasn't in a state when I did them. Which I wasn't about to explain. Though she might have understood perfectly. It was hard to tell.

My doctor still thought Prozac was a good idea.

"I can't afford it," I said.

"I have enough free samples for a month's trial," she said.

"I don't want it," I said.

"Fine," she said. "How about a psychiatrist? They're free."

----------

My new rich-faggot cleaning job was in Strathcona, a half-gentrified area squeezed between industry and skid row. I walked factory streets most of the way, then past old houses, new gardens, green and lovely with odd little parks at every turn. Young lawyers with good taste admired their renos, while their neighbours slept in the parks under newspaper blankets. Men with shopping carts mumbled to themselves. I was invisible.

The condo was all angles and skylights. I wished I lived there, except I wouldn't know how. Stephen was a nice enough guy, showed me around, didn't wrinkle his nose at my outfit or stare at my scars, gave me a key and left. He was fifteen years younger than me and his suit probably cost more than I made in a month. So what? Lighten up, I told myself. He's rich, you're not, big deal, get to work.

The condo was neither a stereotype towels-on-the-floor-guy place or a stereotype tidy-fag place. Stainless steel stove, leather couch, fireplace. Nice. The best thing about it was the fluffy dust behind doors and under furniture like a layer of cloud. Cumulous dust. I couldn't figure out what made the dust go like that—mine was flat and ugly with hairs and sand and paper clips mixed in. I'd never been jealous of someone's dust before.

It was a three-hour job, plenty of time for all the extras. Gave his fridge a fast wipe, empty except for some dead lettuce and an end of smoked salmon starting to curl at the edges. Guess you eat out a lot, don't you, Stephen? In the bathroom, two bottles of prescription tranks: Valium and Ativan, my my. Emptying the waste basket, more secrets: torn paper, six pages with *Dear Bruce* typed at the top and nothing else. Stephen, Stephen, if you ask your cleaner to sort your recycling, she's going to see these things. Vacuuming the closet floor, a bedpan behind a pile of shoe boxes. Don't be fooled by the suit, this boy has secrets big time. Left him a note: I like your dust.

Back home, walk to the kitchen. Walk to the bedroom. Walk to the kitchen, Walk to the bedroom. Go to bed. It's only five o'clock. Who cares.

----------

Get out of bed, turn on the modem. Transferring new messages. Brush my teeth watching the overnight mail come in. Seventy-five messages: Junior, D'isMay, Junior, D'isMay, Junior, D'isMay for half the night. Then Terry and more D'isMay, and then Mei Lin, Howard, Parnell, Charlie, Fruitbat, Mei Lin all on the same subject line: re: sick and tired. Must have been a good fight. Meanwhile my mouth is full of toothpaste bubbles. Go spit. I have four health food store bottles plus the iron pills parked on the bathroom counter beside the toothbrush holder—the Lucy-technique for remembering supplements. Which works as long as you're still habituated to brushing your teeth in the morning. Which I am. Still. Gulp down pills with a swig of wheatgrass juice. Okay, cure me.

Too early to wade through the whole night so I flip to Fruitbat.

from: Fruitbat
to: ThisIsCrazy

```
re: sick and tired
What's going on? Has anyone heard from Junior?
```

Huh?

```
Mei Lin
I've been trying to phone him but there's no answer.
I'll keep trying and let you know.
```

Suddenly my heart is slamming against my ribs. Flip back to the
start: 3:00 A.M. Toronto time.

```
Junior
Sick and tired of the Anti-Poverty Action Group, of the
drop-in centre, of snot-faced legal aid lawyers in suits,
of the cops outside my door, of my life. Is anyone awake?
```

Which tells me nothing. Go to Junior's last post: 3:50 Toronto time.

```
Junior
Why are you phoning Terry?
```

Which tells me nothing. Calm down. Go back to the beginning and
see what it's about. It's probably nothing. I'm sure it's nothing.
Junior's having a bad night, so what else is new? Mei Lin trying to
phone him from California, that's what. Calm down.

```
Junior
I can hear them out in the hallway. Fuck. I can't live
```

like this. Is everyone asleep out there?

D'isMay
Ah, it's the Queen of the Night, with her famous
insomnia aria. "Behold Me, I Am Broken Hearted!" No,
we're not all asleep, some of us are at school trying to
get some work done.

Junior
If you're trying to work, what are you doing on Crazy?
I guess you just had to take a break for a little
homophobic name calling. Fuck off.

D'isMay
Don't get your ass in a knot. Queen is a term of
endearment.

Junior
Not from you. I never gave you permission to call me that.

D'isMay
I'm sorry, I'll never do it again. I'll address you with
terms of deepest respect, like you do when you call me a
liberal sell-out.

Junior
I don't need this. It's the middle of the night, I'm
freaking out, there's a fucking cop outside my door and
the only person online hands me a load of shit. Great.

D'isMay
Is there really a cop?

Junior
Yes there's really a cop. I heard him walk down the
hall, then he stopped in front of my door. Then he
walked away. Then he came back. I have no idea what he's
doing. They have a fucking open warrant. They can do
anything.

D'isMay
Come on, Junior, it's probably someone home late
from the bar, too drunk to remember their apartment
number.

Junior
It's a cop.

D'isMay
Go check.

Junior
Ok I will …

D'isMay
Junior, are you still there?

Junior
It's a cop.

D'isMay
What did you do?

Junior
Shut the door in his face.

D'isMay
Junior! You don't shut doors in cops' faces. You say,
excuse me sir what seems to be the problem?

Junior
Maybe you do, but I don't.

D'isMay
You bet your white ass I do and you should too.

Junior
He's knocking on the door.

D'isMay
What a surprise. You'd better go answer it.

Junior
No way. I'm tired of the police strutting around in
my building, I'm tired of being scared, I'm tired of
everything. I'm going to get a kitchen knife and
answer the door with that in my hand and he'll
shoot me and this whole sorry mess will
be over.

```
D'isMay
Stop it. This is not a game. If it's really a cop
and you wave a knife at him, he *will* shoot. You
ever been shot? Chris at the Paradise still
can't walk right from the time a cop
shot her.
```

At this point I check my mail again. Mei Lin says still no answer. Parnell says he's going to call the Toronto police. Whatever happened has already happened. Hours ago.

```
Junior
So add me to your list. Who cares?

D'isMay
I care. Lots of people care.

Junior
You do not care. You hate me.

D'isMay
I don't hate you, I just don't get along with you.

Junior
Well I don't get along with me either and I'm sick of
it.

D'isMay
Look, Junior, go to the door. Without the knife. If he's
```

there, talk to him. Politely. You gotta cool out this
situation.

Junior
No way. You think I'm just some baby fag from the
suburbs who you can make cute jokes about and never take
seriously. I've had it.

D'isMay
Ok, ok, I'm sorry. Just stay here and talk to me. Is
there something I can do?

Junior
I'd like $10,000 and world peace. And a new government.

D'isMay
Let me phone Terry.

Junior
Terry? In Australia?

D'isMay
Yeah, he should be at the Coalition office. I can get
the number from directory assistance. Hold on, I'll be
right back.

Junior
Why are you phoning Terry?

D'isMay
Hi, I'm back, are you still there? Terry should be
online any second. Because he's your friend, dummy.

Terry
Hey man, what's up? May says you got cops at your door
and a whole lot of other shit. Talk to me.

D'isMay
Junior, are you there?

Terry
What's going on, kid? If you're not up to talking, just
send a few words so I know you're ok.

D'isMay
Where are you? If you're trying to scare me, it's
working real well.

Terry
Fuck this, I'm going to phone him. The Coalition can
pay, I don't care. Do you know his last name?

D'isMay
No. Do you know his first name?

Terry
No. Junior get the fuck back online.

Terry phones Mei Lin who phones Howard who burgles his way in to the Paradise (5:00 A.M., Kansas City) and finds Junior's name (Daniel Zilkowski) and phone number in some devious hacker way. Then Mei Lin phones Junior, etc., etc. for the rest of the morning. I'm checking my mail every thirty seconds now. No new mail. No new mail. In between I write notes to Junior and transfer them to the trash.

```
Fuck you, what are you doing how could you be so stupid?
Do I treat you like a baby fag from the suburbs and not
take you seriously? I suppose I do sometimes. Please
write and say you opened the door and there was no cop,
so you decided to go out for a walk. Or you fell asleep.
Or anything. So we can all be mad at you and not take
you seriously.
```

Finally Parnell comes back. Couldn't get any info from the cops so he started phoning Toronto psych hospitals asking to speak to his brother, Daniel Zilkowski, who'd been admitted last night. After a few "there's nothing in our records," he reached the Petersen Institute where the receptionist said Mr. Zilkowski was not allowed phone calls yet, maybe in a few days.

It's strange to feel relief at the news that Junior is locked up in the same institution where he'd spent too many of his teenage years. He's probably screaming his head off in four-point restraints, but he's alive.

----------

Dr. Lewis found a psychiatrist with room on his dance card for me.

"I sent him a letter and your files and he's agreed to see you. He's quite good," she said.

I wanted to see the letter, know what she said about me, but I couldn't ask. I also wanted to know how she knew that he was quite good, and what it meant, but ditto.

"I tried to find someone in private practice, but they all have long waiting lists," she continued. "Dr. Sullivan works out of the General Hospital Outpatient Clinic; you can have an appointment in three weeks. But the thing is—it's a teaching hospital, so there'll be a resident present for your sessions. Is that all right for you?"

"I guess. Sure. I could give it a try," my mouth said, as my brain spun through all the pros and cons. Pro: I'd always gone to outpatient clinics, didn't know what private practice was like. The thought of seeing a shrink off in some isolated office without hordes of other crazy people close at hand was a little daunting. Did they make you lie on couches? Con: Big shrink plus little shrink equals two against one. And being on a long waiting list had a definite appeal. Maybe I'd be cured by the time my appointment came up. But on the other hand, maybe this shrink would actually help me feel better. Pro and con kept on slugging it out, but my mouth had already done its thing and my doctor was writing down the date and time for me. The General Hospital: I never liked that place.

Jam spent her twentieth year living in the hippie commune and hitchhiking a hundred miles to Vancouver once a week to see a psychologist at the General Hospital Outpatient Clinic. It was the only free mental illness thing she could find, and anyway she was used to hitchhiking.

The psychologist Jam was assigned to was young and handsome and very straight. In those days Jam used the word straight to mean not-a-hippie. She'd never heard of gay lib. It was three years after Stonewall, and she was a closet bisexual with a string of tortured teenage romances behind her. Later, straight meant not-queer except when she was talking with people who worked as prostitutes and then straight meant her.

"Do you think about suicide?" the psychologist asked. John. He wasn't a doctor, so he couldn't be Dr. Andrews, so he went by his first name. "Have you planned how to do it?"

"I think about it, but just as a joke."

"A joke?" he asked.

"You know, like the possibility of suicide is the only thing that makes life bearable. That kind of thing."

He didn't know.

She couldn't explain.

Neither of them understood anything about the other. John thought he was an attractive and successful young man, the obvious object of much transference from his female clients, and Jam thought he was boring. John thought Jam was a disturbed youth with a dead-end life, and Jam thought she was miserable but cool. But because she was going crazy and had come to John for help, John's version ruled.

John said her mental health would improve if she stopped taking illegal drugs and living in a hippie commune and started doing something productive with her life instead.

"Like what?" Jam asked.

"Go to college," he said, because that's what people her age did, where he lived. But Jam hadn't been raised to go to college. She was raised to marry young and be a housewife, which was sort of what she was doing. She baked bread in a wood stove and pumped water to wash the dishes. Unfortunately, she was messing up on the wife part. She kept breaking up with her boyfriends and having miserable one-night stands with women. She knew enough to keep her mouth shut about the women. She knew what happened to kids who got caught out as queer back in high school. Their lives were over.

"What would I do in college?" Jam asked.

"Whatever you're interested in," John said.

Jam pondered that. She was mostly interested in LSD, rock 'n' roll and not being crazy anymore. She didn't see how college would help. John thought she could figure out what she was interested in once she got there. But first she had to learn not to cry and scream and have falling-down fits.

"Find replacement behaviours," he advised. "If you start to feel hysterical, go to your room and scream into a pillow. Or buy some cheap dishes and break them in the basement. Write down what you're feeling. When you're calmer, return to whatever upset you. Soon you'll be able to maintain your calm, knowing that you can release your emotions later, in a safe place."

Jam couldn't afford to break dishes, even cheap ones, but she could afford a razor blade. Cutting her arms was a revelation. The first time, it was the barest scratch. She'd been having a fight with someone in her house and she went up to her room to scream, like John suggested. It gave her a sore throat and not much else. Then she went into the bathroom and took the blade out of the razor that the guys used when they had to get a job or something. Back in her room with the door closed, she stroked the blade across her upper arm. It didn't hurt. A line of blood appeared. She felt dizzy and scared, and then very happy. She washed the blade and put it back. She didn't bother to write down what she was feeling because it was always the same: *hate myself, hate myself*. She didn't return to what had upset her because she didn't want to risk breaking her good mood, so she washed the dishes instead. She was happy all day.

Two days later she borrowed the razor blade again, cut deeper. There was more blood but it still didn't hurt. It started to hurt the next day at about the same time her good mood started to fade. She didn't understand the numbness, the joy. Maybe it was adrenaline or endorphins, her brain flooded with happy chemicals. Maybe it was an emotional release like John had said. It had something to with *hate myself*, but she felt better and that was enough. The next time she was in town, she bought her own razor blade. She knew enough to keep her mouth shut. She wore long-sleeved shirts and told John the replacement behaviour method was working well.

She didn't consider her job until the next week.

Jam's work at the time was two days a week of modelling for art classes at the local community college. Being an art model can be a difficult job, especially for someone who's freaking out. It's a lot like those dreams where you're in school and suddenly discover you have no clothes on. Jam would lose track of herself during long poses and then wake up in one of those dreams. Except she really was sitting naked in the middle of a classroom.

It's also not the best job for slashers, as Jam realized when she arrived at her first class and started to take off her clothes. She had about five little cuts at that point. No one said anything until after the class when three different students asked, "What happened to your arm?" By then she had a good story about picking blackberries.

Anyone who was familiar with blackberry bushes would have known it was a lie, but these were college students.

"I have to get a different job," Jam told John. "If I'm going to college and all." John was pleased to hear she had finally decided to take his advice. He helped her fill out student loan applications and coached her on job-finding. "You can't wear running shoes to an interview," he'd tell her. "Don't put nude modelling on your résumé." She started taking notes in their sessions, bringing her Sally Anne outfits to him for approval. But she hardly ever made it to the interview stage. Mostly they took her application, thanked her and never called back.

"You need to be more friendly," John said. "Smile. Chat to the receptionist."

"What am I supposed to chat about?"

"Anything. Sports, the weather. Regular stuff. And don't stare. Move your eyes around the room. No, not like that—slowly. Lean back a bit. That's good. Now talk."

"Wait, let me write this down."

John thought Jam was the most socially stunted client he had ever worked with, but was hopeful that he could help her adjust. Jam thought straights were weird. Where she came from, small talk revolved around drugs, music and the meaning of life. Still, she tried.

Meanwhile her cuts were getting deeper, and the blackberry story was wearing thin. However, her behaviour was improving. People at the commune were pleased. One of the girls brought her along to a cleaning job in town, showed her the ropes. "The most important thing is to polish the taps. It only takes a second and people are always impressed when their taps shine." Jam put an ad in the local paper:
RELIABLE CLEANING LADY, REASONABLE RATES, EXCELLENT

REFERENCES. She wrote the references herself, they *were* excellent. She got one call, another, another. It wasn't what John had had in mind for her, but it was more respectable than modelling. She wore long-sleeved shirts and always polished the taps.

Jam picked up a brochure from the community college, brought it to John for advice. He suggested art. He thought she was the artistic type because she wore strange dresses. Jam knew it was just what every hippie chick wore, but she signed up for painting because she already knew where the art department was, plus there were no tests.

Later though, when she turned out to be good at painting, she wondered.

----------

Five in the morning, roll over and go back to sleep.

Roll over the other way.

Try not to think about Junior, Roz, outpatient commitment, my past, my shrink appointment.

Pull the covers over my head.

Give up. It's morning. Only six hours till my cleaning job. How shall I entertain myself?

```
from: George
to: ThisIsCrazy
re: Squeegee Amendment
A simple script for anyone who's nervous talking to
government officials:
    Dial 1-800-SEN-ATOR. Press 1 to interrupt
introductory remarks. When asked, enter a ZIP CODE in
```

```
the state of the senator to whom you wish to speak
(a zip code in Kansas, for instance, is 66112). When
asked, choose which of that state's senators by pressing
1 or 2 (Kassebaum is 2). You are then connected to an
answering machine in that senator's office. Leave a
(polite!) one-sentence message about the Squeegee (I
said I was against involuntary services, and for jobs
and homes).
    Do it! It'll take you two minutes.
    P.S. Shut up, Parnell, I *am* against forced
treatment.
```

I could do that. 1-800-SE—nah. I'm a Canadian, they don't care what non-voters think. Parnell ignores the bait, comes back with another telephone good deed for us all.

```
from: Parnell
to: ThisIsCrazy
re: Junior
I tried again this afternoon, but he still doesn't have
phone privileges. It's still good to call if you can
afford it. It lets them know he has a lot of people
around who care about him, which translates into better
treatment.
```

Good idea. It's only 8:00 A.M. in Toronto but psychiatry never sleeps. Scroll back to where Parnell posted the phone number. I need some reinforcements for this call: coffee, open the curtains and let the back yard in. Last February I teased Junior with descriptions of the flowers in my yard, while Toronto was still shovelling snow. Okay, phone.

"Petersen Institute, may I help you?" She sounds just like a receptionist at eight o'clock, already bored and counting the hours.

"I'd like to speak to"—but I can't remember the name. Frantically opening old posts, Mei Lin, Parnell, Howard, hang up. Heart jumping around can't find my breath, room goes dim then too bright colours all wrong walls folding in no air. Panic attack. I recognize it from descriptions on Crazy, you're supposed to breathe slowly and tell yourself it will pass. Okay breathe okay okay.

Then it's over. Fine, you're fine, it was nothing. Flip in Pittsburg sometimes has them for hours. Go to the kitchen. What was I looking for? Oh right, Junior. Back to the bedroom, Mei Lin, Parnell, Howard, then my memory spits out the name. Daniel Zilkowski. Get in bed, pull the phone under the covers.

Dial.

"Petersen Institute, may I help you?"

Hang up.

Let's be systematic about this. Get up. Open Word, new document, save as Petersen Script.

> Hello. I'd like to speak to Daniel Zilkowski. This is his cousin calling from Vancouver. Yes, I'll hold. Yes, thank you. Thank you so much. Thanks anyway. Could you make sure to tell him I called. It's important that he knows his family is with him at this difficult time.

Practise out loud, my voice thin and unconvincing. Again. Better. I'm a thirty-six-year-old white woman living in Vancouver with my husband and two kids. He's a lawyer. I'm a part-time teacher. Special ed.

Voted Liberal in the last election. Sincere. Clueless. Trying to do the family-thing for my poor, messed-up cousin. Dial.

"Petersen Institute, may I help you?"

"I'd like to speak to Daniel Zilkowski. This is his cousin calling from Vancouver."

"One moment please," and she's gone. Yes, I'll hold. Yes, thank you. Seven long-distance minutes with a medley of soft hits from the seventies performed by a string ensemble. Then she's back.

"I'm sorry, he doesn't have phone privileges yet. Try again in a few days."

"Could you make sure to tell him I called? His cousin from Vancouver."

"All right, ma'am."

"Thank you. It's important. That he knows his family is with him. At this difficult time."

"Fine, ma'am."

"Thank you so much. If you could make *sure* he gets this message—"

"All right, ma'am." Click.

Sit there listening to the hiss of long-distance silence, then hang up. That was passable. Like a nervous relative who has never talked to a receptionist at a mental hospital before. She must get that all the time. I wonder if she'll give someone my message. She will or she won't, there's nothing I can do. Close the curtains.

Eventually I go to the kitchen, make more coffee, back to the bedroom, drink it. Back to the kitchen. I could have a new career as a tennis ball. Back to the bedroom.

Open SwordQuest. Oh right, fighting cave bears. Close Sword-Quest.

Open Eudora, more of yesterday's news: Charlie, Chris and Cyber Joe all posted copies of vote-against-the-Squeegee letters to Congress. And then there's Fruitbat. I ponder her post for the sixth or seventh time.

from: Fruitbat
to: Jam
re: life, etc.
Sure I feel bad about what happened to Junior, but he also bugs me. I'm sick of him jumping down D'isMay's throat just because she wants to be an inside agitator instead of a revolutionary. He's so fucking rigid. My way or the highway.

I also disagree with what you said about your life. So what if you don't go to parties and art openings (blech)? So what if you're on the computer all the time? You *like* it. You have a nice place and you can still work enough to pay your rent and buy rice crackers (blech). But what do I know about depression — I've been depressed but never day after day for months. Also, I don't understand why you're not talking to your friend about this stuff. Seems like you two are close.

But then I'm not talking in the Meatworld either. I'm a cranky bitch these days. Withdrawal is taking forever. I'm supposed to pare a tiny edge off each tablet with my pocket knife (very scientific). It's been two days already, when can I pare two edges? Not yet. Ok, Bones, I'll be good. The house is seriously getting to me so I

stay out most of the time. If the library served soup
and had little beds down in the stacks, it would be the
world's most perfect place. From one to four (ten to one
your zone) the computer room is less crowded and I'm
often online. So look me up (Tuesday?) if you feel like
it, and we can have some more or less simultaneous
chatter.

What does it mean when a girl knows what time it is in your zone?
She might have one of those math minds that always knows the numbers. Or?

Did I just get asked on a date?

Tuesday I clean Sam-and-Tina's but I don't have to leave until
noon. I shouldn't log on at ten exactly—too eager. Wait till ten-
thirty, very suave. *Oh yes I did happen to have a moment between
appointments.*

Meanwhile there's today. More coffee. Breakfast. Damn. No food
in the house, and I spent my grocery money on supplements and that
Stephen guy is the only rich faggot I've hooked from the ad in the
*Gay Blade.* Time to change my definition of food. You can't expect
to eat rice crackers and canned chili every day. Rummage in the
freezer. An unlabelled yogurt container full of something yellow.
That'll be dinner. A plastic bag with five curled and frost-furred
pieces of bread. Toast. Perfect. No butter, but hamburger relish will
be nice. Relish is a vegetable.

Back at the computer munching breakfast, I hop onto the Web
and go to the Cyberdyke Personals. I'm going to finish that story
today. Then I can tell Roz and she'll be so pleased that she'll even
explain what her tests are all about.

Suzi is still tanned and fit. Congratulations. Then there's Linda who wants someone in the Liverpool area to do it with her while her husband watches, and Marsha who thinks she might be gay and is looking for a support group in Truro.

Forget it. Trudge down to the Breast Cancer Clearinghouse to see what I can find about this check-up. Download a few likely looking files, close out.

The Breast Cancer Clearinghouse has everything. Lucy sent me there when Roz was first diagnosed. I was impressed, tried to get Roz to look at it with me but after two minutes she got bored, said she could have the same experience with a brochure rack. Roz is not a net-girl, I know. I tried passing on print-outs about nutrition, support groups and the pros and cons of chemo until she told me to fuck off. Then I started reading files with titles like "If the Woman You Love Gets Breast Cancer" for tips on how to not get told to fuck off.

> Be understanding. Love her. Reassure her. Demonstrate
> mutual respect and understanding. Be kind and
> sympathetic.

Kind and sympathetic. That would get me a fuck-off fast.

> Support your partner by accompanying her to her
> radiation therapy appointments. Take her to a wig shop.
> Help pick out some interesting hats.

Or, alternatively, tell her she looks like every other bald dyke on the Drive.

The new files are a mixed bag: diet, exercise, breast reconstruction. Apparently they do that all the time now: scoop the old breast out, leave the skin and fill it with fat from somewhere else. When the surgeon asked Roz about it, she said she wanted cone tits like the hyper-modern queens have.

"After Your Mastectomy" tells me:

> A visit to a new mastectomy patient by a well-trained
> peer support volunteer is welcomed by health
> professionals today. All agree that there is great
> benefit to the patient from seeing an attractively
> dressed, active and well-adjusted woman who says, "I
> have had the same operation."

"Continuing Breast Cancer Care" is not so chipper:

> Doctors often recommend follow-up visits every 3 to 6
> months. Visits may include a complete physical exam,
> blood and urine tests, a mammogram and bone or liver
> scans. These will help the doctor check for the return
> of cancer.

My breasts wince. The return of cancer. Don't say that. I still don't know what to expect at the check-up. I guess I'll just have to sit in some waiting room and wait. I can do that.

Els is at the food store when a travelling sage tells her of a magic sword named Blood Drinker, stolen by thieves and lost to the ages. Oh, I get it: SwordQuest. Seems like a good idea 'cause we only have one fighter, and she has a truly bad sword. Click click to the thieves' guild, poke around looking for clues. But the thieves just want to fight. Ka-pow, Divine Thud, thieves are dust. The Wizard is very cute, especially when she's casting deadly spells. RiverRat follows her around sighing like a fool. Els just wants that sword.

There's a secret room in the Guild Hall with a hidden scroll that tells of a mysterious treasure valley and then bursts into flame like on Mission Impossible. Click click, walk through mountains. I know I've found the right valley because it's full of snakes, long and thick in all shades of smoke and bronze, glistening with muscle. The whole valley is hissing and slithering. Ka-pow, Divine Thud, snakes are slightly slowed. Snake strikes Els, poison 10 points; her icon turns nasty green. Oh no. Wizard casts Cure Poison, Els is cured. Whew.

Snakes strikes Els, Wizard casts Cure Poison. Els is cured. I could do this all day.

----------

8:30 A.M. on Tuesday, two hours till it's time to write Fruitbat. Check mail. The usual overnight gang. Terry is preparing a formal complaint about the executive/asshole. D'isMay says Gina should present it to the board because she won't get mad and blow it. Terry says thanks for the vote of confidence. D'isMay says know thyself, and Gina says she's sure Terry will do fine. Terry says maybe Gina *should* do it and Gina says okay. Then the east coast wakes up, but no Fruitbat. She's being cool, waiting for me to make the next move. Or she's forgotten. Parnell talked to Junior. Says he's doing all right, out of solitary and on a ward with a couple of old friends from last time. Trying to be good, not yell, get out. So far no one's talking shock.

9:00, the midwest is in full swing. Someone at the Paradise wants info on Zoloft, someone in Chicago says it saved their life, someone in England says it nearly killed them.

9:30. Time to start my note.

```
from: Jam
to: Fruitbat
re: life, etc.
Hey Fruitbat, you around?
```

It's kind of short. Sounds anxious, too. Come on, you took small talk lessons, you can do this. The weather. Yes. Open the blind, god it's bright. Close the blind.

```
It's summer outside, blazing on last night's rain, wet
streets steaming. This is a city of flowers, coming in
waves for months now: snow drops, forsythia, cherry
blossoms, clematis, magnolia, honeysuckle, on and on. If
you're going to be depressed, Vancouver is a great city
to go down in.
```

Maybe a bit florid. Depends on what Baltimore is like. People from Saskatchewan don't mind when you talk like that because then they can talk about the big sky and Prairie sunsets. But people in industrial Ontario get huffy and call you names.

```
Of course in the winter it rains all the time.
```

People in Ontario often forgive you if you mention that. As long as you don't say you like the rain or prefer it to freezing your ass for five months out of the year.

```
    I have no idea what Baltimore is like. I know it's in
    Maryland. Does that mean it's hot? Do people have those
    southern US accents? Do *you* have a southern accent, my
    god I didn't think of that, I'll have to start reading
    your email differently.
```

Good enough. Light yet personal. 9:45. Wait another forty-five minutes then send. Fashionably late.

`9:50.`

`Check mail.` George is going to be one of four witnesses talking about the Squeegee at the Senate Labour & Human Resources Committee Hearings on July 27. George? Oh right, he's the director of some enormous mental health consumer group. George. Wow. He'll be the only c/s/x there (of course). And the only formerly homeless person too, no doubt. He wants feedback for his presentation.

`9:58. No new mail.`

10:05. Howard snarking Lucy. Lucy biting back.

10:10. Sarah with three pages of advice for George's testimony. Parnell with five pages. Cyber Joe with eight.

10:11. Okay, mail the goddamn Fruitbat note and do something useful with the rest of your life.

`Send. Check mail.` Fruitbat.

```
from: Fruitbat
to: ThisIsCrazy
re: George at the Squeegee
Congratulations, George! It's good to know *someone*
will be there. How much time will you have? Who else is
speaking? I will definitely put some thought into what I
dislike about outpatient commitment and why homeless
people shouldn't be rounded up and drugged. I'll
probably be able to come up with a reason or two <g>.
```

Writing to the list, the cool bitch. Why why why didn't I wait longer? Okay, I'm not sitting by the phone like some teenager. I'm way too old for this. I should be pursuing my important career. Close Eudora, open Word. Write something brilliant and then go to a cocktail party and name-drop. First line …

Close Word, open Eudora. Check mail. Fruitbat.

```
from: Fruitbat
to: Jam
re: life, etc.
Hey, there you are, from sunny Vancouver to cloudy
Baltimore. Yes, it's hot. Southern accent? Meaning
California? Texas? Georgia? None of the above. I just
have a regular Baltimore accent. And you probably have
one of those cute Canadian accents (grin, duck and run,
as you sophisticated net-types say).
```

Now what? Answer, bozo.

```
from: Jam
to: Fruitbat
re: life, etc.
Yes, my accent is very cute. So how's life in the
library?
```

Send. Regret. I can't believe how dumb that was. Have I ever written two more gooney sentences in my life? Wait an agonizing three minutes, and then her reply arrives.

```
Fruitbat
Life in the library is air conditioned. Other than that
it's pretty slow. How's life in the basement?
```

```
Jam
Life in the basement is very cool. And incredibly
lively. It's only 10:20 and already I've drunk three
cups of coffee, looked out my window and checked my
email twelve times.
```

You can't send that. Start over.

```
Jam
Life in the basement is very cool. And incredibly
lively. It's only 10:20 and already I've had twelve
mainstream publishers offering me book contracts and
five Hollywood stars begging for a part in the movie-
version of my life story. I'm holding out for Margot
Kidder.
```

Better. Which isn't saying much.

> Fruitbat
> Margot Kidder, good choice. Have you ever read _The
> History of Shock Treatment_ by Leonard Roy Frank? I just
> started it.

This conversation is falling apart. I can't think of a thing to say and I haven't read *The History of Shock Treatment*. Come on, come on, you can do this.

> Jam
> I never read it, but I heard him speak once. Are you
> liking the book?

Here I am, discussing literature. John-the-psychologist would be proud of me.

> Fruitbat
> Yeah, it's good. Did you know that the guy who invented
> shock treatment got the inspiration from watching pigs
> being shocked in a slaughterhouse?

> Jam
> No, I didn't know that.

Come on, come on, you can do better than that. We're having a pleasant conversation about shock treatment. This is how people talk, get with the program.

    Jam
    This is a perfectly normal conversation and I can't seem
    to manage it. It's probably a symptom.

No no no. You're not supposed to say things like that. You're supposed to ask about her hobbies and move your eyes around. I can't
do it. Send. You fool, you stupid fool! No new mail, no new mail,
no new mail. She's probably talking to Parnell, I bet *he's* read *The
History of Shock Treatment.* I don't care, people are too much work.
Go put the kettle on. I should eat something. Open the fridge. Close
it again. Food is too much work. Go back and check my mail.

    Fruitbat
    If it's a symptom, the goddamn thing is contagious.

Takes me a minute to work that one out.

    Jam
    Yeah, it's kind of awkward all of a sudden.

    Fruitbat
    You aren't kidding.

    Jam
    So is this a date?

Another bad move, but I send it anyway. I don't care. The kettle is
whistling. I don't care.

Fruitbat
Maybe. I guess so. Awkwardness is one of the big signs
of dating.

Jam
Yeah, I read that somewhere. In a pamphlet, "The Twelve
Warning Signs of Dating."

The kettle is still whistling. Just a minute hold on *shut up*.

Fruitbat
So what can we do about it?

Jam
Be awkward, I guess. I'm real bad at faking it these
days.

Fruitbat
I noticed that.

Jam
You're not so shit-hot either.

Now it's stopped whistling, which probably means the water's all
boiled away, and the kettle's about to melt and set the kitchen on fire.

Fruitbat
True. And I'm trying so hard. But at least you're an

experienced net-dyke. I've never been on an email
date before. I have no idea what you're supposed
to do.

Run to the kitchen no fire *excellent* turn off the stove run back.

Jam
I could make up all sorts of arcane rules and astound
you with my sophistication but the truth is I've never
been on an email date either.

Fruitbat
How can you have an email date anyway? What's the point?
Oh baby, you have such beautiful typing. It doesn't make
sense. How can you be attracted to someone you've never
met?
    And if you were, what would you do about it?

Jam
Hey look, you're the one that asked me on this
date-thing. So *you* tell *me* what the point is.
Was.

Fruitbat
Is. I don't know. The point is maybe it was a dumb idea.
But, ok, I like you.

Jam
Ok, I like you too.

Fruitbat
Ok, now what?


Jam
In my experience of Meatworld dating (which is vast,
it's true) this is the moment when we either die of
embarrassment or start kissing. Do you kiss on the first
date?


Fruitbat
Yes, but I've never kissed on the computer.


Jam
Me neither. I'm trying to imagine kissing you. I don't
know what your lips look like. How do you kiss invisible
lips? You make it up, I guess. We're sitting side by
side on a couch, our awkward first date, and you just
said you like me. So I move closer, put my arms around
you. You don't feel like anyone else, you don't smell
like anyone else. I don't really know you but I want
you. I put my mouth on yours. Your lips are soft.


Fruitbat
Wait a minute. Are you saying you're attracted to me? In
real life.


Jam
I'm saying I'm attracted to you. In real life. And I'm
kissing you. In real life. On the computer.

Fruitbat
Good. I'm attracted to you too. Whoever you are.

----------

The walk to Stephen's seemed longer and trickier today. There was no way around the blocks of lawyers, not enough bag ladies to distract their suspicious glances. Something was shifting. Maybe Cynthia's father had been busy selling houses in the neighbourhood, or maybe it was just me. I walked faster, turned the corner, three more houses, two more houses up the steps key lock close the door behind me. Safe.

"Hi, Stephen," I yelled just in case he wasn't off at work. No answer. Good. Down to business: rags, bucket, vacuum cleaner. Furniture polish, today's special treat. It was the spray-on kind like on TV in the sixties. Clue: Stephen was not a perfect yuppie or he'd have lemon oil with an Italian label.

I was playing sixties TV housewife when someone came out of the bedroom. I jumped, yelled, he jumped, yelled. Oh it's just Stephen, oh it's just the cleaner.

"I didn't know you were here."

"I forgot this was your day."

He was wearing hockey pajamas that could have come from Army & Navy or from a West End men's store where they charge an extra hundred dollars for the ironic detachment. I couldn't tell which, the furniture polish had me confused. Either way, he looked like hell.

"I have a cold," he said. Sure, Stephen. I've used that one myself. I-have-a-cold covers the red eyes and running nose very nicely, but you've been crying.

"It's going around," I said.

"I'll just go back to bed. You could skip the bedroom."

"Sure, no problem. Take care of yourself, eh?"

"Yeah, thanks." He turned, but not before I saw his eyes. Stephen, Stephen, you are in bad shape when a kind word from your new cleaning lady can make you cry.

He went to bed, I went to work, searching and destroying dirt in all its guises. He still had that beautiful dust. He still had Valium in his medicine cabinet, but the Ativan was gone. I considered leaving a note about the hazards of minor tranks, but he probably knew already.

I tapped on the bedroom door when my three hours were up. "Bye, I'm going."

"Bye Jam." His voice was thin and soft. It was hard to feel very sorry for him when there were people sleeping in the park across from his condo. On the other hand, it was hard not to feel sorry for him when he was so visibly desperate. You are not passing, Stephen. I locked the door behind me and steeled myself for the long walk home.

After the first time, Jam thought she'd never go crazy again. But she did.

Jam thought she'd gone crazy before from being in the closet and having low self-esteem and no work to do, and now that she was an almost famous lesbian artist with a feminist analysis, she was safe. But she wasn't.

Dr. Biltmore, her shrink at the Mountainview Hospital Outpatient

Clinic, said she was crazy because of a chemical imbalance. It was the late eighties and most psychiatrists had moved into the prescription-writing business, leaving Oedipus and his buddies behind. Jam had never cared for Oedipus, but she liked Elavil even less. "I feel like a zombie," she complained. Dr. Biltmore assured her that the side effects would pass and gave her a magazine article where science proved bad brain chemistry caused bad emotions.

Jam took the article home. Apparently science had proved many things and the more they proved the less clear things were: chemicals affect emotions, emotions affect chemicals, actions change neurotransmitters and vice versa. The brain wasn't logical in that A + B = C kind of way. Everything was simultaneously cause and effect, feeding back to millions of inputs that became outputs, more like the internet than like third grade arithmetic.

When Jam pointed out this circularity at their next appointment, Dr. Biltmore told her she didn't understand brain chemistry. Jam said, yes, that was what the article seemed to be saying.

"I would be quite concerned if you went off your medication at this point," Dr. Biltmore said. "With your history of self-harm …" And there it was, the threat, naked on the desk between them. Danger to self or others. Don't sass your shrink. Jam backed up, said yes Dr. Biltmore, no Dr. Biltmore, and cold turkeyed off the Elavil without telling him.

Dr. Biltmore enrolled her in the Mountainview Day Therapy Program. Day therapy was a full-time job: nine to four, five days a week, with classes like Self-Esteem, Assertiveness Training and Life Skills. Jam had to quit the rest of her life, which was fine, she wasn't handling the rest of her life very well.

"Hi Trudi? I'm sorry, I'm going to have to book off work for about six months. I've got a grant, we've got that photo installation coming up, you know."

"Six months? Again? Oh dear."

Jam shrugged off the guilt. This was the price they paid for having a lesbian-art-star cleaning lady. There was always a cash-strapped under-the-table exchange student ready to step in for her, and her old job waiting for her after the grant, the tour, the mental health spa.

"Hi, Mrs. Cathcart?"

"Hi, Jam, it's Cynthia." Cynthia. Damn. Lying to unhappy fifteen-year-olds was not the same as lying to your boss.

"Is your mom home?"

"Nah. Just me. Bored. Cranky. I'm grounded, did you ever hear anything so Stone Age?"

"What did you do?"

"Cut school, natch."

"You've gotta work on not getting caught."

"What's the point? I *am* caught, at least till I'm sixteen and can run away without getting dragged back by the cops. It's so humiliating."

It had been more than humiliating, with Cynthia gone for three weeks, Mrs. Cathcart raging and crying, in front of the cleaner even. Cynthia was finally pulled in during a raid on a street-kid squat, locked in her room, social workers and child welfare officers flocking like pigeons to popcorn.

"I met this girl," Cynthia had said, lying on the bed while Jam dusted her blinds.

"You're gay, right?" Cynthia had asked later, when things had more or less settled down.

"So what's it like?" following Jam and the vacuum cleaner around the house after school.

"When did you first know?" leaning on the kitchen counter while Jam scrubbed the stove. Jam talked, brought books that Cynthia hid under her mattress, phone numbers that she memorized and burned. She had a flair for the dramatic. Mrs. Cathcart thanked Jam for taking an interest. "She's such a problem. But she seems to like you."

"So are you coming Tuesday?" Cynthia asked now, on the phone.

"I … no. I've got a … I'm going into this therapy program."

"But you're still coming to work, aren't you?"

"No. It's all day long. I'll be on welfare. But I'll be back at work in six months." Unless Mrs. Cathcart hired someone else. She was less impressed than some with Jam's art career.

"Six months? That's forever!"

"We could get together for coffee on the weekends or something."

"Could we? Could we go to Dolly's on Davie?"

"Sure."

"Could we go to Sappho's? I've got ID."

"I don't know if I'm up for Sappho's."

"Oh." The silence hung between them. "So like you're really … freaked out or something?"

"Yeah. Freaked out pretty well describes it. Don't tell your mom."

"Give me a break. As if I tell her anything. But this therapy stuff is going to help?"

"I hope so."


"But we've got our photo installation in November!" objected Roz. They were sitting on the stairs at the community radio station where Roz's current lover, Doreen, had a late night music show. Doreen had said they could do a photo shoot in the control room if they didn't tell anyone and she could watch. They were supposed to wait outside until Doreen's show was on.

"I know," said Jam, unable to shrug off this guilt. "I can work nights, weekends."

"Doreen is going to love that," said Roz. More guilt.

"I kind of have to do it," said Jam.

"Okay, nights and weekends, whatever you say."

"Are you mad?" Jam asked.

"No," said Roz, "everything's fine except you're pissing off in the middle of a project."

"So everything isn't fine," said Jam, a stickler for details when she was crazy.

"No everything's great. I like my job, Doreen is very hot, our photos are beautiful and you are a pain in the butt."

"Fuck you," yelled Jam, running up the stairs to cry in the community radio station washroom.

"Fuck you too," yelled Roz running after her. They yelled at each other for awhile, then Jam washed her face and they did their photos. That was the shoot when Jam had little cuts all over her legs. When Jam left, Doreen asked Roz about the cuts and the yelling in the washroom, and they ended up having a fight too.

----------

Walk to the kitchen, walk to the bedroom. The telephone is perched on the paper pile beside my computer.

I've been stuck here since getting back from Stephen's. I finally write to Lucy for advice. I know hip urban lesbians shouldn't look to sixty-eight-year-old Christian ladies in rural Virginia for etiquette lessons, but there's no one else.

> How do you ask someone for a favour when you haven't returned their phone calls for two and a half months?

Her reply comes a few hours later.

> Many people would return one or two phone calls and then ask the favour, but that's a form of lying — which adds to your isolation, which is your problem in the first place. And it's sleazy. Just ask her.

Just ask her? Thanks, Lucy. How do I just ask her?

Ring. Ring. Ring. Maybe she's not home. Ring.

"Hello?"

"Hi, Cynthia."

"Jam, hi, how are you?"

"Good, how're you?"

"Somewhere on the road between tragedy and ecstasy. You know. So what's up?"

Just ask her. "I ... have a question. Kind of a long question."

"Great. I love to show off my vast and peculiar knowledge."

"Well actually ..." Spit it out. "It's about phone sex."

"You want to do phone sex? Hey, that would be fabulous! I could put in a word with my boss. You would be perfect. Lots of older women work the lines."

"No, it's not about a job, it's ... it's a little hard to explain. I'm kind of involved with this woman." How to describe Fruitbat? Better not to.

"Anyone I know?"

"No, that's the problem. She lives in Baltimore and I've never even met her, but I think we're, you know, like, doing it."

"Hey that's great!"

"But I've never done that kind of long-distance sex-thing before and well, I thought you could help. Like ... tell me what to do."

"Doing it with someone you know is pretty different from working."

"But I don't really know her, and I've never really ... I don't know." I'm ready to hang up now, but Cynthia's just getting started.

"I've never heard you so flustered. Must be love!"

"It's just—"

"It's so cute!"

"Come on, are you going to help me or not?"

"Anything for love, honey. What do you want to know?"

What do I want to know? I want you to write a script for my life. "How do you start? Like, there you are at work and the phone rings. What then?"

"Let me see. The first thing is to find out what they want. Sometimes they just tell you, 'Suck my cock,' or whatever. Or they'll ask you, 'Are you a blonde,' and you know that means they want a blonde, so you say, 'Yes, I've got long blonde hair.' "

"What if they hate blondes and they're just checking to make sure you're not one?"

"It doesn't work like that. Whatever they ask about, it's what they're looking for. If they say, 'What kind of shoes are you wearing?'

you know it's a foot fetish. Sometimes you need to dig a bit. You can say, 'What do you like to do for fun,' and that tells you what to be. Something they can have fun with. If they say, 'I like hiking,' you can say, 'So do I. I like to go way up in the mountains where there's no one else around. The sun is so hot I have to take off my Helle Henson hiking shirt. All I have on is a flimsy, black lace brassiere and my cut-offs. And then I see you walking down the path toward me.' Like that. You follow the cues."

"What was the cue for the black lace brassiere?"

"Listen, they all want black lace lingerie."

"What next?"

"It really depends on what they're into. What's this girl of yours like? What does she do?"

"She spends a lot of time in the library."

"Ah, the intellectual type. Intellectuals like to figure things out, look below the surface. So tell her, 'I walk into the library wearing a pearl-grey suit. Underneath I have black lace lingerie.' You could take her down into the stacks and read obscure poetry to her."

"Then what?"

"What do you mean, then what? You're an artist, use your imagination. On the phone lines *you're* working on *their* fantasy, and you're also trying to keep them on for as long as possible because they pay by the minute. But in real life it's supposed to be fun. Loosen up!"

"I guess I am nervous."

"This is not like you, Jam. How long has it been since you've dated anyone?"

"Since Alex. Eight months."

"Oh right, Alex. You gave user-friendly a whole new meaning when you took up with her. Forget Alex, you've got better fish to fry.

It'll be great. Relax. Sex is like riding a bike. As soon as you get back on, your body remembers everything."

"Sure, every bike accident you ever had comes vividly to mind."

"That too."

After we hung up I sat there looking at the phone. Fun, loosen up, relax.


Alex took to dropping by Jam's job every couple of weeks. They fucked in Trudi's bed, on the thick imported carpet beside her bed, in her study pressed up against the filing cabinets, on the newly scrubbed kitchen floor, in the hallway under a photograph of Trudi and Allison smiling sweetly at each other.

Jam never knew when Alex might show up, which made cleaning at Trudi's quite interesting, whether Alex showed up or not. She would dress for work carefully, her worn cleaning jeans, carefully laundered, and a flimsy nylon T-shirt you could almost see through instead of her regular cotton. She could feel it whispering against her skin as she scrubbed the downstairs bathroom. "Sex, sex, sex," it said. She didn't see Alex between jobs, didn't even know her phone number. But every once in a while, Jam and Roz had a performance in town and Jam would see her sitting in the back row, staring intently.

When she heard through the grapevine that Alex had started dating a serious young grad student from the Political Science department, Jam assumed the cleaning lady interludes were over. How long can you keep avenging yourself on your ex-lover, anyway? Eventually you find someone else, move on. But three weeks later, Alex walked in as Jam was vacuuming the dining room carpet, grabbed her, kissed her, pushed her onto the floor and boffed her under the table, the vacuum cleaner still growling in the background.

Three months later, Poli Sci was history, replaced by a Communications major, and Alex was still dropping in on Jam. One afternoon Trudi came home unexpectedly, her two o'clock class cancelled. Alex hid under the bed while Jam locked herself in the upstairs bathroom, frantically pulling her clothes on. "Hi, Trudi, I'll be out in second." Trudi hung around the house for an anxious half hour, then went off to a meeting. Alex crawled out, covered with dust bunnies and bruised dignity. "Next time vacuum under the bed first," she said, too grumpy to take up where they had left off. But as she was leaving she turned to Jam. "I'm going to a party Saturday night. Want to come?"

"Sure," said Jam, intrigued.

"Good, I'll pick you up at eight."

"I'm right near the corner of Victoria and Graveley."

"I know where you live," Alex said, and apparently she did. There she was at eight on Saturday, in brown leather pants and a silver-grey sports car. She kissed Jam cautiously on the cheek, avoiding Midnight Plum lipstick and Metallic Storm eyeshadow. Jam was not wearing cleaning lady drag to this party.

They drove deep into the West Side, land of lawns, where Alex's car fit right in. The house might as well have had the architect's name stitched on its butt. The sound of cool jazz and conversation met them on the doorstep as the hostess opened the door, took their coats, showed them to the bar. There was a fireplace at one end of the living room, French doors leading onto a wide deck at the other. Whoever cleaned here was good: the light fixtures had been dusted and the floor had a deep, paste-wax shine. It was a perfect party house if you like martinis and no dancing.

It turned out to be a get-together of the Women Faculty Association with a sprinkling of husbands and boyfriends and a large contingent from Women's Studies, including, of course, Trudi. Alex swept past with a cool nod, Jam on her arm.

"Oh hi, Trudi," Jam called over her shoulder, soaking up every second of Trudi's confusion.

Alex circled, sliding in to chat with the husband of an English prof who just happened to be talking to someone standing beside Trudi. Alex kept her arm draped around Jam, casually stroking her neck, showing off. Scraps of conversation floated by: I liked your paper at the ASSID&D conference, who's on your tenure committee, Betty's never going to finish her thesis.

Jam glanced over, caught Trudi watching Alex, pretending not to. Trudi was angry but hiding it well. Alex was making the most of it, fingers absentmindedly slipping under the neckline of Jam's dress to play with her bra strap. Her nipples hardened with the deliberate display.

Trudi flounced off to the deck where Allison was talking to a well-known closeted history prof, but Alex didn't stop. Her hand shifted to Jam's waist, slowly stroking down her hip, her thigh, back up to feel the shape of her ass. Jam tried to follow the conversation. Someone had stolen someone else's footnote. Or grad assistant. Or something. Her brains were melting and running down her leg. This was way too blatant. She didn't care.

Finally Alex murmured something about freshening their drinks and led Jam toward the bar, veering off into the kitchen and out the back door. Oh my. Down the stairs in the shadow of the deck and into the yard. Cool air of early summer night, faint city stars. There was a brick patio under the deck, chairs and a hammock, darkness striped by party lights shining between the floor planks above, the sound of ice cubes and laughter close as air.

Alex leaned against a deck support, pulled Jam against her. Wait," Jam whispered, carefully removing Midnight Plum with a tissue from the stationery-box-on-a-string that served as her party-purse. Always prepared. Leaned hard into Alex, found her mouth in the dark, tasted lips, tongue, licked eyelids, bit cheekbones.

"Get in the hammock," Alex said. It was hung high, an undignified scramble to get in. Then slowly rocking at Alex's chest height, pushed away, pulled close, Alex's hands opening her shirt, Alex's mouth heating her nipples, then the night air freezing them to tight little knobs, then the hot mouth again. A woman's voice overhead, "I guess you heard Susan got that appointment." Trudi's voice, "What did you expect? She's always sucking up to the Dean." Alex's hands fumbling under her skirt.

"Next time no underpants," Alex said. "Dress like a slut." Jam laughed then gasped, Alex's fingers driving into her. Pushing her away, the hammock arching free, then dropping back, Alex relentless as gravity, harder, deeper, then swinging her out into the night. Trudi's voice, "I prefer the Big Island, not as many tourists." Jam's voice wordless cries muffled by Alex's hand hard on her mouth, hard in her cunt, wave after wave. "Forget Maui, it's completely overrun. You might as well stay in Honolulu."

Alex's voice, "Good slut."

----------

I never liked the General Hospital—too big, too cold, too clean. I had a friend who worked there once, said she was supposed to use a toothbrush to scrub between the tiles. But it was only twenty-five blocks away, which is walking distance if you really don't want to take the bus. I wasn't scared to leave my house. I could walk the back streets to the hospital. Exercise is good for depression. Fifty blocks to and from my shrink once a week, I'd be cured in no time.

First there was my neighbourhood, safe. Old men tending vegetables, young women with hung-over eyes. No one cared what you looked like. They didn't even look. Cut through the industrial zone, empty between shift changes. Cross the park, supposedly full of scary youth gangs, though I've never seen them. Long blocks west, the trees bigger, maple and horse chestnut, meeting in arches over the street. Lawns smooth as Astroturf. Families getting into station wagons pause, look, look away. Their eyes are knives. All doors are locked. Danger, danger. Another block, another family. Their eyes cut through skin and clothes to desperate flesh. Ugly. Get rid of this body so no one can see. Turn down the alley, no one but me and the recycling boxes. Seven more blocks and there's the hospital. I look just like a patient.

It had been nine years since my last outpatient clinic, but the moment I walked in I felt the same rising panic. Calm down, I told myself, you've done this a million times. Yes, and a million times I've been terrified.

The waiting room was low on distractions. There were three posters about depression, all put out by drug manufacturers. *Maclean's* had an article on a big show at the National Gallery in Ottawa, full of important artists I'd never heard of. I should read the art rags more often. I should send our résumé to the National Gallery. Would that make you happy, Roz?

The occasional shrink wandered by, talked to the receptionist, called people in. I tried to guess which was mine. The balding hippie? The bearded Freud clone? Please, not some baby shrink who thinks middle-aged women are pathetic by definition. Please make it some-one older than me.

She was younger, a lot younger, tall and nervous in a white coat.

"Hi, are you Janice?" she asked, reaching to shake my hand. "I'm Dr. Lau, the resident working with Dr. Sullivan. If you'll just come this way?"

Oh right, the shrinklette. I followed her to an office, where Dr. Shrink himself was shuffling papers behind a big desk. He *was* older. He was the Freud clone. You should be careful what you pray for.

----------

When the rates go down on the coast, it's already nine at night in Toronto. I'm ready: phone, phone number and script under the covers with me. This time the receptionist puts me through to the ward.

"My goodness, it's cousin Betty from Vancouver, how nice of you to call." A stranger's voice, a man. Junior. He has a Toronto Jewish accent. I never thought of him as Jewish. Why not? Did I think every-one on Crazy is Presbyterian?

"It's Jam. Hey, how are you? Did you get my messages?"

"Yeah, yours and about twenty-seven others—my brother John in New Jersey, my cousin CloudTen in Denver, my father-in-law Howard on the staff phone at the Paradise while he's supposedly configuring some new software in the office."

"Howard. He's going to get banned someday."

"And my sister in Tokyo."

"Tokyo. Jeez."

"Yeah, I'm Mr. Popularity. The nurses think it's cute. I just hope no one mentions to the parents what a close-knit, far-flung family we have."

"So how are you?"

"I'm all right." The voice sighs. "Slightly more fucked than usual. Locked up, back on lithium, lost my apartment, not a cute boy in sight. The usual psych ward story."

"When are you getting out?"

"Soon, I think. You wouldn't believe how good I'm being. I don't recognize myself."

"Do it, boy. Kiss all the ass you can. Suck up now, scream later."

"I'm trying. The lithium helps. Everyone likes me better on lithium. I'm a polite corpse."

"Not *everyone*, asshole."

"Everyone who's not a nutcase. So how are you? Killed any trolls recently?"

"No trolls, but lots of snakes."

"Ah, Jam, your life is so exciting."

"Things have been picking up a bit lately. I'm kind of having an affair."

"You are? Shit! That's fabulous! What's she like? Where did you meet her?"

"It's … Fruitbat, actually."

"Fruitbat? You and Fruitbat? Steamy! Tell all. Does Crazy know?"

"No, and don't you tell them either!"

"Why not?—Oh horse-fuck, it's the nurse with the meds wagon— yeah okay, just a minute—sleeping-pill time, shit, I want to hear the dirty part. What do cyber-dykes do in bed? —Just a minute, okay? Back off—"

The line goes dead. Oh Junior. Please don't be yelling at the nurse. Please be a polite corpse for a few more days, weeks, whatever it takes.

Maybe by then I'll have figured out what cyber-dykes do in bed.

Lie with the covers over their heads listening to the cut-off silence of the long-distance line.

The silence clicks into a dial tone.

Some people like lithium. Some people say it has few side effects. Twenty percent, according to Lucy. Others say it's worth the side effects. Others say it's not. Some people get so sick even their shrinks think they shouldn't take it. Twenty percent, according to Lucy. Others find it an excellent means to off themselves, since the therapeutic dose is so close to lethal.

My new shrink wants me on lithium, I can tell.

He wasn't a listening-type shrink. He fired off sets of questions and interrupted my answers while shrinklette took notes.

"Do you have trouble concentrating, making decisions, talking to people, working? Are you losing weight, losing friends, losing sleep? How's your sex life? Are you always tired? Do you fret about the past, present, future?

"Do you have periods where you're very energetic, talk fast, make big plans? Do you need little sleep, blow your budget, make rash decisions?

"Do you have more than three showers a day, wash your hands a lot, check over and over to see if you've left the stove on and locked the door and remembered your wallet?"

It's the diagnosis quiz. I tried to tell the truth, but it's hard to tell the difference between truth and what I've read in the Diagnostic and Statistical Manual. Tired equals Major Depression. Big plans is Bipolar Affective Disorder. Checking doors is Obsessive Compulsive Disorder.

"These other breakdowns you've had, were you anxious, hyper, restless? Energetic, irritable, talkative?"

Bipolar Affective Disorder. Again. Damn! Bitch-face Dr. Lewis told him about my father. Well, what did you expect? How to answer? Tell the truth: yes, no, yes, no, yes, no. Those aren't the answers he's looking for. You're being uncooperative.

"But you decided to become an artist during your first break-down. So it was a time of creativity, you felt special, talented."

He was working very hard. He really wanted manic episodes. I wouldn't mind one myself, it would make for a change. But the best he could get was, "Yes, sometimes I've been very happy." At the end of my quiz he asked shrinklette if she had any questions.

"I was wondering … if there's anything in your life right now that you think might …"

She had a warm, open face. I hadn't noticed before. She was really very nice. Wonderful, in fact. I felt like I was going to cry.

"Maybe it has something to do with being middle aged. Don't a lot of middle-aged women get depressed?"

"It could be connected to middle age, yes," the shrink interjected. "You seem to have a pattern of mood swings that no doubt started in your childhood. We often see that pattern, where manic phases dominate until middle age and then the depressive episodes become more severe. Winston Churchill was a good example of that. His manic energy helped win the war, but he spent the last years of his life so severely depressed he never left his bed."

I hang up the phone, kick off the covers, sit up. Enough of that dial tone. I can leave my bed whenever I want. I've got places to go, things to do. Yeah, like what? Go for a walk, sure, get some air the night is young. Okay so put on your shoes. Okay lock the door behind you. Okay.

It's raining. I should have worn a coat. The sidewalk is shiny, street-lights set the trees on fire. Lean on the gate, watching. Headlights burn cold, white streaks down the street. I never noticed that before.

I had told Dr. Shrink I didn't think I had mood swings. He said it was hard for a layperson to self-diagnose. "Probably you're not aware of how your behaviour appears to others, especially in a manic phase. That's very common. Is there someone you're close to who might have insight into that? A family member or friend?"

"Roz," I said doubtfully. "I've worked with her a long time."

"Good. Ask her if she'd be willing to come in and talk to us. To give us her perspective."

"You mean here, at the clinic?"

"Yes. I'm sure she wants to see you get better. Dr. Lau will set up the appointment for you."

Shrinklette smiled encouragingly. Roz. Jesus.

"And after that," Dr. Shrink continued, "we'll discuss treatment options. Prozac would be useful for the depression. But without something to control your mood swings, it could throw you into another manic episode."

That was when I knew he was thinking lithium.

Another car drives by. I really like the headlight thing. I could walk down to First Avenue where there's more traffic, or the park where there's less. Or just around the block. But I can't seem to get beyond the gate. When my clothes are soaked through, I unlock the door, go back to bed.

When her six months of day therapy at Mountainview were up, Jam was still crazy and there was nothing left to try except more Elavil and signing herself into the psych ward. She went for a walk instead, turning corners at random, trying to out-walk the *hate-myself* that was hot on her heels. The night was dark and warm until she hit downtown, and then it was bright.

There's really nowhere in Vancouver that's all that dangerous, or everywhere is, depending on who you are and what you have to do. At that time there were only seventeen unsolved murders of prostitutes in the Downtown Eastside, but there'd be three more by the end of the year and five the year after. Jam didn't think about those dead women when a car turned in front of her, blocking the crosswalk, and a guy leaned out and asked if she was working. She just thought the guy must be pretty out of it to get the fashion codes so wrong. She told him no, walked around his car and across the street. The car slipped back into its lane and drove slowly down the block, keeping pace with her. She figured he was just going in the same direction as her, but it made her nervous so she turned the corner. He turned after her. She turned around and walked in the opposite direction, losing him for a block, but then he was back. That's when she started thinking about the dead women. That's when the *hate-myself* caught up with her.

The Downtown Eastside stays awake longer than most of

Vancouver, but it was finally asleep now. The only person she had passed in blocks was a singing drunk guy. She had liked the way his voice echoed in the empty streets, asserting his presence, his humanity. Now she was aware of the long, dark alleyways and wished the singer was there instead of the quiet car. But. She could turn again, turn down the alley, walk past the rows of dumpsters, see what came after her. The alleyways of the Downtown Eastside were, if not dangerous, then uncertain. You never knew who's private business you might interrupt. But. Maybe that car had some business to take care of with her, would take care of her, give her what she deserved. She who wrecked every relationship. She who fucked girls and made pictures of it. She who was crazy for no good reason again, again. Whatever the car wanted with her, she did deserve it. She turned.

The alley was narrow between old buildings, slit of sky above crossed with wires. There was a crow on one of the wires, black against the black sky.

"Go home," it said. "Go home now."

It was only the second hallucination she'd had in her life, but unlike the piano in the woods she recognized it as a hallucination immediately. "Jesus, now you're really crazy," she said. Behind her the car turned. There were dumpsters, some blue, some grey, trash spilling out of them. It was very dark. Her shoes made a soft, gritty sound with each step. The car kept its slow deliberate pace. She didn't know what he wanted. *Hate-myself,* her footsteps said. In the dark she saw a man leaning against the side of a dumpster, eyes closed, mouth open. Then she saw a woman kneeling in front of him, working at his open fly. The woman looked up and met her eyes.

"Get out of here," the woman said, and Jam started to run. The car picked up speed, but she was near the end of the alley, then she was on the street then there was a twenty-four-hour café and she was in a booth, shaking.

"Coffee, please," she said to the waitress.

Jam slept late the next morning. When she woke up there was a crow sitting on the foot of her bed. "Oh no," she said, pulling the covers over her head. She thought about the psych ward. She risked a peek. The crow was still there, tilting its head to look at her from one round eye, and then the other.

"You'll be okay," said the crow.

Jam lay there thinking about her non-options. Everyone said if you were going to sign yourself in, you should do it at Sacred Heart, not Mountainview.

"You're okay," said the crow.

"Thanks," Jam said. She thought about all the stupid things she'd ever done and the dreary mess she was making of her life.

"Hey, jerkface," said the crow. "You're not listening. I said *you— are—o—kay.* You're not so bad, you're fine, get it?"

"I'm not sure," said Jam.

"Read my lips," said the hallucination. She would have pointed out that crows don't have lips, but she was too tired. The next time she opened her eyes the hallucination was gone. "I'm fine," she told herself. She'd done affirmations in Self-Esteem class, pretending to believe that she wasn't a fucked-up nutcase, but it had never worked for her. However, she'd never been called a jerkface by a hallucination before.

"I'm fine," she said. And for some reason, she was.

----------

from: Jam
to: Fruitbat
morning
It's one o'clock on your ocean, ten on mine. Slow time
at the library. Slow time here too. I've had a raucous
morning lying in bed since five telling myself to get
up. Why do I tell you these things? Depression is not
very attractive.

from: Fruitbat
to: Jam
whoever you are
It's almost one o'clock here in sunny Baltimore. Maybe
you're still asleep or off at a cleaning job. Or maybe
you're checking your mail, kinda looking for me like I'm
kinda looking for you. Looking for your lovely typing,
that is. Mmm, nice ASCII. But if you walked in and sat
down beside me, I would never recognize you. Will this
get less strange?

Jam
re: whoever you are
Hey, you're there! I don't think it'll get less strange.
Probably more strange in fact. Are you up for it?
    What if I did sit down beside you?
    I'm strolling through the computer room in the
Baltimore Public Library. I'm looking for obscure
poetry, but there's nothing in the card catalogue, so I
decide to do a Web search. I log onto a computer: it's

Freenet so it takes awhile. I glance at the woman on the computer next to me. Mmm. Interesting. She looks up, catches my eye, takes in my pearl-grey suit, very conservative, but with an edge of danger in the lacy camisole underneath. I let my eyes linger. Definitely interesting.

Fruitbat
re: morning
Ah, you *are* looking for me. Good. Why do you say depression is unattractive? Is this a proven fact? I think we'd better conduct a scientific study. I could crawl into bed with you and complicate your attempts to get up. It could be a *very* long research project.
   Depression is a slippery word. I never know if you're using the common-language term for feeling shitty or giving yourself a psychiatric label. Maybe I'll crawl into bed and lecture you, would that be attractive?

Jam
re: morning
I use the word depression in its slippery sense, a description of how I feel, subliminally shaped by drug ads and my new shrink. So lecture me. If you can keep your head clear of that shit, you're a miracle.

Fruitbat
re: whoever you are
Why are you wearing a pearl-grey suit? Do you actually

own a pearl-grey suit? This is a whole new side
of you.
P.S. What's a camisole and why is it dangerous?

Jam
re: whoever you are
I don't own a pearl-grey suit. I was trying for subtle
and intriguing. Guess it needs work. A camisole is a
small leopard with long teeth often found under the
suits of subtle and intriguing women. What do you want
me to be wearing?

Fruitbat
re: morning
Keeping my head clear of that shit is no miracle. It's
work, especially with my body twitching from drugs and
my mind slowed to quarter speed. When/why did you
acquire a shrink and how is he/she?

Jam
re: morning
Why do you keep saying how slow you are? You seem
pretty fucking fast to me. You must have been a real
speed freak BC (before chlorpromazine). As for the
shrink, I acquired him/her just this week and he/she
is, well, mixed. He (shrink) is pretty scary, she
(student shrinklette) is actually quite nice, even
asked me what was going on in my life.

Fruitbat
re: whoever you are
What do I want you to be wearing? I dunno. Whatever
you're wearing is fine. I'm not exactly dressed for a
formal occasion myself. So what *are* you wearing (that
pearl suit has me a bit nervous).

Jam
re: whoever you are
What if I said I'm wearing black lace lingerie?

Fruitbat
re: morning
Damn right I was fast: 95 words a minute. 110 with
typos. As for your shrink situation, sounds like good
cop/bad cop. You know you're in trouble when you feel
*grateful* for a (student) shrink asking how you're
doing.

Jam
re: morning
110? That's scary. I favour the two finger method. In
typing, that is.

Fruitbat
re: whoever you are
You're sitting at the computer in black lace lingerie?
Are you folks having a heat wave or what?

Jam

re: whoever you are

I was just trying to ... oh forget it. No black lace
lingerie, no heat wave. I'm wearing jeans and a T-shirt.
I've worn the same thing every day and slept in it every
night for the last three weeks. Sexy, no?


Fruitbat

re: morning

I'm still a ten-finger typist, but let's just say I've
been perkier. One of the wonders of email is you can't
tell how fucked up I am. You don't see me shuffling and
shaking, you don't see me rewrite each sentence three
times. It's easy to pass in cyberspace. And if my
replies come slowly, I can blame it on Freenet. Which is
in fact quite fast.


Jam

re: morning

You rewrite every sentence three times? Why do you
bother? I'm not such a nor-melle that you need to sweat
to pass for me.


Fruitbat

re: whoever you are

You sleep in your jeans? Man, you *are* down.


Jam

re: whoever you are

So what.

Fruitbat
re: morning
You're not a nor-melle, but if you knew me in real life
I doubt you'd be interested. But since we're not too
likely to meet, it's not an issue.

Jam
re: morning
You are really arrogant. Oh sure, *you* can be cool
about me not getting out of bed on a bad day, but *I*
could never deal with your Thorazine shuffle.

Fruitbat
re: whoever you are
So, nothing. What colour is your T-shirt?

Jam
re: whoever you are
Kind of a pale green, with Miami Beach written on the
front.

Fruitbat
re: morning
Ok yes, I'm arrogant. I'm also feeling sorry for myself.
Another attractive trait. Bones has me cutting down so
tediously slow, it feels like I'll never be off. So I'm
being a bitch. Sorry.

Jam
re: morning
Apology accepted. How's the withdrawal going?


Fruitbat
re: whoever you are
Ah, Miami Beach, dig the irony. Pull your shirt up. I
want to see your breasts.


Jam
re: whoever you are
Getting pushy, aren't you? I've never flashed my chest
in a library before. There, look all you want.


Fruitbat
re: morning
Withdrawal is the shits. I'm twitchier than ever. But
Bones says I might just be naturally twitchy. Not
everything I feel is because of some drug reaction.
Thanks, Bones.
   Have you ever been on psych-meds?


Jam
re: morning
I was Elaviled during my second breakdown but it was so
hideous that I stopped. They say Prozac is better. You
ever done anti-depressants?

Fruitbat
re: whoever you are
Ok, run your hands over your breasts really slowly. I
want to feel you. I want you to feel my hands on you
stroking your nipples. Mmm, I think they're getting
hard. Are they hard?

Jam
re: whoever you are
Oh yes, they're very hard.

Fruitbat
re: morning
I don't know what all I've been on. In the hospital they
didn't exactly do formal introductions. Fruitbat, this
is Haldol. Haldol, Fruitbat. But I don't think those new
anti-depressants are as clean as the drug companies
would have you believe. You should read Breggin:
_Talking Back to Prozac._

Jam
re: morning
I'm waiting for the interactive CD-ROM.

Fruitbat
re: whoever you are
I don't believe you. I don't believe you even pulled
your shirt up. Did you?

Jam

re: whoever you are

No, I didn't. I was just … I don't know. Typing. Now I've
pulled my shirt up for real. You and the librarian can
go ahead and stare at my tits except I'm wearing a bra.


Fruitbat

re: morning

Did you ever take neuroleptics?


Jam

re: morning

No. I've avoided drugs except for that Elavil episode.
Oh yes, and my wild youth spent pursuing street drugs.


Fruitbat

re: whoever you are

A bra? Let me guess: black lace.


Jam

re: whoever you are

Black satin, actually. With lace at the edges.


Fruitbat

re: morning

So you've never been locked up or force-treated?


Jam

re: morning

Nope. Quiet little outpatient, that's me. Knock on wood.

Fruitbat
re: whoever you are
Ok, black satin, fine, it's lovely. Take it off.

Jam
re: whoever you are
There, it's really off and I'm really touching my breasts.
And my nipples are hard. *Really* hard. Are you satisfied?

Fruitbat
re: morning
What was Elavil like anyway? How long did you take it?

Jam
re: morning
How long did I take it? Take what? Sitting here with my
shirt up, you staring, fingers flicking my nipples, the
other hand, my hand, trying to type some conversation
about psych drugs? It's no longer morning, whoever you
are. I can't take it.

Fruitbat
re: morning
Good. It's midafternoon. I want my tongue on you.
I want your hands on me. I'm so turned on I can hardly
sit still but the librarian is staring. Now unzip
your jeans.

Maybe the Wizard likes RiverRat, even though RiverRat is only Level Two and a bit of a dork. Maybe Els is in love with the woman in the food store in Taro. Meanwhile there's a secret cave in the snake valley with another self-destructing scroll. If you seek the Sword, beware Vrstilmn, evil sorcerer of the Barrens. The Barrens. Click click, a long ways North to where there's not much of anything, which I thought was the programmer getting bored, but apparently it's the Barrens.

The tower of the evil sorcerer isn't hard to find because there's nothing else, but it's in a lake of fire. Ah, right. I was wondering what the Wizard's Firewalk spell was for. There's a little sizzling sound at every fire step they take, but they make it to the front door uninjured. Locked, of course, and while Els is trying to bash the door in, the Wizard's Firewalk spell runs out. Aoww! 7 points damage. Re-cast Firewalk just as a squadron of Mung Demons swoops down on them. Creepy laughter rings from the tower walls: "Puny mortals, your bones will be my toys."

The evil sorcerer Vrstilmn.

----------

Morning of Roz's tests, I'm supposed to meet her at the bus stop on the Drive at ten. Roz's car is a bit on the wrecked side if you're picky about things like smashed-in doors, broken headlights and green goo dripping from the whatsit.

The bus is no problem. Rush hour will be over, it will be half empty, we'll sit by ourselves in the back. No one will stare, it'll be fine. I haven't ridden the bus in months. Maybe the fare's gone up, I don't want to have to ask the driver. Or Roz. Probably it's still the same. Or it'll say on the fare box. I can't do it. Too many people, unpredictable. It'll be fine. No.

Call Roz.

"Hi, I'm running late, let's take a cab. I'll pay."

"Late? We don't have to leave for another hour and a half!"

"But I have a shit-load of stuff I have to get done."

Pause and then Roz says, "I can take the fucking bus to my fucking tests. It's breast cancer, not a broken leg."

"This is pure selfishness. Help me out."

"Okay, okay. Taxi, ten-thirty. We'll split the fare."

Half a taxi there and back is eight dollars. If I eat beans and rice till my next cleaning job, I'll be fine.

What next? My clothes are all wrong. You should always dress respectably when dealing with the medical profession, even if you're just the friend in the waiting room. My blue jeans are grey, my Miami Beach T-shirt has a wilted lettuce look. Sniff. Oh god.

Check the closet. Black pants, white shirt—long sleeves but summer-thin. Good. Shower first. Walk to the bathroom, look at the tub. Walk to the bedroom look at the clothes. Walk to the kitchen, look at the stove. Make tea.

It's stupid to worry about clothes when your friend is being tested for cancer. Who cares about clothes? The lump of organic deodorant is still in a bag on the table. Rub it into my armpits, then all around under my T-shirt for good measure. Cool sting on my skin. There's still the short-sleeve problem. Back in the bedroom, try the white shirt over Miami Beach. Looks dumb, and it's too thin. Too thin for what? Protection. In the closet is a long black coat, cotton, no lining, a bit odd for midsummer but not too bad. I can say I have a chill. Reverse hot flashes. Something.

It wraps around me hiding everything. Good.

Roz's test was at the Sacred Heart Hospital, third floor. I'd always felt more comfortable there because it was the city's main AIDS hospital, and they seemed to take queers in stride. No one had batted an eye when Roz had listed me as her next-of-kin last winter before the operation. They'd assumed we were lovers, so we were still, in a sense, in a closet. Roz's real lover said she was her sister. They'd been together for three months, broke up two months after the operation. She really wasn't next-of-kin, but neither was Roz's father except in the legal sense, which said I was no one, a friend.

The waiting room was a calm green. There was a picture of Jesus above the receptionist's desk. He was pointing to a big pink heart open and glowing in his chest, smiling kindly like an ad for a double bypass. We sat side by side in a row of other wait-ers. It seemed like the perfect time to ask Roz to go with me to my shrink. But Roz seemed to think it was the perfect time to grill me about my non-writing, and she beat me to it.

"So how's butt-fucking?" she asked, loud enough to startle the matching business girls sitting on either side of us.

"It's all right," I said. "I'm not feeling very inspired." That was my new line—the rough draft one was getting a bit worn.

"Get inspired then," said Roz. She's not really into the delicate mystery of the muse.

"I'm trying, but ..." But what? "I'm not sure what this show is about, you know? How is it different from the last one? What's our reason for doing it?"

"I just want to do something," Roz said.

"But what's the unifying theme that pulls all the separate bits together?"

"I just want to do something."

"Maybe the theme is …" My tongue refused to supply the rest of the sentence. Our performances were pretty chaotic but they were usually about *something*. They were usually about what was happening in our lives. Tell the truth. Scare yourself.

"Maybe I should keep working on that net-sex story," I said.

"Fine. I'll bring over my new stuff this week, and we can see what we have."

I was grasping for a reason why next week would be better when a woman in a white uniform came to the door and called Roz's name.

Net-sex. Let me eat your pussy. This week. Great.

I picked up an old copy of *Newsday:* "Generation on the Edge: The Boomers Face Aging." Apparently everyone born between '45 and '58 was white, affluent, college educated, spent the sixties being hippie radicals, the eighties amassing large amounts of money and the nineties ruling the world. It didn't say what we were doing in the seventies. Inventing Classic Rock Radio, I guess. Switched to *Chatelaine:* chartreuse was *the* In colour this summer, which meant I didn't have to take off my Miami Beach T-shirt till fall. Excellent.

Maybe when Roz got back I'd ask her about seeing Dr. Shrink. I could make it sound like a wacky adventure. I could say … what could I say? Hey Roz, let's hang out in another hospital, want to? I'm seeing this weird doctor, it'll be a blast. I picked up *Maclean's,* couldn't concentrate, put it down. It was the smell. The same smell as the surgical ward last winter, my first visit after the operation. Hey Roz, let's hang out in a hospital. Roz groggy from morphine. I had brought books and deli food, tried to have a conversation. Yeah, I'm working on the budget for the grant, it's going fine. No, I didn't forget misc. expenses—you're not the only one who can do a budget. And all the while the shrill voice of a woman one curtain over, "Can't we wait till my husband gets here?" Then the soft murmur of her doctor. Then the woman, "What does that mean?" Murmur. "Inoperable?" Murmur. "Then what can you do?" Murmur. "What do you mean?" Murmur. "Are you saying I'm going to die?" Murmur. "But do you mean I'm going to die?" Murmur. "Oh no. No." Murmur. "Can't you do something? Isn't there anything?" Then the doctor's voice raised. "We're all going to die sooner or later."

"Let's go somewhere else," Roz had said, pulling herself awkwardly out of bed. Crossing the ward, leaning on her IV pole with every step, refusing my arm. The woman's voice following us down the hall. Sitting in the visitor's lounge, drinking coffee from the machine.

"Shit," Roz said, eyes bleary, tongue thick with drugs.

"He should have waited for the husband," I said.

"Shit," Roz said.

Now sitting in the waiting room I heard the woman's voice. Oh no. No. Wondered if Roz heard her voice every time she came back here. Wondered why I ever thought she should come to the General with me. Wondered how long these fucking tests were going to take.

----------

Rain washes the pollution out of the sky and stops sometime in the night. What time is it? What time is it in Baltimore? What time is it in Washington—hot damn, today is the Squeegee hearing. Check mail.

Twenty-six go-George-go posts and one newbie begging for help unsubscribing because he can't deal with the Crazy volume. Parnell even called George "old friend," which I guess they are in a way. One from George in the Washington dawn.

```
from: George
to: ThisIsCrazy
Squeegee Day in D.C.
Greetings from our nation's capital, city of pomp and
poverty. I spent the night on the 27th floor of a velvet
hotel, while people below searched trash cans for food
in the 100 degree heat. Ten years ago I was down there
too, scraping for survival and trying to avoid the
hospital, crueler than the streets in my experience.
Today I put on my suit and prepare to trade handshakes.
First breakfast, then the air-conditioned taxi to the
Dirksen Building where homelessness is an abstraction
for polite debate. I'll probably spend a total of 10
seconds breathing the real air of this town. Wish me
luck, folks.
```

Toss off my own go-George. Send. The hearing will be over by the time he reads it. Now get to work. Three hours of hot sex writing before my cleaning job. Open Word. There's pages of lesbian+sex downloads, all still less than inspiring, but I'm having my own net-affair now, and I can write about that.

I met her on the crazy-people's list and I liked her right away. She was

What, she was what? Time to seek inspiration. Open Eudora. `Mailbox: Fruitbat Save`. The amazing thing about fucking by mail is you then have a written transcript to pilfer from. `Whoever you are,` yes, that was *très* hot.

> `You sleep in your jeans? Man you *are* down.`

Well, maybe not that one.

> `So did you ever take neuroleptics?`

How do you write about the erotic bonding possibilities of unpleasant psych-drug experiences? You don't. It's been a long time since Allen Ginsberg howled for Carl Solomon and madfolks were almost respectable, in some circles at least. Nowadays there's something seriously strange about being turned off by Suzi "tanned and fit" and turned on by Fruitbat "do you really want the whole pitiful story of my incarceration?" Dirty girl talking to herself in the park, picked up by the cops and spat out into a psych home—how can she be the sex interest in a story unless you're going for that creepshow thrill? Watching weirdos doing it. *Shut up, don't talk about my girlfriend like that.*

> The cigarette burns on her arms comfort me.

Maybe I'd better go back to science fiction butt-fucking. Maybe I'd better go back to Eudora—dear Fruitbat tell me again why there's nothing wrong with us.

> `Check mail 1 out of 15, 2 out of 15, 14 out of 15,` mostly Squeegee Day in Washington, including Fruitbat's.

```
Fruitbat
Tell 'em, Cyber Joe.
```

Scroll back an hour and a half to Cyber Joe.

```
Cyber Joe
This is what I would tell them if I were there: How
can I get better when I'm too sedated for anything
but bouncing between the Clubhouse and my boarding
home cubicle? Guess it's not as messy as being homeless,
guess that's what counts. Out of mind, out of sight.
```

Yeah, tell 'em. I can't even tell Roz.

Close Eudora, open SwordQuest.

Fighting in the lake of fire is painful. The Wizard keeps forgetting to recast Firewalk, and there are lots of burned feet and evil laughter. Plus the Mung Demons have this deadly-breath-thing. I'm getting to hate that Vrstilmn guy. We get dusted seven times without getting a foot inside the tower. Then suddenly it's dark out. Check mail. George is back.

```
from: George
to: ThisIsCrazy
re: Squeegee Day in D.C.
Sitting in my hotel with my laptop wishing I still drank
(no I don't I really don't). It all went so fast. I was
on first: I started out by telling the committee not to
do it and then I suggested four or five safeguards to
prevent the worst abuses since they no doubt *are* going
```

```
to do it. The last word was given to a famous
psychiatrist who said that mental illness causes
homelessness — not .02 percent vacancy rates and
5-year wait lists for subsidized housing like we have
in New York. Sure, if they'd just take their drugs the
housing would appear. I feel sick. I can't wait to
get home.
```

I guess we're going to lose. Open SWORDQUEST.

----------

Open Word: Net-Sex, draft one.

> *Peter:* Let me eat your pussy
> *Jam:* Hey Peter, you want my pussy? Come and get it.
> *Peter:* Spread your legs for me.
> *Jam:* You like what you see?

This is incredibly boring. Change margins. Walk to the kitchen, look out the front window. Walk to the bedroom, look out the back window. Change typeface.

By the time it's noon and late enough to call Cynthia, I've worn a track in the linoleum. Dial. Answering machine. "Hi, I'm not here. I'm somewhere else having fun. Without you." Beep.

"Hi, Cynthia, this is Jam, I—"

"Hey girl. For you I'll pick up the phone even at this uncivilized hour."

"I'm honoured."

"Really, I just want to hear the dirt. How was your date?"

"Oh right, my date. It was … good actually. Great. I think it's going to work out."

"That's so kewl. I feel like the midwife at the rebirth of romance. Did she go for the black lace lingerie?"

"I'm not sure. She had it off me pretty damn fast."

"Mmm hot. Give me the blow by blow."

"Actually … I have to ask you a favour."

"What's up?"

"This is a bit strange …"

"Hey, for the woman who bought me my first Brazen Bronze eyeshadow I can do strange."

"I'm seeing this shrink—"

"Oh dear."

"And he wants me to bring in Roz so he can question her about my behaviour. But you know Roz. She'll call him by his first name, or make him call her Dr. Rosenthal. She'll tell him he's full of shit, and then I'll really be in trouble."

"So what are you going to do?"

"I wondered if maybe—if you would come. And say you're Roz."

"I see what you mean about strange. Why don't you just tell the shrink she can't come?"

"The thing is, he's decided that I'm a manic-depressive except he's having a hard time finding the manic part. So Roz is supposed to come in and tell him what he wants to hear so he can prescribe all these different drugs. *She* wouldn't say I'm manic, because I'm not, but I can't ask her to go to the General. I can't."

"Maybe I'm oversimplifying things here, but if the shrink isn't listening, maybe you should fire him."

"I guess. But then I'd have to go on someone else's waiting list for months. And he has a student shrink who might be okay."

"Is this like before, in the day program? Are you feeling really messed up?"

A long second of silence. She had been fifteen when I went into the day program. By the time I was out, she had turned sixteen, left home, moved in with her girlfriend, dropped out of high school, gotten a job at McDonald's. We had never talked about it. I don't know what she thought then, what she's thinking now. People don't like it when you're too messed up, I do know that. Another second, another.

Find a cheery voice, "Hey, you're right, it's way too complicated. And unnecessary. I can just—"

"Shut up, I'm thinking."

I shut up.

"Am I supposed to be thirty-nine?" she asks finally.

"I didn't give him any details. He just knows I work with Roz and she's the only one I've been seeing in the meat world, I mean, the real world."

"I could probably do thirty. A young-looking thirty. Does he know what you guys do?"

"God no. He knows it's art, that's all."

"Can I be a painter?"

"Whatever."

"Great. I'm Roz, I'm a painter. So what's he going to ask me?"

"Stuff about mood swings. Does she spend months depressed and then suddenly stay up all night, talk fast and think she's god, that kind of thing."

"Do you?"

"No."

"So what am I supposed to tell him?"

"I don't know. The truth, I guess."

"Pretend to be Roz and tell him the truth. I'm not really following this too well. Back up a sec. What are we trying to achieve here?"

"I guess I want him to stop thinking I'm clueless about my own life so he can listen to what's actually going on and maybe help."

"Sounds like you want a major personality make-over for the guy. I'm not saying I couldn't do it, but maybe we should go for door number two."

"I want him to stop thinking I'm in danger of talking too fast, so he can stop pushing lithium on me."

"Lithium's bad?"

"It can be. It is. I don't know."

"So what should I wear? Can I be butch? No, I'd better be femme for the shrink."

"You're not supposed to seduce him, Cynthia."

"Sure I am. Ever so subtly. Play out his important doctor fantasy but distract him from the lithium."

"Wait a minute, I don't think you should—"

"Listen honey, when it comes to men, you're not even an amateur. You may be my childhood mentor but the day I take lessons from you on manipulating straight guys is the day I hang up my telephone."

It's true, she has a lot of experience. But not with shrinks.

"Where is this place? Do you want a lift?" she says.

"Sure, thanks." I manage a few minutes of small talk, then we hang up.

Now what? Oh yeah, write that story. Check mail first in case there's anything inspirational along the cyber-fuck line.

Downloading: 1 out of 82, 2 out of 82. That's what you get for not checking first thing in the morning. 5 out of 82, 6 out of 82. Sigh. Go do something. What? Wander aimlessly. 47 out of 82. Think of it as meditation. 63 out of 82. Open the curtains, watch the roses climb up the back fence. 81 out of 82, 82.

Number 37 is Fruitbat.

> Another Baltimore heat wave, sleeping naked imagining you sweating with me, skin to skin. It's been so long since anyone's touched me except orderlies at the hospital throwing me into seclusion. I fall asleep thinking of you and dream of them. Why are you so far away? Why do I like you so much?

Write something.

> Oh bat-girl I like you too. Nothing is wrong and I still can't cope with my life.

You can't send that. Sure I can, why not. Open, send, close. There. Now write her something longer, better, more reasonable. No, you're supposed to be writing a story.

> dear Fruitbat.
> dear Fruitbat.

Okay read your mail. Squeegee Day in D.C., Alternatives Conference, Fuck Off Howard. Lots about Terry's job, oh yeah, they had the board meeting finally, how'd it go?

```
from: Gina
re: Terry's job
I'm writing to report on last night's board meeting
because Terry can't. He no longer has access to the
staff computer. He's no longer on staff. He got fired.
    Yes, he called the executive director a pasty-faced
toad-fucker, but the asshole was baiting him. Yes, he
threw a cup of coffee, but he didn't throw it *at*
anyone. But the board voted to fire him, 4 to 3, just
like that. I can't believe it.
```

The next post is Gina again saying she's too pissed off to work so she's going to play International Liaison till her shift is over. The next is Gina saying is anyone there please talk to me. The next is Gina asking why the net is completely dominated by sleeping Americans. The next is Gina saying she's quitting the Coalition, bye gang, it's been good. Eventually the east coast comes online, Parnell, George, Lucy, then Sarah, Howard, Mei Lin, MadMax. Sympathy, advice, anger. But Gina is gone.

----------

Morning. Put the kettle on, go back to bed. Make coffee, go back to bed. Cleaning job in two hours. What to wear? Grey turtleneck over Miami Beach. Coat over that. Fine, get up. Why? Okay, don't.

To lie in bed, perchance to fret, aye, there's the rub. I have to do something about my life. How long can I just drift along like this, how long will I? What if we don't get the grant, what will I do for money? What if we do get the grant, how will I write clever stories, stand up in front of people and talk about sex. I hate sex.

Actually I don't hate sex. The thought propels me out of bed to download my mail. `1 out of 43, 2 out of 43.`

Lots of `Terry's job.` No Fruitbat.

```
from: MadMax
to: ThisIsCrazy
re: Terry's job
What's the big fuss, Terry? You can still work at the
Coalition as a volunteer. Or collect welfare, kick back
and go to the beach. Maybe it's time for the old guard
to move over and give someone else a chance.
```

```
from: Paradise/Howard
to: ThisIsCrazy
re: Terry's Job
It's winter in Australia and Terry's no longer online,
pee brain.
    In America it's summer, 200 people died from the heat
in Chicago over the weekend. Most at risk are those with
medical conditions, including "the mentally ill." Let's
all go to the beach.
```

Jesus, two hundred people. Roz used to live in Chicago. I should call Roz. Hi, I was just reading about people dying and I thought I'd phone.

No.

Hi, Roz. I was just wondering, have you heard back from those tests yet? Dial. The phone rings, rings. Finally I give up, scan the rest of my mail for Gina, Terry, Fruitbat. No luck. I should work on my story. What story? I could go back to bed. Take the phone with me and call Junior. Forget that the world is going to hell in a shopping bag and I have no money.

It's a different receptionist, says Junior's gone home. Suddenly my script no longer works.

"Already? That's great," I blurt.

"Signed out this morning."

"But I thought he lost his apartment."

"I don't know about that. He's staying with his parents."

"His parents?" His parents? "Do you know why ... are you sure ... what's their phone number?"

"I'm sorry, I can't give it out. But you're his cousin, surely you—" Hang up.

Directory assistance. How many Zilkowski's can there be in Forest Hill anyway? Three.

New script.

> Hello, is Danny there? This is Janice Johnston. Yes, Danny and I were in high school together. That's all right, I'll call back later. When do you expect him? Okay, thanks, bye.

The first Zilkowski is an answering machine. Sid and Shirley can't come to the phone right now. Beep. The second is a woman's voice, cautious.

"Yes, he's here, may I ask who's calling?"

"It's Janice Johnston, Danny and I were in high school together."

"What do you want?"

What do I want? What do you mean what do I want? I want to talk to Junior. "I'm just … on the grad reunion committee."

"Well, all right."

Muffled voice, her hand over the phone, then the strange voice I still don't think of as Junior's. "Hello?"

"Hi, kid, it's me."

"My high school reunion?"

"Jam."

Long pause, then the voice, cool and polite. "Not exactly. Not at the moment."

"In other words your mother is standing there listening to every word."

"That's right."

"Jesus. So how are you?"

"I'm not sure."

"How long are you at your parents' for?"

"It depends."

"On finding an apartment?"

"Not that."

"Is it some kind of condition for your release?"

"Yes, that's right."

"Shit."

"Yes. I agree."

"And the lithium?"

"That too."

"Shit, shit, shit."

"Exactly."

"And your mother's monitoring your phone calls. Great. Are you back online at least? Can we email?"

"I think so. I could be. When did you say the reunion was?"

"How 'bout tonight?"

"Not really."

"Tomorrow?"

"Further."

"Monday?"

"Probably. What time did you say?"

"Ten?"

"Oh no, not at all."

"Midnight?"

"Your time."

"Right. Monday, midnight on the Pacific. This sucks."

"That's right."

Dial tone. I forgot to tell him about Terry and Gina. But maybe he doesn't need bad news. Is that patronizing or considerate? I don't know. Go to work.

The walk to Stephen's was hard even with my black coat over everything. I rushed through factory streets, turned at the park, woman with a briefcase walking toward me, eyes down. I looked back as she passed, caught her looking back. She sped up, looked back again as she unlocked her car. Two men stood talking on a new porch, natural cedar, very nice, their eyes tracking me down the block. This neighbourhood was getting very tense. The man passed out on the park bench ignored me. Three blocks to go. I tried distracting myself with possible getting-past-the-gatekeeper scripts, in case emailing Junior didn't work and I had to phone again. "This is Janice Johnston, sorry to bother you, Mrs. Zilkowski, but ..." I muttered silently. Then recklessly out loud. The laws of sanity are so flimsy when you get right down to it, so easy to cross over. Louder. "I hate you, I hate what you keep doing to him," for two blocks scaring lawyers—*hey boy, just look how close that edge is*. A rush of power, then my own fear. Stop it stop it. I'm an artist, I have a career, an apartment, a computer. No one crosses over until they have to. People get punished for scaring lawyers.

Stephen was wearing the suit again, putting papers in his briefcase.

"Hi, Jam," he said. "I'm just on my way out. To work." His hands were shaking. Cutting back on the tranks, are we, Stephen? Good for you.

"Anything special?" I asked.

"Special?" he asked with an edge of panic.

"Special cleaning. Like extra. Like wash the windows, make sure to vacuum the closet floors, that kind of thing."

"Oh yeah, right. I mean no. Whatever."

He stood there holding his briefcase. Looked at his watch, looked at me.

"You're going to work," I said.

"Oh right I ... sure sorry bye."

"I'm having a real peachy summer myself," I said. "Ain't life grand."

He looked at me startled, started to laugh, then put his hand over his mouth. Then we both were laughing, the kind of laughter that goes on far too long and stops in abrupt embarrassment.

"I ..." Stephen said.

"Yeah," I said.

He stood there, looked at me, looked at his watch.

"Work," he said. "Right."

----------

Cynthia probably *could* pass for thirty in her natty businessgirl suit and careful makeup. She looked how I was supposed to look in the failed pearl-grey library fantasy, which made me even more nervous than I already was. The contrast with my black coat and unwashed hair was rather striking. We sat in the waiting room, her trying not to giggle, me trying not to bolt. Eventually shrinklette appeared and was duly introduced.

"Dr. Sullivan will see you now," she said. When I stood up, she added, "Just your friend for now. It won't take long."

Cynthia gave me a reassuring wink and sashayed off to the inner sanctum. She didn't look anything like Roz. Her purse matched her shoes.

I sat, mind racing stupidly, squirrel in a cage. She'll be fine calm down check out today's literary offerings. *Cosmo:* "Are You a Good Lover?" Two pages of true/false, do you compliment him on his sexual performance? are you willing to try new positions? Stood abruptly, walked to another chair. *Time, Maclean's, New Woman.* Another chair. The receptionist was watching me.

Maybe I was having symptoms. Maybe it *was* a manic episode. Or maybe I was sick of reading old magazines. Tried to remember if it was okay to pace in an outpatient clinic. Probably not. Pretended to look at the posters. One was the "Twelve Signs of Depression," just like that pamphlet. There were drawings of little depressed people acting out the different signs: tired, anxious, suicidal. I scored high but not as high as on "Are You a Good Lover?" Maybe I was in the wrong business.

Finally Cynthia/Roz came back followed by Dr. Shrink himself, patting her shoulder as he thanked her. What the fuck did she say?

"If you wouldn't mind waiting while I talk to Janice?" he asked and swept me off to his office, shrinklette trailing behind.

"I hadn't realized about your lover," he said, seating himself in the chair next to mine. I preferred him behind his desk.

"My lover?"

"The university professor. Who died of breast cancer."

"Oh right, that one," I said. Damn, Cynthia, what did you say?

"Your friend thinks that's the explanation for your depression, the natural grieving process. An easy conclusion to draw, I suppose. But given your history, I think the crisis of your lover's death was a trigger rather than a cause. You'll continue to cycle in and out of depression until we address the underlying condition. Prozac for the depression, with lithium to prevent a manic rebound would be the standard treatment. You'll have to have regular blood tests to check for lithium toxicity. Dr. Lau will explain all that. I've written you the prescriptions you'll need."

Shrinklette smiled encouragingly. "It's very effective," she said. "You'll see."

Winding through rush hour on the way home, Cynthia alternated between cursing the traffic and cursing Dr. Shrink. "I thought I had him! I thought he was really listening!"

"Shrinks are noted for listening closely in order to tell you that you don't understand what's going on. They teach it in shrink school."

"And that junior shrink! Why did you say she was good? She just sat there taking notes like his little lackey. I bet he sends her for coffee."

"She has to do what he says, it's like being in the army. She's okay. I think."

"Well he's a jerk," she said, leaning on the horn for emphasis. "Anyway, you don't have to fill that prescription."

"Anyway, I'm not going to. Why did you tell him that dead lover story?"

"I thought he would back off on the chemical imbalance stuff if you had some tragedy he could focus on. Silly me. Hold on, I'm going to run this light. And besides, I always wanted to give Roz's breast cancer to Alex."

"Dress like a slut," Alex had said. Jam knew that *didn't* mean dress like one of the girls who froze their butts on rainy street corners north of Hastings. It meant dress like a lesbian university professor's idea of a slut, post-modern and deconstructed. She considered her closet. She had excellent sex clothes, scrounged for photo-shoots, then recycled into real life. Basic black leather mini-skirt, goes with everything: good. Basic bustier, looking more like a dyed-black fifties long-line bra than the slinky numbers sold in Luv Shops; sort of a retro-bondage look, beaded with tiny brass safety pins. Good. Basic black tights with holes, basic boots. Jam posed in front of the mirror. Hmm, kind of mid-eighties. The mid-eighties *were* the last time she and Roz had done sex-as-fashion photos. Jam changed the boots for fuck-me pumps, the tights for stockings, edge of garter just visible. It could pass for eighties nostalgia. In fact, it could pass for anything with Trudi, who wasn't exactly cutting edge.

Check the mirror again. Hmm. The scars were a problem. Jam

had long black gloves from Value Village, but not quite long enough to cover them all. Maybe a little gold enamel paint on the ones that still showed, simultaneously hiding and flaunting, not bad. What else? Perhaps a studded leather collar? No, too over the top. Ah, but this one: ancient orange velvet with rhinestones, used to belong to a standard poodle. Yes.

Alex picked her up at nine wearing the same brown leather pants as last time. Butches can do that.

"Good slut," she said, flicking Jam's nipples under the bustier until Jam was breathless, then running her hands up under Jam's skirt. "Lose the underwear," she said. Why not? Jam removed her panties, then Alex's leg was between hers, wet snatch riding on slick leather thigh until her knees were buckling and Alex said, "Come on, we'll be late for the party."

It was a long drive through the rain up into the north shore suburbs, Alex's hand on Jam's thigh just above the stocking line keeping her wanting it. Then they arrived: the British Properties, richest suburb in B.C. The hostess greeted them at the door, wife of some guy from the chemistry department, took their coats, flinched as Jam's came off revealing too much of everything. Jam didn't mind. It was Alex's gig.

In the living room was the surprise: no Trudi.

No Women's Studies department.

It was another kind of university party, men and wives. The famous closeted history professor was there, but no other dykes as far as Jam could tell. Suddenly she wasn't sure what game they were playing. Danger, danger, said her head. Fun, fun, said her cunt.

The host offered them drinks. He'd already had a few himself.

"Oh my," he said, staring at Jam's cleavage. "Nice ... dress. Where'd you find *this* one Alex?" He laughed. Alex laughed. Jam didn't. She was suddenly afraid Alex would tell him. I found her scrubbing Trudi's floor.

"Picked her up on the corner of 10th and Fraser," Alex said. She laughed. He laughed. Jam could have told them that the whores were chased off Fraser two years ago, but she wasn't fast enough. Alex was walking off, saying, "Hey, are you going to show me that new CD player you've been bragging about?" and Jam was left standing alone in the middle of a party of strangers. With no underpants.

She got herself a drink, tonic water, keep your wits about you, and found a wall to lean on. It was a fairly prominent wall. If Alex was trying to shame her, she wasn't going to hide in a dark corner. She would display her shame, open her body to the covert glances, enjoy her shame, turn it to pride. Whore bitch cunt lesbian cleaning lady.

Performance artists usually come to terms with public humiliation early on in their careers.

After ten minutes of slow sipping, the host wandered up to her. "So where did you two really meet?" he asked. His eyes kept flickering back to her cleavage. Alex was watching from across the room.

"Alex is one of my clients," Jam said. "I'm a professional dominatrix."

"Oh," he said backing off fast. "Fascinating. Well, hope you're having a good time."

More slow sipping. There *was* someone she knew. A sessional from the Art department who she'd met at a dozen openings. Sometimes he recognized her and sometimes he didn't. It was like a barometer of her current art world standing. At the last opening she'd had to remind him who she was. "Oh right, you used to do that performance thing," he'd said.

"I still do."

"Really? I didn't think anyone was into performance anymore. I'm doing interactive video—like my piece in the Seattle Art Museum, but more stripped down." Openings could be vicious. She and Roz had never performed in a museum.

Suddenly Jam was ready to go. She looked around for Alex, saw her talking to a woman who looked more like a student than a wife. Alex turned, caught Jam's glance, stared expressionless for a moment, then turned back to the student. Maybe she was Alex's new grad romance. Maybe that was who the show was for. Or maybe it was a fuck-you to her boy-colleagues in the Chem department. Or maybe it was for Jam. Who could tell? Whatever it was about, Alex clearly wasn't going to take Jam home just yet. She was on her own.

Jam settled herself on a more obscure wall as far away as possible from the interactive video jerk. Sipped her drink. Felt the eyes slip over her. I am not a social reject who no one will talk to. I am a warrior, enduring this.

Alex was still talking to the student. Or whoever she was. Still watching Jam.

Jam's tonic water was getting low. She stopped sipping, pretended to be absorbed in watching the bubbles. It was like grade school recess. I'm really very busy trying to walk all the way around the cement edging of the playground without falling off. You wouldn't believe how beautiful these bubbles are. I can tell Roz about this tomorrow, turn it into a joke, a story.

Then another university boy, this one younger, shyer. "Can I get you a drink?" he asked.

"I have one," Jam said.

"Oh yeah, you do ..." He was struggling but Jam wasn't in the mood to help him out. "Aren't you an artist?" he finally managed.

"Yes," Jam said cautiously.

"I thought it was you. I saw your show 'ForPlay' at the York Theatre. Actually I wrote a paper on it, 'Queer Culture Jamming: Poaching in the Preserves of the Avant-Old-Guard.' I'm in graduate school, Art History department, queer theory. Richard Wilbur." He stuck his hand out. Jam shook it. She was not an over-the-hill has-been, she was queer history.

"I always wanted to ask you," he said, "I mean, is it okay—are you sick of talking about 'ForPlay'?"

"It's fine," Jam said. He was not staring at her cleavage. He was not trying not to stare at her cleavage. He was not the party social worker who goes around being nice to all the losers. He was waving his hands around and talking too fast. He was a gayboy academic and she loved him. Alex was watching.

"I always wondered if you were referencing Foucault. I said you were, in my paper. I found quotes in *Madness and Civilization* that really fit, and my prof gave me an A, but I always wondered ... were you?"

Alex was watching, closer now.

"Yeah, Foucault, for sure," Jam said.

"That's what I thought." He grinned at her. She grinned at him. Alex was standing next to them now.

"Hey Alex, you didn't tell me there were queer-theory boys at the U.," Jam said.

"Queer theory is everywhere," Alex said, putting her arm around Jam's waist. "So is queer practice." Pulling her close.

"There's not too many of us at the U.," Richard said. "In theory, I mean." Alex ignored him, ran her hand over Jam's ass. Her cunt remembered the smooth leather. Nasty, but you turn me on. She wondered if the dominatrix rumour would circulate—*Professor Donaldson pays someone to tie her up and whip her.* Probably. Served her right.

"So are you guys working on something new? I wrote a paper on them," he explained to Alex. Alex stared past him.

"We just got back from touring," Jam said, "but we have a few ideas. We're applying for a grant."

"And speaking of touring, go get your coat," said Alex.

"Yes ma'am," Jam said. "Sorry, Richard, duty calls. Nice to meet you."

Hallway, coats, door. On the front steps Alex grabbed her, pressed into her. It was still raining, porch light silvering the air.

"Watch the lipstick, tough guy," Jam said.

Alex passed her a handkerchief. "Get rid of it."

Jam wiped carefully, Black Raspberry, then dropped the handkerchief on the ground. Littering in the British Properties, probably a hanging offense.

When they reached the car, Alex leaned her gently against it, kissed her hard. "No sudden moves," Alex said. "Car alarm."

Jam stayed as still as she could while Alex pulled her coat down around her shoulders. Cold rain slicked her skin under Alex's hands. Alex's knee pushing her legs wide, cold hand sudden in the hot of her cunt. "Don't move," Alex said, starting a slow irresistible rhythm deeper deeper. The other hand on her breasts, making them cry out, deftly undoing the fourteen little hooks down the front of her fifties retro-bra, letting it fall to the ground, rain on skin, hands hard. Alex stepped back, looked at Jam, fingers still working her tits, her cunt.

"Women over forty should never wear bustiers," Alex said. Jam flinched away from her, setting off the car alarm. Alex watching with a slight smile like a butch Mona Lisa. The alarm pulsing behind them. Jam twisting away, stumbling in her heels, remembering to walk not run, too late.

Alex following.

Jam found her balance, slapped the next car, the next, setting off car alarms all down the block. Fuck you, British Properties. Curtains twitched. Alex paused, retreated. Fuck you. Jam managed to get her coat buttoned, should have picked up the bustier. Should have laughed and traded insult for insult, invulnerable. Should have stared back, chin angled just so, like Roz when she dropped the pink bathrobe and walked across the floor.

She hadn't forgotten she was over forty when she put on that outfit. She'd had nearly two years of *gee, you don't look forty* to burn it into her brain. It was supposed to be a compliment but it wasn't a compliment, it was a threat. You couldn't be a rebel art grrrl at forty. You were supposed to have a teaching job, or a show in a museum, or disappear.

By now she was blocks away, her feet hurt from walking in heels, she didn't know where she was. She could, in fact, disappear. She had twenty dollars in her party purse, she could walk to somewhere new and stay there, start over as someone else. Okay. She turned the corner, walked down a different street. It was the same as the last street—dark, wet. Turned down the next street, walked a block, stopped. Cul-de-sac. Looked up at the big house where the street ended and knew it wasn't where she was supposed to start her new life. Walked. Eventually lights cars stores, took a bus to another bus, got off somewhere else. Found herself at dawn back in Vancouver on a park bench beside an old man who kept falling asleep in the middle of his life story.

It was cold. She went home.

----------

Els hits Mung Demon: blam blam. RiverRat casts Flame Cloud: whoosh. Wizard shoots Death Arrows: thunk thunk. Mung Demon is slightly slowed. Mung Demon breathes on RiverRat. Danger danger. Maybe I should go back to the orcs. I really want to kill something.

Cup of coffee, check mail. The headers stream by: Rory, Flip, MadMax, Lucy. Fruitbat. Ah.

> from: Fruitbat
> to: ThisIsCrazy
> Meds again again
> It's 11:30 pissing rain in Baltimore. Cut my meds back
> another notch, had a screaming fight with Phil at the
> house and can barely sit still. Walked all the way
> downtown to the library which helped but then I had to
> wait 45 minutes to get on a computer. Jesus. My heart is
> jumping like I gotta run, yell, pace the floor, some-
> thing, but you're not allowed to pace in the library,
> it's sit still or back out in the rain.
>     Charlie says:
>     >You should really be withdrawing under medical
> supervision.

```
Thanks, Charlie.
    Howard says:
    >When I came off of Haldol I tapered down over two
months and it was still hell.
Yeah, Howard, I know what you mean.
```

And another one, off-list

```
from: Fruitbat
to: Jam
G'morning
You are asleep. You West Coast types are lazy and
backwards.
```

Eleven-thirty Baltimore. Three hours ago. Damn.

```
from: Jam
to: Fruitbat
Hey bat
Are you still around? I'm here, trying to work. Will
check in on the hour. Talk to me.
```

Work. Open Word, stare at the blank screen. Good start. Change the margins, font, type size. Stare at the screen.
    Three o'clock Baltimore. `Check mail.`

```
from: Parnell
to: ThisIsCrazy
heat deaths
```

I read the following paragraph in the newspaper this morning: "In Milwaukee, officials said heat caused or contributed to 60 deaths. Among them were 18 people who were taking anti-psychotic drugs that block the body's ability to release heat, said Medical Examiner Jeffrey Jentzen."

18 people dead from what drug companies call a side effect. How many of them were ever warned this could happen? Were offered alternatives? Were pressured, coerced or outright *forced*? If the Squeegee goes through, the government will be *rewarding* states for pushing anti-psychotics down people's throats.

It's 85 degrees here in Newark this morning. 98 in Chicago. How many people are dying?

So that's how people die of mental illness in heat waves—it's the drugs, the fucking drugs. Anti-psychotics are for "schizophrenics"— Haldol, Thorazine, Stelazine. JJ in Kansas City. Cyber Joe in New York. Fruitbat.

Check mail. It's only been a few minutes, but there are already five posts saying christ no, saying goddamn drug companies, saying what can we do? Three of them are from people on neuroleptics. No Fruitbat. Check mail, four more. Check mail, six.

Look, there's nothing you can do. You have no control over heat-waves or the less advertised effects of major tranquillizers. You're supposed to be writing.

Okay.

No new mail.

Come on. You told Roz you were working on something. Pull out that Mrs.-Stella-non-story-thing.

Jam would check. Yup, four condoms, what a guy.

It's not so bad, it just needs something lesbian.

Sometimes Jam's girlfriend would drop by Mrs. Stella's in the afternoon. The doorbell would ring and when Jam answered it, there she'd be, leaning on the door frame trying to look suave.

Then what?

Then they fuck. Fuck fuck fuck. The end.

Four o'clock Baltimore. Check mail. No new mail.
Maybe coffee would help. Drug myself into some semblance of life. Methedrine works better—where are you now that I need you? Kitchen. Kettle. The watched pot never boils. Fine by me.
Five o'clock Baltimore. Check mail.

```
Sarah
re: heat deaths
I was on Thorazine for seven years, no one EVER told me
about the heat problem. I'm re-posting George's
congressional email list. Everyone who hasn't written
about the Squeegee should do it, and everyone who has
should do it again. Goddamn.
```

Maybe I should move to St. Louis and help Sarah save the world. She could tell me what to do. Lift one foot. Put it down. Lift the other foot. Oh Sarah, you're so organized.

It's another country, there's nothing I can do.

I should get organized. I should clean my desk: eight inches of unsorted scripts (the before-cancer tour), grant drafts, old calls for submission that I was going to submit to—really, someday—out of date now. And staring at me from the top of the heap: two squares of doctorly scrawls, Prozac and lithium. My prescriptions.

The books say that when you're stuck, you should just make yourself write, write anything, get the words flowing and see where they go. Okay, flow.


Babblebabblebabblebabblebabblebabblebabblebabble


Stop it. You can do it. Just do it.

Six o'clock Baltimore. `No new mail.` I should write something for Roz. I should call Roz and find out about those tests. Yes. Ring. Ring. Ring. Ring. Where the fuck is everyone today? Hang up. I should wash my dishes. I should fill the Prozac prescription, maybe I'd feel better. I can't remember why I didn't want to.

```
from: Jam
to: Flip
Private
I need some advice but I'm not ready to talk about it on
the list — people would just jump on me. Especially
Parnell and Fruitbat. What's Prozac like? How much do you
take? What side effects do you get? Does it actually help?
```

All my doctors say it's great but they aren't on it — or
maybe they are, what do I know? I can always stop, right?

Seven o'clock. No new mail. Fuck this. I go onto the Web and search
Prozac. There are 2,489 documents with the word Prozac. Good. A
familiar calm settles over me. This could keep me occupied for days.

"The Prozac Café" seems to be an online chat group featuring
someone named Laurie Lust. I could research my cyber-sex story
there. Some day.

"Prozac, Is It for Me?" looks better:

If you have been seriously asking this question, then
the answer is probably yes. As opposed to days past when
medication was given only to those deeply depressed,
today psychiatrists are treating young, active, healthy
people who are burdened with anxieties and feel they
could be performing at a higher level. The vast majority
of people claim to feel less oppressed by life and
generally happier.

Less oppressed, more happy. I could do that. Maybe I'll take Prozac
and get a real job. As a researcher. And function at a much higher
level. Next hit:

Sales of anti-depressants have been increasing by about
45 percent a year.

Yeah, yeah fine, I know. "Psychopharmacology Today" is a bunch of
doctors trading drug stories:

Subject: What to tell patients
I usually tell patients who are starting Prozac that
they are unlikely to experience any side effects
(instill positive expectations).

Few side effects—that's what my doctor said. "Don't believe everything your doctor says," Parnell whispers in my ear. "Shut up,
Parnell," I tell him. "I'm doing research."

Subject: Bruxism
The mouth guard used by football players, which costs
$2.00 in NYC, works very well for bruxism induced by
Prozac.

It's good to know there's a simple cure for bruxism if I should get it
from my new life-enhancing drug. Next hit:

Adverse Signs and Symptoms: insomnia, agitation,
pacing, hostility, anxiety, violent thoughts and/or
behaviour, suicidal thoughts or behaviour, muscle
twitching, panic, convulsions, cold sweats, sexual
dysfunction, confusion, drowsiness, nausea,
superhuman strength-energy, hair loss, heart
flutters, skin rash, vision problems, altered
personality ...

Superhuman strength and altered personality sound pretty good, but
as for the rest, there's quite a few that I manage to produce all by
myself. In fact, they're the very things Prozac is supposed to cure me

of. Parnell would say, "I told you so." Fruitbat would say, "Don't be a fool."

"But probably those are all really rare side effects that almost no one ever gets," I answer back. "And what if it works? What if there was just a pill, and I could take it and everything would be different?"

Eight o'clock. No new mail.

Nine o'clock. Transferring new messages. Flip, Parnell, Fruitbat. Ah.

from: Fruitbat
to: Jam
I'm back
again. Where are you? In another country, another world.
I've been walking around. And around. It's still raining
and I'm soaked to the skin. But the library is warm and
I'm nearly alone except for about twenty other people
with nowhere to go, hanging out, reading, sleeping,
waiting to get online. And the librarian watching to make
sure we don't break anything or disturb the normals.

Got a note from that asshole Bones who says I should
go back up a notch till the jitters stop and then try a
smaller decrease. Fuck him. And fuck Parnell and his
fucking newspaper clippings. Distract me.

Raining, she said it was raining.

from: Jam
to: Fruitbat

    re: I'm back
    Yes, I'm here in another world where it's still
    daylight. Fuck Bones for sure. Seems to me it would be
    better to tough out the withdrawals and get off sooner.
       How hot does it get in Baltimore?

Click on send and off it goes. Check mail. Nothing. What did you
expect it's been ten seconds. Check mail. Nothing. Check mail.

    Fruitbat
    No, Bones is right. I have to do it gradually or I'll
    get caught. The weather in Baltimore is the weather in
    Baltimore. Can we please talk about something more
    interesting? I can't stand people fussing at me. You're
    not being very distracting.

It could almost be Roz with her stiff butch pride. But it's not Roz,
and there's another post right on the first one's tail.

    Fruitbat
    Sorry. You're not fussing, you're worried. I'm worried
    too. And furious. It's so easy for me to imagine those
    people. I hate it.

I know.

    Jam
    Hey kid, it's ok. I can do distracting. Want to hear my
    great literary output of the day? "Babblebabblebabble-

babblebabblebabblebabble" Moving, eh?

Send. As a distraction it rates pretty low. Let's see, I've done flowers, weather's off limits, sex would be kind of tasteless in the face of all that death. The amazing dust at my cleaning job?

> Fruitbat
> Sounds like you're having a non-brilliant day yourself.
> Are you still trying to write a sex story? Maybe I could
> help …

Maybe sex is not so tasteless. Good.

> Jam
> Let's see … sex story … where to begin?

> Fruitbat
> Begin anywhere, just can we please forget the suit this
> time? I don't do social workers.

> Jam
> It wasn't a social worker suit. It was very sophisti-
> cated. But ok, I'll leave it at home. I'm in Baltimore,
> the rain has stopped and the night is cool velvet. I'm
> walking in the park. It's late, too late to be in the
> park alone. Maybe I'm a bit nervous. There's someone
> walking toward me. I relax a bit when I see it's a woman.

Cool velvet, a bit pretentious maybe. Too late now. Put the kettle on.

Sure you relax. She's small and skinny and dressed out of a dumpster. You probably think she's a panhandler.

I think she's cute.

You are weird. Ok. I walk up to you and look into your eyes. "Spare change?" I say. I *am* a panhandler.

Somehow I thought you had something different in mind when you asked to be distracted. But hey, if cyber-spare-changing is your thing, whatever. I look through my pockets and find a couple of loonies. Then I remember I'm in another country and search again till I come up with an American two. You probably think I'm a dork.

I think you're cute. But there's no such thing as an American two.

Ok, two ones. So what are you going to do about it?

There's nothing I can do about it. I just asked you for money — that already defines our relationship. There's no way I can ask you for a date.

You're so literal. This is a fantasy. Here's what happens: You look at the bills, then you look at me and start to smile. "Can I buy you a coffee?" you ask. I'm alone in a strange city. "Sure," I say.

One minute. No new mail. Two minutes. No new mail. The kettle is whistling. I go to the kitchen, pour water into the teapot.

If you had given me a five I could have taken you to a groovy cappuccino bar, but as it is, we go to a smoky little cafe. I'm doing this total butch number, holding the door open for you, ordering the coffee. You're half-charmed, half-irritated.

Yeah, you're pushy, but two can play that game. "So, do you always pick up chicks in the park?" I ask.

"Not always. But you were looking for me."

You are so smug. I think someone needs to take you down a peg or two. I volunteer for the job. "Oh, is that what I was doing? I thought I was looking for the bus stop."

"The bus stop is right outside. There'll be a bus any minute. See you around."

"Yeah well, I gotta finish my coffee."

"Yeah, well, you'd better hurry … if you want to catch that bus."

"I don't run for buses," I say, taking another slow sip. "Or for pushy butches who think they should always be in charge."

Her reply comes fast and angry, an electronic slap in the face.

> Look sweetheart, the day you are as out of control of
> every goddamn thing in your life as I am will be a brand
> new fucking day in your life.

What do you know about my fucking life and what I control? I write, and then delete. I get to decide if I'll have oatmeal or freezer bread for breakfast. I get to decide whether I'll take drugs that could kill me.

> You're right. I *was* looking for you. I don't care
> about coffee. I just want you to take me somewhere and
> kiss me.

No new mail. I pour the tea. It's cold. No new mail. I drink it anyway.

> Right. Let's go somewhere. And where *exactly* am I
> supposed to take you? I live in a goddamn psychiatric
> boarding home.

Fuck you, I write and then delete. Walk into the kitchen. Walk back.

> And I live four thousand miles away. I've never even met
> you. It's all impossible. Let's talk about the Squeegee
> Amendment.

Check mail. Her reply is already there.

I'm sorry. It's the withdrawals.

I know.

Ok. Forget the Squeegee. We're back in the park —
there's forest and no one else around. You're looking at
me with those wary what-next eyes, but I'm tired of
games. "Come here," I say. "I know what you want."

It smells like spring and wet earth and green things. I
walk slowly toward you.

I pull you into me, kiss you hard.

Your tongue is hard in my mouth. I'm shaking under your
hands. You're shaking too.

I'm shaking so hard I can hardly type. I lean you
against a tree, my hands up under your sweater your
breasts are so soft

I can feel your cunt pressing against me. You have no
cool left. I tease my hand between your legs. Mmm, your
jeans are wet. You want it bad.

Oh god yes

I undo the snap and slowly pull the zipper down.

```
oh god
```

```
I slide my hand into your pants, slowly tangling through
your pubic hair, slip into the wet of your cunt and then
pull back.
```

```
Jesus god fuck me now bitch the library closes in
five minutes
```

On the ground now, the smell of wet earth and sex, my hand is full in her and she twists under me gasping, her hands hard on my shoulders pulling me deeper deeper, her voice on my computer screen oh god oh god oh god

----------

"This isn't working," says Els.

"We need a plan," says the Wizard.

Click click, sneak around to the other side. Sizzle sizzle, Firewalk to the back door. Locked, plus a squadron of demonettes. Thud, kapow, dead demonettes. They aren't very tough. The Wizard grins wild and lovely in the glow of the firelake, but this probably isn't the right time for RiverRat to declare her undying love. Bash bash, the door falls in. Excellent. They're in the evil sorcerer's kitchen surrounded by scullery giants, much tougher, armed with carving knives and meat cleavers, an out-of-the-fire-into-the-frying-pan situation. `RiverRat casts Ice Bolt,` once, twice, then the computer choir sings "`Cool!`" and RiverRat is Level Three. More strength more stamina more spell points. Maybe the Wizard is impressed. Or maybe she's busy ducking cleavers.

Wake up hot and sweaty, sun through the curtains glowing red like my own little hell. What time is it? Eleven forty-nine, says the clock. Digitals are so irritating. Trudi-and-Allison's at one, I have time. Coffee. Ah. `Check mail`. Weather report from Fruitbat, thank you thank you, 82 degrees.

Breakfast. Nothing. I should go back to the bulk food store. Soon. Meanwhile it's quarter after, lots of time. Call Roz.

I'm so used to the phone ringing in her empty apartment that her voice startles me.

"Roz?"

"Yeah, hi. Jam, great, I was going to call you."

She was going to call, what does that mean, is it good or bad just ask. "What did they say?"

"What did who say?"

"The tests!"

"Oh right. The tests said I have to go back and get more tests. How's your net-sex story?"

"Why do they want more tests?"

"Because they love tests. How's your story?"

"But did the first test show ... something?"

"Look, are you going to tell me about your story? It's almost August and we need to start pulling things together."

"I want to hear about the fucking tests!"

"Fine. I'll tell you about the tests then you tell me about the story. Deal?"

"Deal. What happened?"

"There's a swelling on one of my lymph nodes. It could be anything, they don't know. So we're doing more tests. Did you finish your story?"

"What kind of anything?"

"People get swellings sometimes, from infections or whatever. Sometimes it's from cancer."

"So what do they think?"

"They think they want more tests. Beyond that, they're not committing themselves."

"When?"

"Three weeks."

"Jesus."

There's a moment's silence while my brain bounces back and forth between it-can't-be and it-must-be, and Roz's brain does whatever it does when faced with this.

"Did you finish your story?" Yes, of course. That's what Roz's brain does.

"Yeah, I did. Yeah." The words come out with no forethought and hang there.

"Good. So how is it?"

"It's ... strange."

"Strange like how?"

"Well, the characters are ... Net-sex is strange, that's all."

"Is this the voice of experience?"

"Kind of."

"Yeah, right, I 'kind of' fucked someone on my computer. This is going to be a bizarre show. When can we get together?"

"Let me get my date book." I sit with my hand over the mouth piece, mind spinning. Now I have to write that story, I have to. "Sorry Roz, can't seem to find my book and I have to go to work. I'll search my paper piles tonight."

"Call me. I wouldn't want to show up unannounced and interrupt a hot date, Jam humping her keyboard or whatever you do."

"Fuck off."

"Bye."

Damn, I'm late for work and no-breakfast is now no-lunch. I could stop at the corner store on my way to Trudi-and-Allison's. Or maybe not. Maybe Trudi will be out and I can find some freezer bread or something, she'll never know. Grey turtleneck over Miami Beach, coat over that, what else? My hair—check the mirror, kind of daunting—who cares, you're late she probably won't be home.

But Trudi was home. She and Alex were having lunch as I walked in.

"Hi, Jam, long time," said Alex smoothly, as if eight months never happened, eight months and one night when I walked away.

"Hi," I said, willing my body to walk into the room, willing my stiff lips to smile. Jesus my hair. Trudi was watching, her head cocked to one side like a chicken deciding whether to peck another chicken into bloody ribbons.

"Hi, Jam," she said, "how are you? The kitchen floor really needs scrubbing and could you be sure to dust the living room blinds?"

"Sure," I said keeping my eyes on Trudi not wanting to see what was in Alex's smile. Remembering the well-laundered jeans and nylon T-shirt of last year, the Metallic Storm eyeshadow. "Anything else?"

"No, that's fine." Dismissed. Maybe I was supposed to be shamed by being sent off to scrub the floor while Trudi and our mutual ex lingered over lunch, or maybe she was just being businesslike. I couldn't tell. Probably she couldn't either. I was just glad to have something to do somewhere else.

I shut the kitchen door but could still hear them as I gathered my supplies, laughter and the clink of silverware. Moving quickly, bucket, rags, cleanser, fled to the upstairs bathroom locked the door. I looked worse in Trudi's mirror. Ran my fingers through my hair tearing out tangles. Flushed torn hair down the toilet, wiped the smudge off my cheek okay good. But the coat, I couldn't scrub Trudi's kitchen floor wearing a coat. I could say—no, there's nothing to say, you have to take it off you look like a bag lady. Took it off, hung it on the towel rack, my body cringing exposed in the grey turtleneck. Get used to it.

I did a very thorough job upstairs hoping they'd leave before I came down, but no. Downstairs, scraps of conversation momentarily drowned out by the vacuum cleaner, the rush of water in the scrub bucket.

"Stewart was impressed with your paper."

"Was he?"

Stole bits of lunch-fixings as I cleared the counters, wiped them down. Rosemary bread and three kinds of cheese, I hadn't eaten like that in weeks. Months?

"Said it was good for a girl."

"You're making that up!"

Trudi had my favourite lemon-scented organic cleaner, saving the earth every time you scrub your floor. She had a yellow, plastic scrub brush, good enough but nothing to write home about. There was something soothing about the hot water, the swish of the brush, eye-to-eye with the white tiles. Floor-level is a unique perspective that many people miss out on. I would be fine if I could scrub floors with the door shut forever, life a muted conversation in another room. But no. Trudi and Alex had to come in, footprints on the wet floor, dishes in the clean sink. Had to stand there and watch me on my knees, had to talk to me.

"So, whatcha been up to?" asked Alex, leaning against the counter as if she was settling in for a good long chat.

"The usual," I said. Just go away just go away I can't play these games anymore.

"You still doing your art stuff?"

No, I've become a professional nutcase. "Sure, Roz and I are working on something for the Performance Festival."

"Fabulous," said Trudi. "What are you going to do?"

Roz is going to stand on the stage and yell at me for being a fuck-up, the latest in avant garde entertainment. "Can't really talk about it yet," I said. "Work in progress you know."

"In other words she has no idea," said Alex. Ha-ha forced myself to laugh with them, good line. I could scream at her instead or stand up and leave or heave the bucket of wash water over her pressed pants. I could smash the dirty dishes against the stove and scream scream scream never stop screaming. And then. Then you would be in real trouble. After forty, women are more likely to lose their sanity hearings; it was in a study Parnell posted. Hold fast to the scrub brush the swish of bristles over white tile the hot water cooling now. Hold fast.

----------

Midnight Monday, time for my email date with Junior. Where are you? D'isMay reports on an argument with her Abnormal Psych prof about whether dissociation is a disorder or a talent. She (talent) whipped his ass. In her version at least. Then there's a Coalition header.

```
Dear ThisIsCrazy
My name is Billy and I'm on the board at the Consumer
Coalition. I'm supposed to be the new International
Liaison, but I'm not very good with computers. If you
get this message could you please write back so I'll
know I'm doing it right? Thank you.
```

I should write him a welcome to Crazy, but I don't feel very welcoming. I want Terry and Gina back. I want Junior.

12:15. 12:20. If this were the Meatworld I wouldn't start to worry for at least an hour. If this were the Meatworld I'd be asleep.

12:30. No new mail. My lithium prescription is still staring at me from the top of my paper pile, but my other prescription has been transformed into a little bottle of pills. *Prozac: take two daily with food.* Sixty dollars, ouch. I have to find another job or three. Or get that grant. But I don't believe in the grant anymore, not since Terry was fired. The two seem connected, as if Terry getting fired was a signal the world had shifted beyond the point where badly behaved lesbian artists could still get grants. Roz, Roz, Roz.

12:45. No new mail. Standing in line at the drugstore, I had told myself that filling the prescription didn't mean I was going to take the pills. Maybe I'd just look at them. A sixty-dollar knickknack to decorate my computer. Maybe just having them around would be a placebo. Placebo does very well in all the drug tests. Sixty dollars, yeah right.

12:50. Maybe lithium has cured Junior's insomnia, and he's fast asleep. Maybe lithium will cure all his problems, and he'll find a new apartment and do a withdrawal with Bones and then go back to being sleepless and hard to get along with because he prefers that to being drug-normal and why shouldn't he? 12:55. Still not time to worry. Re-read Fruitbat's morning post.

> Another rainy day in Baltimore, 79 cool degrees, but who's counting? Thinking about you last night. Yes, and the night before. Keeping very still as you fuck me slow and hard. Not letting my breathing change as I cum, in this little room with three other women who are also pretending to be asleep. Why do we work so hard to hide what we all know? That we're lonely and horny and jerk off in the dark.
>
> No, don't tell me what you look like, I don't want to fill in hair/skin/eye paint-by-numbers on your imaginary body. Don't even send a picture. I don't want to pretend that you're my Meatworld lover and we'll be together someday. Even though I ... love you? I can't tell the difference between love and desperation these days. Maybe there is no difference.
>
> This is what I want. I want you to be thinking about me at 8:00 P.M. your time one week from today. And the week after that too. It'll be 11:00 my time, safe, lights out. I want you naked on your bed with your hand in your cunt, cuming for me. I want you to cum really loud. I want you to scream for me.
>
> Ok?

Okay.

Yes. Slip my hand into my pants as I check the mail one more time.

Junior
Hey sorry I'm late. I had some trouble accessing my
account and then there were half a million Crazy
messages that downloaded onto my father's hard drive
and I had to delete the evidence. Are you there?

Ah Junior, your timing could be better.

Jam
 Hi, I'm here. How are you doing?

Junior
Fucked. Why didn't you tell me about Terry?

Jam
Sorry. I forgot.

Junior
How could you forget? I'm cut off from fucking
everything and you just kind of forget to mention that
my friend got screwed.

Guess lithium hasn't cured him after all. What a relief.

Jam
Our last conversation was pretty bizarre if you'll
recall. Don't yell at me because you're mad at the
stupid Coalition. Or your stupid parents. Or the stupid
universe.

Junior
The universe isn't stupid, just people.

Jam
At least you're out of the bin.

Junior
The bin was more straightforward. No one pretended to
love me.

Jam
Ah kid … is there any way to get out of there?

Junior
My case manager says I can move to a psych home. I have
my name on a couple of wait-lists in Parkdale. Yeah I
know they're hellholes, but I'll have phone privileges.
And I can do library Freenet. And take the bus to cruise
Queen's Park.

Jam
You could cruise hot boy-sites on the net on your
father's account and stick him with the bill.

Junior
I'd be too nervous. Even talking to you is scary. It
reminds me of being 14 — step out of line and it's off
to the shock doc.

Jam
But you're not 14 anymore.


Junior
But he's still Mr. Normal and I'm just his faggot mental
patient son. Or maybe I'm being paranoid, I don't know.
Listen, I should go. I'll keep in touch.


Close out and sit staring at the blank screen till the screensaver
comes on. I forgot to tell Junior about the heat deaths. He'd want to
know. Parnell will tell him, go to bed. The screensaver is set for
Warp: stars zooming by as you hurtle through space. You can make
the stars go faster if you want. Go to bed. I could look up heat death
on the Web. Go to bed. *Prozac: take two daily with food.* Go to the
kitchen, yesterday's red beans and rice. Okay.

----------

Prozac day one: Nothing. Unless the small gathering of tension at
the back of my neck is something.
Prozac day two: Headache. Nausea. Or maybe the nausea is from
the brown rice and pickle casserole I ate for dinner.
Prozac day three: Headache. Nausea. Colours brighter. Brain ...
strange. But your brain is always strange if you pay too much
attention to it.
Prozac day four: Headache. Brain strange. Can I still think? I
think so. But how would I know if I couldn't?
Prozac day five: Mild headache.

Prozac day six: Nothing
Prozac day seven: Nothing.

Dr. Shrink was mad that I didn't get the lithium. Told me all the bad things that were going to happen to me from not following orders. Euphoria, wet dreams. I told him I didn't have any money left after the Prozac. He sent me out to the waiting room and shrinklette went to check their sample stash. But I forgot to wait.

Shrinklette phoned me at home "I'll leave the lithium at the front desk, you can pick it up tomorrow." She sounded irritated, like she was tired of being ordered around by Dr. Shrink and ignored by non-compliant patients.

"Okay," I said. But it's a long walk to the clinic.

----------

Jam and Fruitbat are lying in bed waiting for 8:00 P.M. (11:00 EST). Fruitbat is wearing flannel pajamas: blue washed to grey with a pattern of faded trout, pinned at the waist where the elastic gave up. Jam is wearing nothing. Naked on the bed with hand on snatch, as promised. At almost-eight the sun is just setting, and twin rectangles of grey light glow in the basement dark: window and computer screen. At almost-eleven it's pure night, lights out in the psych home, Sally who gets sleeping pills is starting to snore. Fruitbat reaches out slowly, barely rustling the sheets. Finds Jam in her bed, soft skin— no, she's in Jam's bed across the continent with mountains and the Pacific ocean.

Jam is in Fruitbat's bed and they have to be very quiet. Other women are asleep around them and if they get caught ... what? Something bad. Jam is Fruitbat's lover from outside, who somehow snuck in. Or maybe she's another resident. Yes. She's one of the women sharing Fruitbat's room, but there are five of them, not three. The room is just big enough for five single beds with a bit of space between. In real life there'd have to be somewhere to put your clothes, but this isn't real life, it's Jam's fantasy and she's lying in the bed next to Fruitbat's, thinking about her, wanting her.

Fruitbat is Jam's lover in the little apartment with the garden in back. It's like Fruitbat's old apartment only nicer. Jam takes care of the garden. They have jobs, money, eat in restaurants. Jam is lying naked on the bed. Fruitbat is standing watching her. "Come here," Fruitbat says.

Jam has been watching Fruitbat for days, weeks. She is silently seducing her. Jam is the only open queer in the psych home, other women avoid her. But Fruitbat stays up late to sit beside her watching TV in the living room, which is the group therapy room from Jam's second breakdown. They have group therapy in the psych home too. Other women confess their sins, but Fruitbat is silent, gives the shrink nothing.

Fruitbat is wearing jeans and a cool shirt. "Come here," she says, and Jam gets up, puts her naked arms around her. She's probably taller than Fruitbat—most girls are. She's older too, that's okay. An older femme, experienced, wily. She used to go out with a university professor until Fruitbat stole her. "I'm going to take your woman," she said to the professor at the bar one night. How could she say that, it's too stupid. But the words rush in her cunt, she says it again, "I'm going to take your woman." The professor laughs. Jam, standing beside her, looks Fruitbat over, considering. Later Fruitbat comes over to their table, asks Jam to dance. The professor still thinks it's a joke.

Jam is lying in the narrow bed trying to hear Fruitbat's breathing, fighting waves of fear and desire. Is she still awake? Does she want me? How can I touch her, how can I not? She knows what I am. *Lezzzbian. I hear you're a lezzzbian.* She could be a straight girl behind that toughness, she could be a jerk. Or she could be waiting, cool butch scared to move. Jam throws the covers back, goes to Fruitbat's bed. Knows where it is even in the pitch black room. Like an infrared sensor Jam can feel the sleeping bodies around them. Jam kneels by the bed. Fruitbat is awake, she can tell by the breathing. Jam reaches out. Fruitbat is still, allowing the touch. Shoulders, arms, breasts, Fruitbat sleeps naked. Hips, legs, wet wet hole. Finally Fruitbat cracks. "Get in my bed," she whispers. "Now." Jam slips out of her pajamas into the bed. No fast exit no easy excuse. Desperate skin, legs winding around her. The smell of her hair, the taste of her cunt, starving for it and trying not to creak the box spring.

Fruitbat leads Jam out onto the dance floor, puts her arms around her. It's a slow number. Jam moves with her, soft breasts under some sleek femme-thing. The professor knows nothing about this woman she thinks is hers. Fruitbat knows. "Come home with me," she says. "Just like that?" Jam asks. "Yes," says Fruitbat. And then they're somewhere else in bed and Fruitbat is lying on top of Jam. Maybe she has a dildo on, sure, a dildo, slow easy strokes deep into Jam's cunt and Jam gives everything moaning calling her name, Deb, god Deb please yes. Trying to be quiet as her body screams in the narrow bed.

Jam cums loud in the basement, imagining herself silent. Wow, she thinks, incredible. Says it out loud. "You're incredible." Fruitbat smiles in the half-light, kisses her. Jam can taste her tongue, then can't. Tries to hold her solid while Fruitbat flickers in and out and finally evaporates.

----------

Prozac day 10: Nothing.
Prozac day 11: Nothing
Prozac day 12: Nothing
Prozac day 13: Nothing
Prozac day 14: Nothing
Prozac day 15: Nothing
Prozac day 16: Nothing

Dr. Shrink was pleased with my lack of side effects, says it's normal to still be depressed. I may not get my brilliant new personality till week three. Told him I hadn't had a chance to pick up the lithium. Dr. Shrink very stern. Shrinklette walked me out to reception, watched me put the cardboard sample packs in my purse.

"I don't really want to take it," I told her.

"I know," she said. "You're still depressed. It's hard to do the things that will make you feel better. It's hard to believe you'll ever feel better. But you can. You will."

The samples stare at me from on top of my computer. So what's my next excuse? Maybe I should just take them, it would be easier. Calm rational voice in my head says *kill yourself*. That would be easiest of all.

----------

Morning, ten o'clock. No new mail. Close out of Eudora, open Word, stare at the blank screen. Good start.

Eleven o'clock. Parnell, Charlie, CloudTen, Charlie, Parnell. Fighting about something. Two in Baltimore, no Fruitbat. Back in Word the screen is still blank. Another exciting day in the life of an artist. Open net-sex downloads. Nah. Open Mrs. Stella. Nah. The last time I talked to Roz, I asked if she wanted me to come to her tests and she hung up on me. Called me back and yelled about the Performance Festival and hung up again. Called back and I asked about the tests again and she said they were two days ago. Why didn't you tell me? And she said, why should I you're not my mother. I asked when she'd get the results. We really need to start rehearsals, she said. I said, give me a few more days I'm onto something.

Open science fiction butt-fucking. Nah. *Kill yourself,* says the voice that seems to have taken up permanent residence in my head, the sensible almost soothing voice. *Kill yourself,* good idea.

Twelve o'clock. Parnell is talking about burning the Squeegee Amendment on the steps of the Lincoln Memorial.

One o'clock. Lucy is looking up D.C. court cases involving disturbing the peace and fire. Back to Word, sort through last year's files. Misc. Rejects has the beginning of an abandoned story.

> Judy stretched her long runner's muscles on a bench outside the English Bay Beach House. Sunset was her favourite time to run the long stretch of seawall around to Third Beach and back.

God, that's bad. What was I trying to do? I take out the first "long" and change the second "stretch" to "miles." It doesn't really help.

But still, I could work on it. What happens? She jogs along the seawall, we already know that. We know she runs one hand through her sun-bleached hair, gazes pensively at the mountains and picks up another long-legged jogger. Probably wearing tight satin shorts and $200 shoes, looking like something out of *Personal Best*. And they fuck, no excuse me, make love in the sunset with the warm breeze caressing their soft, unblemished skin. Pass the puke bag.

Stop it. Write the story. For Roz.

So. She runs. And she comes to a deserted strip of sand. And sees a woman. But there's nowhere deserted near the Beach House. It's all urban shoreline with traffic and high rises pushed close up. No deserted strip. Judy runs and sees a woman.

The woman is lying in the sand. At first it looks normal. A woman lying in the sand. Then Judy realizes what she's seeing and adrenaline kick-starts all her nerves. The woman is naked. She's looking up at the empty sky. Her hand is on her cunt, moving in slow circles. She's moaning. Her bare limbs twitch to the rhythm of her hand.

"Crazy," Judy thinks. "A crazy person on the beach. I should call the cops." But she doesn't. She slows down, stops, stands watching. The woman doesn't seem to see her. She doesn't seem to see anything. Her hair is matted like it hasn't been brushed in days. Or weeks. There's sand in her hair and sticking to her sweaty skin. Judy can see her cunt. It's pink and moist.

Judy is sweaty too, from her run. Her Nike T-shirt and Adidas shorts are damp. She really should go. She walks a few steps closer. There's a fresh cut down one of the woman's arms, scabbed over with sand. She's probably one of those homeless people who was let out of a mental institution, Judy thinks. She read about that in the newspaper. She should call the police, or an ambulance—someone official who will take this woman back to where she belongs.

Stop it. She picks up a woman in satin shorts.

The woman's hand is moving faster now. Two fingers slide deep in her cunt, hold for a gasp and then pull out. Over and over, in and out like an insistent machine. Her mouth is open wide, crying, sobbing, pleading. Her legs are thrashing in the sand. She's like a marionette with a clumsy operator jerking her strings. She's like an animal caught by a confused, instinctual imperative. Sex is like that. That's why you should only do it in private.

That's why you shouldn't leave your house. You're not in control these days, it's not safe.

Judy wonders who she should call. She has a quarter in her fanny pack, along with her plastic bottle of electrolyte replacement drink. She's prepared. She has a subscription to *Runner's World*. But she just stands there watching. Her cunt is wet. She feels how she could walk down onto the beach. She feels how she could do anything to this woman. She could kneel by her side and touch her naked breasts, slap her face, anything. But the woman is crazy, and Judy doesn't really want to touch her.

Judy walks down onto the beach and stands looking at the woman. She nudges her with the toe of her shoe. The woman doesn't respond. She's lost in the sky. Judy walks to the tide line and picks up a stone, ocean smooth in her hand. She throws it, hard. It hits the woman in the ribs. She's a good thrower, fast and accurate. She pitches for a dyke baseball team. They all wear matching uniforms: green and yellow. She throws another. It hits the woman's breast.

Why are you writing this? You can't show this to Roz or perform it on stage. No one will laugh, it's ugly.

Tell the truth. Scare yourself.

The woman gasps, doesn't turn, doesn't stop the hand's in and out. The stones hit with a hard thunk: her ribs, her face, her cunt, her legs. At every hit the woman flinches, cries out. In between stones are different cries, a different twitch of limbs as her hand works. The sunset is glorious overhead. Judy has a quarter in her fanny pack. Soon she'll call the cops.

No. Don't.

Go into the kitchen. Find my hairbrush under a pile of unopened mail and brush my hair. Hard. It's matted like it hasn't been brushed for days. Weeks. I should wash it. But I don't want to take off my clothes. Shove the dirty dishes aside and wash it in the sink. Dry it with a dish towel. Go back and save my story. What am I saving it for? Who am I going to show it to? No one never never. *Kill yourself.*

Three o'clock. No Fruitbat.

Four o'clock. No Fruitbat.

Five o'clock. No Fruitbat.

----------

After the scullery giants come the trogs, then the slime toads and the harpies. Find a staircase go up it, evil laughter: "Puny mortals, your hearts will be fish food." Bigger meaner monsters, blood everywhere. Another staircase, another. How tall is this stupid tower anyway? Vrstilmn keeps laughing. He's a real creep.

Fire alarm, no, the doorbell, no, the phone. Pick it up. Jesus, what time is it?

"Hello?"

"Hi, Jam, it's me."

Cynthia. 1:07 P.M. I must have fallen asleep.

"Hi, Cynthia, what's up?"

"Nothing, just calling. How's the evil shrink and his tricky minion?"

"They're fine." Pause. Guess I'm supposed to say something else. "I'm fine too. How are you?"

"Great. I met this fabulous new woman at the bar. Whew. Amazing. We should go to the bar sometime, want to?"

You've got to be kidding. "Sure, sounds good, but actually by the time the bar is jumping I'm fast asleep. Life over forty. Gotta love it."

"How 'bout coffee then? At The Place?"

"Sure, The Place, soon. I'm working on this story-thing right now, but next week, absolutely, I'll call you."

"Okay, we're on. So what's the story about?"

"I can't really talk about it yet. Work in progress. You know."

"Maybe next week you can read it to me."

"Next week, great."

Hang up. What was that all about? Please god, don't let Cynthia turn into a social worker.

Get up, coffee. More coffee. Brush your teeth, no I can't. Brush your teeth, you still brush your teeth, no I can't. *Kill yourself* says the voice, calm and reasonable. No, brush your teeth.

```
To: Fruitbat
Subject: strange
Hey bat-girl. What's the difference between hearing
voices and having random strange out-of-the-blue
thoughts in your head?
```

Send. Check mail. 27 messages. Still no Fruitbat. I stayed up till two reading Australia, Japan and lots of Junior forgetting to worry about his parents waking up. It's my new thing, stay up late *and* wake up early, nap and be a zombie in between.

```
Junior
re: international liaison
Billy, I gotta apologize for my rude welcome the other
night (day). I guess I kind of flew off the handle. I
thought you were some compliant consumer-clone Mr.
Executive had brought in. But any friend of Terry's,
etc. How's he doing? Say hi for me, ok?
```

Billy's trying to organize a meeting of Coalition members to figure out what to do about the Mr. Exec situation. Right on, Billy. That's what I wrote him, "Right on, Billy." I couldn't focus enough to write any more. Then I fell asleep, then I woke up again at six. And again with Cynthia.

```
Hey bat-girl, where've ya been?
```

Transfer to trash. It hasn't even been two days, I'd never be so uncool in the Meatworld. But in the Networld things are so tenuous. She could be hit by a car and I'd never know. Never. She'd just be gone, evaporated from my computer screen, and I wouldn't know if it was her way of breaking up or what. Maybe this *is* her way of breaking up. Maybe it's the heat wave. Shut up. Anything that can happen can happen to you. Shut up.

*Kill yourself*, says the voice in my head, but it's cool and distant and I'm too tired to figure out how to go about doing it.

----------

This time it's the alarm clock: 8:30 A.M., have to be at Stephen's by ten o'clock. `Check mail,` no Fruitbat damn you. Ten new messages, but I can't be bothered. Sit there considering the lithium on top of my computer instead. Then it's past ten, must have fallen asleep again again. Better phone. What do I tell him? The dog ate my homework. No dial tone. Oh right, I unplugged it. After Cynthia.

"Hi, Stephen? This is Jam. Sorry, I slept in, just saw the time, I'll be over as soon as I can get there."

"That's okay. Just let yourself in, whenever."

That was easy. `Check mail,` no Fruitbat.

Breakfast. Why does cheap food always require cooking? I could make a big pot of oatmeal and eat it all week. Good idea. Maybe tomorrow, but I have to eat something now so I can take my pills. Search the depths of my cupboards—flour could make pancakes, no, too much work. Evaporated milk, no I'm not that far gone. Jesus, where did this come from—package of candied something-or-other, red and green for fruitcake maybe. It'll do. Kind of thick and sticky hard to chew, but not bad. Fruit is good for you. Okay, two pills $2 each, delicious. Fill in the drug-journal.

Prozac day 18:

What do I feel? A glimmer of energy hope life? No. What then? No headache nausea bruxism sexual dysfunction. This would be a lovely time for sexual dysfunction, Fruitbat. No evil manic episode even though the lithium is still untouched. Bad dog.

Prozac day 18: Nothing

Nothing is an active state, mind running in circles unable to focus because everything is equally flat. Except for a few very sharp things. Nothing has no horizon—when you're there it's everywhere. Eleven-forty. I must have fallen asleep. Now someone's knocking on the door. Now they're knocking on the window. Now they're saying hey Jam are you in there, getting more and more irritated. Roz.

When I opened the door, some of her irritation left. Maybe 15 percent.
  "You look terrible," she said. "Have you been sick?"
  "Yeah, that evil flu."
  She pushed past me into the kitchen, put on the kettle.
  "I've still got germs," I said.
  "I'll bet you do." She gestured to my unwashed dishes. "Looks like you have a whole germ factory going. You trying for a Martha Stewart Seal of Disapproval here?"
  "You should have phoned," I said. Then wondered if it made any sense: Martha Stewart Seal of Disapproval, you should have phoned.

Do those things go together? No. I should have told her I was going for the Seattle grunge look. She always insults my housekeeping. It's a game, lighten up. But she was already running with the next thing, her irritation back up to 95 percent.

"Yeah sure, I should have called. I *did* call. You should have answered your fucking phone."

"Oh right. It was unplugged. I forgot."

The kettle was whistling but she ignored it. "I've been calling since yesterday. The grant letters are out, Rosemary told me. She was rejected."

"Wow. Too bad."

"So ours hasn't come yet?"

"I don't think so. I'd better check." The kettle was shrill in the background, made it hard to think. I turned it off, looked for tea bags. Found an empty Red Rose box.

"So check already!" Roz yelled. Irritation 100 percent. And rising.

"Oh right, sorry." She followed me outside, up the front steps, inside the main entrance. The landlady had left my mail in a stack on the table by the front door as usual. There was quite a bit of it. Roz grabbed it out of my hand, sorted through, ripped one open.

" 'We regret to inform you.' Damn damn damn."

"Wow, too bad," I said, following her back down to the kitchen.

"Damn," she said several times more. Then she kicked a chair. It fell over very satisfactorily, she picked it up and sat down. "So what are we going to do?"

"I don't know," I said. Maybe there was herbal tea somewhere. I started opening cabinet doors.

"We're committed to the Performance Festival with or without the grant. We just have to think up some cheap tech effects."

"Right," I said. There was a tea bag back behind the old yogurt containers. Smelled like dust. Probably chamomile.

"We could look through our videos, see what we could recycle. Maybe we could pool our money for a few nights at the video co-op and re-cut old footage."

I couldn't find the teapot, washed out a mug, put in the tea bag. What else? Oh yeah, water. Put the kettle back on.

"We need to have a meeting, look at our writing, think about structure. Whatcha doing this afternoon?"

"Oh god, my cleaning job, I forgot."

"How about tomorrow then?" She followed me into the bathroom where I checked the mirror, ran my fingers through my hair till the worst clots were gone.

"Tomorrow?" she repeated.

"Yeah, I guess, sure." She followed me into the bedroom where I turned on my modem. The lithium was still sitting there. `Config PPP. Check mail.`

"Print me out what you've got so far and I'll take it home and read it," Roz said.

`1 out of 18. 2 out of 18.` Sarah, Howard. What did I have that I could show her? Mrs. Stella, net-sex downloads, the woman on the beach. "I have to format it, I don't have time right now."

"I don't need it formatted."

`9 out of 18. 10 out of 18. 11 out of 18.` Tom, JJ, MadMax.

"I have to go to work. I don't have time."

Then Roz was yelling, "Fuck you! You can look at your fucking email but you can't print out stories for me. Are we still working together? Did you quit and forget to tell me?"

I could feel how much she wanted to lash out and hit me. It was like when we were breaking up. But she never let herself hit people, it was something you could count on. She walked out, slammed the door instead. The kettle was whistling.

16 out of 18. 17 out of 18. No Fruitbat. And the lithium was still waiting.

By the time I got to work it was two-thirty. Stephen had left a note and cheque under a rainbow flag fridge magnet. Hi Jam, gone to work, how are you. Hi Stephen. What should I do about Roz? *Kill yourself*. Oh shut up. Scrub the bathtub. The water in the toilet was bright chemical blue. With pee it would be turquoise. Good thing I'd gone to art school, took Colour Theory. What about Roz? Maybe she'd never speak to me again. But Roz wasn't the not-speaking type. Scrub the sink. Had I done the tub already? Do it again.

Vacuum the living room. Someone had swept out the fireplace and made a sort of flower arrangement but not with flowers. A sticks and stones arrangement. Carefully dust around it. Knickknacks on the mantelpiece: an amethyst crystal, onyx ashtray, clay vase—Bizen, by the look of it—good thing I'd gone to art school. Ugly brass tray, probably a valuable antique. As I lifted it to dust underneath, the tail of my rag upset the vase. Fumbled for it, missed, watched it fall, hit the floor and roll, spilling dirt across the carpet. Unbroken, thank god, Bizenyaki is expensive. Knelt to pick it up—jesus what a mess, what was in it? Ashes. And a few charred bits of bone. Oh shit. His lover or his best friend. Shit.

"Sorry, sorry, sorry," I whispered to the ashes as I scooped them into the vase. Urn. Put it back on the mantelpiece, there, good as new. Except for the ash I couldn't scoop out of the thick weave of carpet. Oh god.

I could just leave it, write a note: Dear Stephen, sorry I spilled your friend. Didn't know what you'd want to do with the remains of his remains, so I left them. Then what would he do? Clean it up himself, alone in the house on his hands and knees with death in all its messiness? No. Turned on the vacuum, sucked it up. Afterwards nothing showed.

Okay, dust the bedroom. Then what, vacuum? How could I vacuum a bunch of dirt up into the bag with Stephen's lover? Of course, it was already full of dirt before the lover even got in there. No, not dirt. That cumulous dust. "It's Stephen's special dust," I told him. "You'll like it." Finished the bedroom, washed the kitchen floor, rinsed the mop, put rags in the laundry and I was done. Except—what to do with the vacuum bag? I couldn't just put it in the trash. I couldn't leave it for Stephen to throw out, not knowing what was in it. I could bury it. That would work. Take it home and bury it in the back garden. At night, so the landlady doesn't ask about it. Fine.

I put in a fresh bag and walked home with Stephen's lover. Put him on top of the computer with my lithium. Death in a sample pack, meet death in a bag. The therapeutic dose of lithium is very close to the fatal dose. Everyone knows that.

----------

Jam is lying on her bed waiting for 8:00 P.M. (11:00 EST). A week ago, Fruitbat had told her to be there: 8:00 P.M. Thursday, take your clothes off and think about me. Jam supposes they still have a date, even though she hasn't heard from her in four days.

"Hey Bat," Jam says, and Fruitbat is in her bed. Arms, lips, I love you.

Fades out mid-kiss. Jam keeps trying for awhile, but her clit is numb. *Kill yourself,* the voice says, *kill yourself.* She lies in bed listening to it till she finally falls asleep.

----------

Thursday was Trudi-and-Allison's. I phoned first, got an answering machine and figured it was safe. Floated through looking for imaginary dust and trying to stay awake. Then Trudi showed up, but alone, alone thank you. Hi Jam, air kisses, chitchat. Prayed that the earth would open up and swallow me but no reply. Then remembered my imaginary horrible flu and Trudi backed off—proper respect for germs, not like Roz.

When I got home there was a plastic bag on my door handle, papers inside.

`Check mail.` Thirty-seven messages, no Fruitbat. Open one at random.

> Paradise/Howard
> TV makes you think there are a hundred murders a
> night, when really there are way more suicides. What
> would it be like if all the shows that revolve around
> killing each other were about killing ourselves?
> Weird.

Hi, Howard. Okay, look in the bag. Pages of handwriting. Roz. Maybe I'll have a nap. Lie in bed making up answers to accusations she might have written. Get up. `Check mail.` No Fruitbat. Okay, look at Roz's pages. One long story, one short note.

Hi Jam. I'm still mad at you but we have a fucking performance to put together. So. Here's a piece I've been working on. I thought it would be good intercut with something of yours for a back and forth between two different approaches to sex, like we did in "ForPlay." What do you think?

Of course. Roz isn't the letter-fight type. She likes it loud and in person. Take the story to bed fall asleep instead. Or maybe it's not sleep. It's more like those dreams where you're trying to run away from something, but your body is stuck in slow motion. Something frantic inside of something frozen. Wake up, read Roz: a cynical young femme playing in a country and western bar band picks up a butch who's at the bar with her mother. They end up kissing in a cubicle in the women's can, with a conversation about makeup happening outside their stall. The femme finds it quite instructional, until the butch (packing, of course) pushes her against the door and shows her what a mighty dildo can do. Also quite instructional. Very hot. No one has breast cancer. I try to imagine it intercut with woman-on-the-beach. A different approach to sex. No.

Then someone is knocking on the door. Answer this time, slow motion body opening the door, but it's not Roz it's Cynthia.

"Hi Jam," Cynthia said. She was holding a big, awkward flat of little leafy plant-things. She looked like she might drop it at any moment, so I let her in.

"Look what I got!" she said, dumping the flat on my kitchen table. "This woman at the phone-lines, her husband works at a nursery and she was giving them away for free. They're lupines. In spring they have yellow flowers.

"Great."

"So like I have nowhere to put them at my place so I thought maybe we could plant them in your back yard. Okay?"

I couldn't tell whether she was asking a favour or offering occupational therapy. But I definitely owed her. "Sure," I said.

"Super. Let me wash my hands. Got any tea?"

I didn't understand tea and hand washing as a prerequisite for plant planting, but I wasn't following anything very well these days. Cynthia washed in the kitchen sink without remarking on the dishes situation and sat chatting as I searched for a tea bag. I heard a lot about her co-workers on the sex-lines, her new girlfriend, her old boyfriend. It had nothing to do with me, required nothing from me. Eventually I found a bag of (mint?) tea, heard about her mother, her older brother, her views on the federal deficit. Eventually she decided it was time to plant.

"Let's hit the dirt," she said cheerily.

"First I gotta just ..." I couldn't remember the word, but Cynthia didn't seem to need a word. She followed me into the bedroom.

Check mail. Lucy, Frank, JJ.

"Nice vacuum cleaner bag," Cynthia said.

"Yeah well ..." I said. Flip, Rory, Parnell.

"Are you taking this stuff?" Cynthia asked, reaching over me for the lithium. "I thought you weren't going to."

"No they ... gave it to me. But I'm not taking it." Maybe tonight though. Maybe tomorrow.

"Why don't you just throw it out?" Cynthia asked, juggling the sample cases.

"I don't know," I said. I want them. Don't want them. Want them. I could have said, "Did you ever feel as if knowing you can check out is the only thing keeping you alive?" And she could have said, "Yeah, been there, it sucks." If she were someone else, she could say, "Sometimes it's like waves in and out: want, don't want, want. But if your out is so close at hand, one wave can suck you under before the next wave washes in. Been there too." And I could say, "Yeah, it sucks." And she could say, "Hold on for the next wave. I need you." And I could say, "I'm trying."

"Well, don't let them push you into anything," Cynthia said, returning the samples to the top of the computer.

Fran, David, Cyber Joe. No Fruitbat.

"Do you know anything about TV weather?" I asked.

"You mean like weather reports?"

"Isn't there a weather channel? That tells you the weather everywhere? I need to know the weather in Baltimore."

"Ah, Baltimore, your girlfriend. Can't you just ask her?"

"No, it's a ... thing."

"Okay. Baltimore weather. It's my mission and I shall succeed. I'll call you when I find it."

"Thanks." Sit slow-motioning for another minute and then float back to the kitchen.

"Do we need a trowel or anything?" I asked.

"Beats me," said Cynthia. "What do I know about gardening?"

The soil was soft and wet and we dug it up with our hands. We planted the lupines under my bedroom window where I could watch them from the computer. Cynthia wasn't talking at this point, just clowning around. Smelling a handful of dirt so deeply she breathed some up her nose, snorting and laughing. She painted a dirt-moustache on her upper lip. I watched, dug, planted. Nothing seemed to be required. Afterwards she washed her hands again but left the moustache, strolling down to the Drive to see who she could shock. Bye Cynthia.

Back inside check mail. 1 out of 11, 2 out of 11. The good thing about doing your mail so often is it takes less time to download. Open the curtains look at the lupines. Hi, guys. Turn back in time to see her name scroll by on the download list: Fruitbat, Parnell, Sarah, Starlight, Fruitbat, Jenny, Cal. Her first post is to ThisIsCrazy.

```
Fruitbat
test
Well guys I'm fucked. Went for my blood tests at
Baltimore State like the committed little outpatient I
am, second time since I started withdrawals. First time
I got through fine, but this time I flunked. It was the
fucking slow beginning of a fucking slow withdrawal, but
it registered on their test. Of course it did, what was
I thinking? I was thinking if it was gradual enough …
No, I wasn't thinking I was just … fighting. Sorry to
have wasted your time, Bones.
```

Her second post is to me.

```
Got my wish. Off Thorazine. Once-a-week injections now,
high dose Haldol, drooling and shuffling. You wouldn't
like it. You really wouldn't. No charity, please. It's
been fun.
```

I wait for the next one, the one that says sorry, it's the drugs, talk to me. It doesn't come.

Walk to the kitchen walk to the bedroom walk to the kitchen. Maybe I should kill something.

On the fifth floor is Vrstilmn, laughing and summoning undead armies. Ghosts, ghouls, ghasts, hundreds of them. The Wizard takes out the first wave with a Divine Thud, after that I can't be bothered. Watch skeletons hack and smash while Els and RiverRat and the Wizard stand around. Eventually all three icons turn into skull-and-crossbones, no one left to cast Resurrect. I'm tired of that game anyway.

----------

What time is it? Open curtains, grey light, early or maybe it's going to rain. Good, the lupines need it. Guess I could water them, but they've got to learn to live in this world. You can't count on meat-creatures with watering cans to solve all your problems. The clock says 5:27—8:27 Baltimore. Is the library open yet? I don't know. Check mail: 1 out of 14, 2 out of 14. Say good morning to Stephen's lover. *Good morning*, he says. *Good morning*, says the lithium, *maybe today is the day*. 13 out of 14, 14 out of 14. No Fruitbat. Billy, Junior, Billy, D'isMay, Junior. Later. Coffee. Fall asleep on the kitchen table, wake up, 7:43—10:43 Baltimore. Check mail. No Fruitbat.

New message. Same as the old message I've written and trashed five times already.

```
Bat stop it don't go away you don't have to. I'm too
fucked up to know how to tell you. I know the drugs are
hard for you but it's not charity I need you there's
this voice.
```

Trash. You can't say don't leave me I'm too fucked up. You can't.

```
I know the drugs are hard
```

Good, then what?

```
but
```

The screen glows white and flat you can't get past the glass float deeper into the glow lose yourself in electron pulses you can't it's too flat.

```
there's never been charity between us never you know it.
Don't go away.
```

Send. Are you still going to the library checking your mail what are you doing? Stay in air-conditioned rooms as much as possible. Please.

Fall asleep wake up what now? Pee. Toothbrush reminds me to take my meds. Force-feed oatmeal. Prozac day 20.

What time is it? Check mail. Parnell says why didn't you tell us about the blood tests. Howard says of course there were blood tests, there had to be something, an instrument of monitoring and coercion, or it wouldn't be the psych system we know and love. Bones says I don't understand why they gave her Thorazine and blood tests in the first place, injectable Haldol is much more common. Cyber Joe says maybe she didn't do well on Haldol when she took it before. Jim says if she had a bad reaction before, why would they give her Haldol now? Howard says that's got to be the stupidest question I've heard all day. Sarah says we have to keep the pressure on the Senate or hundreds more folks are going to be where Fruitbat is right now. JJ says where *is* Fruitbat, I hope she's okay. Me too, JJ.

Check mail. Nothing. *Kill yourself*, the voice says, but Stephen's lover is guarding the lithium. *No*, he says.

*Kill yourself, no, kill yourself, no, kill yourself, no.* At this rate I'll die of boredom. Look up suicide on the Web.

> If you are depressed and have thoughts of suicide, you
> must see a doctor. Most people can be treated with
> medication.

Yeah yeah yeah I'm being treated and what a treat it is. I don't know what they're so excited about. It's like the car accident: live, die, live, die, if we had gone through the guardrail, it would already be over with.

The best page is on suicide prevention self-help:

> I've discovered through recent suicidal difficulties
> that if I smoke a cigarette, I can convert my desire
> to kill myself quickly into a more long-term
> death-wish.

Good idea. But I've never smoked cigarettes, and I'd have to go to the corner store to get them. Cold oatmeal could be seen as a slow route to suicide. Try it. Hmm, kind of like suicide by eating wet cement, but I don't think it'll actually do me in. Do I take my Prozac now? No, you already did that. Or maybe that was yesterday who knows what day it is? Could take the lithium, maybe it's time.

*No.*

Shut up, you're just a bag of dirt. You AIDS guys think you know everything about life and death.

*I know more than you,* Stephen's lover says, which is true, there's no answering it.

Maybe later, I tell the lithium. `Check mail.` Bones says he once knew a guy who moved to another state to avoid his outpatient commitment order—that meant he had to cold turkey his drugs, but sometimes you gotta make those choices, not that Bones would ever encourage anyone to break the law. Junior's is a private post in the middle of the day—taking chances, boy. Wants to know if I'm all right. I should write him.

`Dear Fruitbat`

It's only been a day, I can't send note after pitiful note come back please.

Then it's dark again when did that happen must have fallen asleep. Is it time to take my Prozac no it's the phone. Pick it up without thinking.

"Hello?"

"This is your evening weather report calling. Daytime high 87 degrees, overnight low 83."

"Baltimore."

"It was on TV just like you thought."

"Thanks. 87, jesus."

"Anytime."

"Really? Tomorrow? Can you?"

"Sure I guess. Are you okay?"

"Fine. I just woke up. I'm a bit …"

"So how is Baltimore? Tell all, honey, it's the price of your weather reports."

"I can't right now, Cynthia, I just … woke up."

"Okay, but you owe me."

I do. Thanks, Cynthia. Bye.

`Check mail.` Coalition/Billy, D'isMay, Junior, Coalition/Billy, Coalition/Terry, D'isMay. The night shift.

```
Fruitbat where are you damn it tell me what the Haldol
is doing. We can scream about it together don't go away
because you're hurting it's stupid where are you?
```

Trash. *I'm here,* says the lithium. *I'm waiting.* Yes, but what kind of death are you? Hours of screaming pain while my insides disintegrate I could do without. *Picky picky,* says the lithium. Where could I find out? None of the suicide pages had anything about comparative methods. Probably no one on Crazy would tell me either. Jerks. Maybe I could get Dr. Shrink to tell me, he wants me to take the lithium.

Maybe this is my manic episode, punishment for not following doctor's orders. Jesus Christ, maybe it is.

```
Dear Bones maybe I'm manic after all what do you think?
My nerves are very fast but I keep falling asleep. Or
something. I don't know what manic feels
```

Then I must have fallen asleep because now I'm awake again, still
dark. Raining now. The lupines will like that. See I told you, you
don't need me. Try to think what else to ask Bones but I fall asleep,
wake up.

```
is it because of the Prozac am I really
```

Send. Check mail. No Fruitbat. Coalition/Billy, Coalition/Gina.
Gina? Gina's gone. What's going on? Scroll back to the start of the
night.

```
Coalition/Billy
takeover
We did it. I can't believe we did it. We walked into the
Coalition, told them we were occupying the office and
they could stay or leave. Louis kept saying we couldn't
and Terry kept saying we could and then they just left,
except the people in the drop-in who wanted to stay and
watch TV. So now the door is locked and we sent out press
releases on the computer. And we have sleeping bags and
food and we're staying till the board meets our demands.
```

Have they been talking about this for days or is it a surprise? I
can't remember. I can see them, tiny people on the other side of the

spinning globe, barricading their tiny drop-in centre. It's daylight there and in D'isMay's tiny Tokyo.

```
D'isMay:
re: takeover
Whoooheeeeeeeeeee! Can you hear me shouting my fool head
off? Billy Billy I love you. Tell Gina to get her ass
online. I *missed* you, girl!
```

Oh right, Gina's there and Terry. I get it.

```
Coalition/Billy
re: takeover
Oh no, Mr. Exec just called. Gina's talking to him right
now, she keeps saying, "Fine, call the police then."
```

Then Junior comes on, writing from the time zone before Mr. Exec and call-the-police.

```
Junior
re: takeover
You did it! You did it! Ah god there is justice
somewhere on this earth. Give Terry a big hug for
me, or pound him on the back or whatever you tough
Aussie guys do when you're so happy you can't
STAND it!
```

I don't like this thread anymore. I don't want to sit here in Vancouver listening to the cops coming for Terry with Junior at his parents' house watching it all go down. *Kill yourself*, says the lithium. Open up the first cardboard sample case. Seven little pills, each in its own blister of plastic. I like blister packs, I like pushing the pill through the foil backing. *No*, says Steven's lover. I'm just looking, I say. Put my tongue on the pill: bitter. *No*, says Steven's lover. *Yes*, says the lithium. *It's genetic*, says Dr. Shrink. *I'll call the cops*, says Mr. Exec. *Go barefoot*, says Fruitbat, but she's not here she's gone. *Kill yourself.*

*No*, says Steven's lover, *no no no no* it's too fucking noisy in here I can't stand it get out.

Out to the kitchen open the door. Night and rain. Inside they're still arguing. Out to the front gate, streetlights caught in wet tree branches far away noise of cars on First Avenue going home. Late. Lean on the fence and watch. Car turns down my street, headlights do that glaring-thing I like. I could open the gate and walk into that glare, walk forever. Then the car is gone. Wait for another watch it wait again watch. It's nice out here far from *yes no yes no*. I could walk into that glare. But the gate is shut.

When I wake up I'm in the back yard. Fruitbat is squatting on the ground, looking in the basement window. *Oh there you are*, she says. Hi, I say. *Come here*, she says. We're on the ground by the lupines and she's taking my clothes off. Rain and mud and her hands on my skin. She's lying on top of me under me inside me kisses burn like headlights unfreeze my tears dissolve into rain I scream for her push my hand into her as she opens and opens and I feel her heart beating deep in her cunt.

----------

The phone rings. Rings. Rings. What day is it? Check mail.

> Sarah
> re: test
>    I'm worried about Fruitbat. She hasn't been online
> for two days and that blood test hit her pretty hard.
> I know she's probably just taking a breather, adjusting
> to the injection, but ... Anyone have any idea how to
> contact her in the Meatworld? Mei Lin? Parnell?
> Howard?

Midwest U.S. online, I must have fallen asleep.

> Parnell
> re: test
> Does anyone know her name or which psych home she's in?
> Baltimore must have dozens.

> Mei Lin
> I contacted Baltimore Freenet but the sys admin won't
> give me any info because it's not an emergency. Howard?

> Howard
> She's not as connected as Junior. I'm trying.

Then there's Lucy writing privately: Have *you* heard anything
from Fruitbat, I know you two were close, are you all right?
And Junior again, another daring daylight post: Are you ok? I should
write.

Hey Bones,

The lithiums are all out of their blisters now, lined up in front of my monitor.

> I don't know what manic is. Or not. But if the Prozac is making me manic, should I stop? And if the lithium is

If one is close to toxic, two will probably do it, three to be sure—or all of them, why not, what am I saving them for?

> Parnell
> re: test
> I found the Baltimore Yellow Pages online and I've got a list of psych home numbers and my concerned relative act. But I need a name.

> Sarah
> re: test (and the Squeegee)
> Seems like we're always strategizing from hopelessness. Why? What does this do to our organizing? How many of you have put off writing to the Senate because you think we don't have a chance on the Squeegee? What happened to Fruitbat is exactly what the Squeegee is about. Three days and we still haven't heard from her. How many people do we have to lose?

Shut up, Sarah. Shut up shut up.
*Kill yourself.* The lithium voice is far gentler than Sarah's. Sort

back through old posts till I find the Labour & Human Resources Committee address. New Message. Stare at the screen.

    Dear Senators,

I'm a foreigner, what do they care? What was I doing? Writing to Bones.

    Dear Bones if the Prozac is making me manic then will
    the lithium

*Kill yourself.*

    Dear Senators,
    Don't

*Kill yourself.*

    Don't

*Come on,* says the lithium. Seven tablets. I arrange them in a circle like petals around an empty centre. Pick off a petal, put it in my mouth. She loves me. Swallow. She loves me not.

*Stop it,* says Stephen's lover. Voice like a whip, I must have nodded off.

*Put the lithium in the bathroom,* he says. *Put the toothbrush in the trash.*

What?

*Put the lithium in the bathroom. Put the toothbrush in the trash.*

It doesn't make any sense but I do it anyway. Easier to follow instructions. Lithium in the cabinet behind the bathroom mirror, toothbrush in the pail under the kitchen sink.

Toothbrush. Did I take my Prozac what day is it? Back to the bathroom, two Prozacs and a glass of water. *Come on.* The lithium is in the cabinet behind the mirror door. *Come on.* Stephen's lover is not as loud in here. The face in the mirror is tired, too tired. Open the cabinet door, turn the face to the wall. Behind the mirror is the lithium.

Behind the lithium is my razor blade. *You know me,* says the razor blade. Yes, I do. Shut the mirror on the lithium voice. The too-tired woman is back, holding a single edge Schick. My favourite brand. First she makes a razor-line all the way around her arm. Blood bracelet just below the elbow. For safety. The line you can't cut past. Skin separates in a perfect ring, disconnecting the forearm. Cut deeper till you feel something. The blood is so fast. It's never this fast.

```
Dear Senators,
Don't
```

I wake up bleeding on my keyboard. Fruitbat is crouched by the basement window looking in at me.

"Open the goddamn door," she says.

Float to the hallway trailing red. The door knob is slippery, blood on both hands.

"What the fuck are you doing?" she yells. Roz.

"Hi," I say.

"Jesus Christ," she says, "you're going to the hospital."

"It's okay," I say, "I didn't cut below the line."

She barges past me, barges back. "Do you have bandages, sheets, anything?"

It *is* bleeding a lot. Only three gashes but they're deep. I guess we should do something. "Butterflies," I tell her.

"What?" she says.

"Butterflies. Those little ..." I can't remember the word, Roz's panic is rising by the second, makes it hard to think. "Little bandaids," I finally manage.

"Bandaids?" Roz yells. "You can't fix that with bandaids." She is so loud. Louder than Steven's lover. She follows me into the bathroom. "Oh god," she says. Blood on the sink. Bandaids are on the shelf above the lithium. My hands are too slippery. "Open the little ones," I tell her, sitting on the toilet and holding out my arm.

"You need stitches," she says. No help. I wipe my hands and arm, tear open a bandaid with my teeth and manage to get it on reasonably straight one-handed: crossways to the cut, pulling the edges of flesh together.

Roz gets it then, takes over, four butterflies on each cut, talking all the time about stitches and the hospital.

"It's all right now," I say, but she's not listening. I can't go to the hospital, Roz, it's not safe, you don't know what you're doing. But she's relentless, calls a cab, wraps my arm in a T-shirt.

"Where are your keys? I need your keys," hustles me outside and locks the door behind us. Wait on the curb, Roz cursing the minutes. Cabby pulls up, opens the door for us, then freezes as he sees my arm but Roz pushes me in.

"I won't let her bleed on your fucking upholstery," she says. "Sacred Heart. Emergency."

I have to pull myself together. Have to think. Calm and careful. I can do hospitals. Stay focused. Stay awake.

Then Roz is throwing money at the cabby, dragging me through the big doors like a hurricane until she hits the first layer of bureaucracy and everything slows right down.

"Name?" asks the woman at the emergency desk.

"Janice Johnston," says Roz.

"What seems to be the problem?"

"She seems to be bleeding," says Roz through clenched teeth.

"Let me see," the woman says, and I unwrap the T-shirt. Oozing cuts, she doesn't even blink. "What happened?"

"She got cut," Roz says.

"I cut myself," I say at the same time.

"We'll need some information for our records," the woman says.

I re-wrap my arm, drifting a bit while Roz recites my vital statistics. Date of birth, family doctor, drug allergies, current medications. Roz gets most of it right.

"That's it then, take a seat. The doctor will be with you soon."

All around are clumps of people, some whispering, some whimpering, some watching hockey on the wall-mounted TV. Uniforms bustle by. In the world of emergency my seeping wounds are no big deal. A woman in white calls my name.

"Here," Roz says. "She's here."

"Hi," the woman says, "I'm Nurse Phillips. Let's take a look at that arm."

"Finally," says Roz, following.

"Just Janice for now," says Nurse Phillips.

"I'm her partner," says Roz.

"Just Janice."

"I'm her partner!" Roz's voice is rising. You'd think she'd know how to act in hospitals after cancer.

"She has to talk to me alone. In case ..." I can't find the word but Roz gets it.

"They think *I* did that to you?"

"They just have to check. It's ... a thing they do."

"Routine," says Nurse Phillips.

"Yes," I say. Routine, that's the word.

The examining room is small and bare, two chairs, desk, examining table. Nurse Phillips washes her hands in a sink in the corner and unwraps the T-shirt.

"It wasn't her," I say.

"I didn't think so. You could use a few stitches."

"Can't I just have butterflies?"

"You'll scar more," she says, wiping the blood away with wet gauze.

"That's okay," I say.

She pulls off the bandaids, wipes some more, pulls the wounds shut with proper butterfly bandages, wraps gauze around it all.

"So what happened?" she asks, opening a file on the desk. She seems nice—relaxed and practical like someone you could really trust. But she's taking notes and it's stupid to trust someone just because they wash your arm. Especially in a hospital.

"I was feeling down. I cut myself."

"Are you suicidal?"

"No." You have to tell them no. She wants more she's waiting. An explanation, something safe and known and pre-approved. "It's a ... obsessive compulsive disorder, my doctor says." Yes, good. "I'm on

Prozac but it hasn't kicked in yet." Perfect. It was on the Web, Prozac for OCD. "I'm sorry."

"How are you feeling now?" she asks.

"All right. Shaky. I didn't mean to cut that deep."

"The psychiatry resident will see you in a few minutes. Would you like to wait in here where it's quiet?"

"Sure thanks," and she's gone. Little white room, nothing in it, harder to focus. Maybe Fruitbat is sitting in a white room too, waiting for someone to decide her fate. In or out. Maybe we could be in together that wouldn't be so bad, me a lithium zombie, her with a Haldol drool.

Door opens. Roz.

"Hi," I say.

"Hi," she says. She's gotten quiet. Good. "How are you doing?" she asks.

"Okay."

Silence till the resident comes in. Young, even younger than shrinklette—looks fifteen. Introduces himself shakes hands even. Dr. Something. He has the file the nurse was writing in, sits down and looks through it.

"You're taking Prozac?"

"Yes." Roz looks startled says nothing. Good Roz.

"Is Doctor Lewis prescribing it for you?"

He's got the intake form too, family doctor: Arleen Lewis. "Yes," I say, keep Dr. Shrink out of it as long as I can. "For depression. And OCD, 20 milligrams. But it hasn't kicked in yet."

"How long have you been taking it?"

"A month." I think.

"Any side effects?" BabyDoc isn't even looking at me.

"No."

"A month is a long time, it should be working by now. What does Dr. Lewis say?"

"She said it might take awhile."

"Okay. Up the dose to 30 milligrams and see Dr. Lewis as soon as you can. Monday, if possible. I'll send your file along."

Dr. Lewis, Monday, file, he's letting me go. I start to relax but he's not done.

"Do you have suicidal thoughts?" He looks at me now.

"No. This wasn't suicide. It's just ... cutting."

"Yes, I understand. I'm concerned about you hurting yourself again though. The higher dose of Prozac may be all you need, but it will take awhile to come into effect, and it's a long way till Monday."

Oh god second thoughts. Danger to self or others how to convince him?

"I can stay with her till Monday," says Roz. Thank you thank you.

"Good," says BabyDoc. "Make sure she gets that appointment." Why do they think a doctor's appointment is going to fix everything? I don't care just get me out of here.

"Meanwhile I've got some tranquillizers to help you through the weekend."

"Okay." Sure anything. He hands the bottle to Roz, my keeper now. "Maybe she'd better have one right away," he says.

Roz passes a tablet. It's the melt-in-your-mouth kind, Ativan probably, can't cheek it and spit it out later, oh shit I'm already having a hard enough time tracking. Then we're shaking hands again. Roz leads me back to the waiting room pay phone cab I made it.

----------

Keys, door, Roz is my keeper.

"Do you want some tea?" she asks.

"I just need to lie down." In the bedroom close the curtains get in bed, dark except for the stars on my computer screen. Roz lies down beside me, arms around me, body calm and undemanding as ex-lovers can be, her one breast soft against my chest. Something lets go inside, then another and another how many things knotted tight for how long? I skim across sleep, soft voices *kill yourself kill yourself* lapping in like waves quiet and distant. The smell of her skin warm breath on my neck familiar safe.

Roz being Roz, this doesn't last.

"Do you know there's a vacuum cleaner bag on your computer?" she asks.

"Yeah."

Quiet again for a minute.

"Can I get you anything?"

I know that restless, driven mind. Give her something to do. "Tea would be nice." Chill where her body has been, pull the covers over me make my own heat. Wave after wave. Footsteps.

"I can't find any tea."

"Oh right. I'm out."

"I'll go get some. Will you be all right?"

"I'll sleep."

"You sure?"

"Sure."

Footsteps, door. Get up, check mail. No Fruitbat. Scan the test thread. No one's heard anything. Lucy says maybe she'll take the bus to Baltimore tomorrow, it's only a two-hour ride. But Lucy, you never leave your cabin except for Wednesday shopping, Sunday church. Parnell says sure, ask everyone in the library, why not? Voice in my head says *now, now, come on,* the lithium in the bathroom go look, yes it's still there. Razor blade is gone, Roz probably. *Come on.*

*No,* says Stephen's lover. Maybe later. Maybe soon. Back in the bedroom open the curtains, lupines, open my post to Bones.

How can you tell

Sound of the door, back in bed fast, eyes shut. Footsteps.

"Is black tea all right? It's all they had."

"Sure fine." Drift till the tea comes. Sip. Drift.

"You're freaking me out," says Roz. Jolt awake.

"Huh? Why?"

"You seem so out of it. You can hardly talk. Are you okay?"

"I'm fine it's just …" What, it's just what?

Wake up. Tea is cold and Roz is sitting at my computer.

"What's all this stuff about lithium? Are you supposed to be taking something else? Who's Bones?"

Life is so complicated.

"Lithium. I took it. But I'm not really manic. Or I don't think … Bones is a doctor. I was asking him."

"I thought we just did the doctor. You got an Internet shrink too?"

"No he's … different. He knows a lot."

"I'm glad somebody does. What about the Prozac? Shouldn't you take that now?"

"I took it." I think.

"But you're supposed to increase your dose."

"Oh right. It's in the bathroom."

She's gone a long time. If she brings me lithium, that will be that. Unless two isn't enough or the one I took before was too long ago— so many variables, live die. It's the Prozac. Swallow with tea, drift.

"How do you send stuff?" Roz asks.

"Send what?"

"Email. I clicked on send and nothing happened."

"You gotta be connected."

"So how do I get connected?"

Pull myself up. Config PPP open send. Roz makes me write it all down. Then she makes me write down the check mail routine. Then she lets me go. I go. Deeper, further. The waves wash over me, pull me under. *Kill yourself. Come on.* It would be easy. Where are you going, Roz would say. I gotta pee, do you mind, I would say. Then I'd be in the bathroom with the lithium no razor to distract me so easy.

*No,* says Stephen's lover.

What's it to you? I'm just your boyfriend's cleaning lady plus I spilled you on the carpet.

*Oh you know us AIDS guys, a bunch of little cheerleaders for life. I'm in favour of cleaning too.*

"You have a zillion messages," says Roz. "Who are all these people?"

"It's a Listserv."

"A what?"

"Listserv. You write to the list and everyone gets it. Then they write back and everyone gets that. ThisIsCrazy."

"It sure is. Oh, here's one from you. Last night. 'Dear Bones.

Maybe I'm manic after all what do you think?' It's the same as the other one, except even less coherent. I went ahead and sent your other one, I hope that's okay. And I added the emergency ward stuff and asked the doctor guy what I should do. And then I did the check mail thing and got a zillion messages. How do you cope with this shit?"

"You look for names. Fruitbat. Is Fruitbat there?" I get up and look over her shoulder. No. "There's Bones, see? from: Bones / to: ThisIsCrazy. But look for Fruitbat, I need to talk to her. Follow the threads."

"Follow the threads. Great. You are making no sense."

"Here—re: test."

"I get it. And yours is re: manic."

"Do you think I am?"

"I think you're a mess. Or maybe you're fine, what do I know? Tell me you're fine."

"I'm fine."

"Great."

I have to pull myself together, fix this situation. Can't trust Roz, have to get in control before she does something. But my nerves can't seem to register her as a threat, or maybe control has slipped past my grasp.

"Cyber Joe, CloudTen," Roz is saying. "Why do they have such weird names, are they retro-hippies or what? Here's Bones again, good."

"Good," I murmur, waves washing over me. Drift down further under the ocean now away from the tug of lithium surf, fish with strange eyes Stephen's lover laughing in seaweed drag, but Roz as usual has to give me a blow by blow of her every thought pulls me back over and over.

"The Dr. Bones guy wrote three times asking what was going on with you. And the Junior guy is jumping out of his skin worrying. How long will it be till they get my letter?"

"Seconds. Minutes. Days. It depends."

"Perfect. Modern technology at its finest. Maybe I should call the guy at emergency."

"No, he doesn't ..." What to say, how to convince her? "Bones is better." Please Roz, don't, you've got to be careful, I can't deal with them.

Roz is on the phone. "Someone else will have to chair it then, I can't come, I'm tied up all weekend. No, not that kind of tied up, family crisis." Not emergency. Thank you, Roz. "Forget it, you do it." Hangs up swearing.

Sink down again caught in the surf dragged in and out crashed onto rocks. Then Roz's voice again, again.

"What a jerk. Who is this guy? He got my message, but he says I don't know anything, he needs to talk to you."

"Who?"

"Dr. Bones. He says you have to tell him exactly what's going on. I already told him! Asshole."

Bones. And Roz. Oh dear.

*Life is supposed to be complicated,* says Stephen's lover.

"I should. Talk to him. Yeah."

"Fine, talk to him, be my guest," says Roz, vacating my computer chair and stomping off to the kitchen. Drift. Then she's back "You talk, I'll type," she says.

"Tell him …" Tell him what? The undersea the waves the rocks? "Ideation, method. No plans. Don't need plans. Just need to get up and walk to the bathroom."

"Wait a minute, how do you spell ideation?"

"I-d-e-a-t-"

"Okay, okay, got it. I hope he knows what you're talking about 'cause I sure don't. What the hell is it?"

"Thoughts." Thoughts voices waves. When the intake worker at Mountainview asked if I was suicidal, I told her I had ideation only, nothing to worry about. She didn't like that. Patients aren't supposed to use the jargon.

"Okay, I sent it. Asshole."

"Is Fruitbat there?"

"No," Roz fiddles some more, leaves, comes back, "Do you want some lunch?"

"I guess."

Leaves, comes back. "You have no fucking food in the house."

Leaves. The room is very still, hum of the computer, undertone of distant traffic.

*So what's it like being dead?*

*We're not supposed to say. Meatworld folks are supposed to wonder and not know.*

*Guess I'll find out.*

*We all find out, eventually.*

Comes back. "I got sandwiches from the corner store, egg salad. I have no idea how old they are." Passes me plastic wrapped bread.

"Thanks," I say, drift.

Then Roz is shaking me. "Hey, wake up, are you all right?"

"I'm just sleepy."

"When did you last eat?"

"I'm not sure."

"Sit up. Eat." She unwraps plastic, I force myself up. I manage half a sandwich, she supervises a round of tea drinking and then she lets me go. The surf knocks me down, I breathe sand and bitter water for awhile. Then Roz again.

"He's back. He says what else?"

"What else what?"

"Besides the ideation stuff, I guess."

What else. Nothing. Nothing. "I'm ..." Tired. "Can't focus. Too many things." My blood is fast. "My blood is fast. Does that make sense?"

"No," says Roz, typing. " 'And my observation, Dr. Bones, if you can be bothered listening to me, is that she's having a hard time talking and she seems to fall asleep with her eyes open.' Okay, here's another one, someone called Flip, re: manic. He wants to know how much Prozac you're on. He says I should take you to emergency. 'We've just been to emergency, and they fixed the dose: 30 milligrams a day.' God, these people are irritating. Now the doctor's back, good. 'It really sounds like a bad Prozac reaction. She should start tapering off.' Off, on, what the fuck! Can't these shrinks make up their minds?"

"It's not science." And I wouldn't exactly call it art either. Sarah said that. If the shoe doesn't fit, don't wear it. "Is Fruitbat there?"

"Fruitbat. I'll check. No. The Bones guy asks if you have a doctor you trust?"

"No."

"Okay. 'No.' Now someone else says it sounds just like what happened with her husband on Prozac. Now he's on Paxil and doing better. Are these people all hets or what?"

"Mostly."

"Here's the doctor again. 'How long has she been at 30 milligrams?' 'Five hours. The guy at emergency raised her dose. It was'—what was it before?"

"Twenty. Four weeks. I think."

"'Twenty milligrams for four weeks. She thinks.' "

"Why?"

"Why what?"

"Why is it the Prozac?"

"I'll ask. So is this doctor guy het too?"

"I don't know. Probably."

Drift again never far from the surface. Occasionally there's a new episode. Like a soap opera. If I get bored I can channel surf. Roz-on-the-Net Channel. Smell-of-the-Pillow Channel. Under-the-Ocean Channel. Kill-Yourself Channel. Talking-to-Fruitbat Channel.

*Where are you?*

*Somewhere.*

*Are you still alive?*

*I'm not sure.*

"Flip says he doesn't know about the sleeping thing, but he knows four different people who've gotten suicidal on Prozac. 'If she wasn't suicidal before starting Prozac it's definitely something to check out.' Yeah, but she's not suicidal, asshole."

"She," I say, "Flip is a she."

"Flip is an idiot," says Roz.

Eventually there's dinner, red beans and rice. Thank you. Roz leaves, comes back. The phone rings. Roz answers, murmurs a bit, listens, murmurs.

"Do you want to talk to Cynthia?"

Hesitate, then hold my hand out for the phone. I owe her.

"You still want to know the weather in Baltimore?" she asks, subdued.

"Yeah. I do."

"Partly cloudy high of 79, low of 75."

"Thanks."

"Do you want me to come over?"

"No, that's okay. Roz is … all I can handle right now."

"Call me if there's anything."

Eventually I have to pee for real. Roz has cleaned up the blood. *Hurry*, says the lithium. *There's not much time left.* The woman in the mirror stares at me. Turn her to the wall. I could take one more, leave it to chance: yes-no, enough-not enough. I could take one every time I pee until I'm dead or Roz figures it out. *That's fair*, says the lithium. Stephen's lover says something else but he's too far away. Bitter on my tongue. There.

Float back to bed, wait and see. Under the ocean Stephen's lover is mad at me. Roz leaves, come back takes off her jeans gets into bed with me. "Do you want pajamas or something?"

"No."

"At least take off your shoes." Oh right, I don't sleep in my shoes, I'm okay. Take my shoes off, sit on the edge of the bed. Do I have to pee? Maybe. Yes. Walk to the bathroom, pee. Maybe I should get that blue stuff Stephen has. *Come on*, says the lithium. The face in the mirror is no one I've ever seen before. *Go back to bed*, she says. I go back, get under the covers, curl around Roz. I think she's asleep, she's so still, then she rolls over and puts her arms around me.

"Are you going to be all right?"

"I don't know," I say. I nestle closer, the familiar feel of her body against mine, meat to meat. We drift together for awhile, pretending to sleep. Familiar silence, don't ask don't tell. It's a form of lying, Lucy would say. Shut up, Lucy.

"Did you hear about the tests yet?" I ask the darkness.

"Not yet."

"I hate it."

"Yeah," she says. Rolls over. Rolls back. "I'm tired. I'm always fucking tired. I've been tired since the stupid surgery if you really want to know."

"Yeah."

She sits up suddenly, turns on the light. "Let's not do that stupid show. We can just cancel out. It's not like it's the week before and all the posters are up."

"But you wanted to do it."

"I want to do something, something besides waiting around. But I'm not really into this show and neither are you. So let's do something else."

"Like what?"

"Like I don't know what. Something real."

"I'm not doing too good with real these days."

I feel the laughter in her chest. "Okay, I'll do something real, you do something unreal."

"Virtual," I say.

"You got forty-seven emails overnight. Don't these people ever sleep? Don't they have jobs or friends or anything to do with their lives?"

Answering seems vast and complicated. Some of them have a lot of energy. Some of them live in Australia. Some of them don't have jobs or friends. So? "Is—"

"Fruitbat. No."

Go pee. Lithium time but that woman is still there. *"Make some coffee,"* she says. "Okay," I say. Kitchen kettle coffee filters. Sit and drift till the kettle screams. Pour wait pour. *Come on, do it. You're running out of time. Come on, you know you want it.*

Back to the bedroom with two cups. Roz is at the computer, grunts thanks.

"Bones says you should cut the Prozac to 20 mills for today, and then cut another half cap and let him know how it's going. Are they allowed to prescribe on the computer like that?"

"I don't think so," I say. "But it's more like advice." Take my coffee back to bed tired from my big outing.

*Good morning,* says Stephen's lover. *I wasn't sure you were going to make it.*

"Good morning," I say.

"Good morning to you too. It's quarter past twelve," says Roz.

"Would you ... can you ask about Fruitbat? If anyone's heard?"

"Okay."

*So what's it like being dead?*

*There's no coffee, you wouldn't like it.*

"Great coffee," says Roz, reading my mail. Is Fruitbat there? No. Try to dive down to where the fish are phosphorescent with big eyes but I'm caught in the surf again *come on* lungs fill with panic *so easy* the waves suck me back, crash on rocks, suck crash till Roz's voice pulls me out.

"Bones says Prozac stays in your system for a long time and you shouldn't be left alone while you're still suicidal. 'She's not suicidal.'"

Get up, go to the kitchen. Stop it, Bones. You can't tell those things to normals, you can't. *Come on. Hurry.* Go to the bathroom look in the mirror. *Go back to bed.*

Shut up all of you.

Go back to bed under the covers. Drink some coffee try to think.

"He says you *are* suicidal, I should check the bathroom. The boy is not listening. 'I did check the bathroom, there was a razor blade and I threw it out. She told the other shrink it was just slashing, there's a difference you know.'"

Good Roz. Don't panic.

"He says I should ask you what's in the bathroom."

*Go ahead, tell her, tell her everything,* says Stephen's lover.

*Why should I? What do you know?*

*More than you do.*

"Lithium."

"Right, that other drug you were supposed to be taking. 'Lithium.'"

*You were never supposed to take it.*

"He asks how long you've been taking lithium."

"I just took one. Yesterday. No, there was one before that. Two."

"He's back. He says I should look for pills in the bathroom and flush them. I'm sick of doctors. Do you want them flushed?"

*Yes. No. Yes. No.*

"I guess. Sure. Why not."

Footsteps, the roar of surf in the toilet bowl. *Come on.* Stop, I changed my mind, don't leave me I need you. Chase the lithium through the sewers. Bipolar alligators turn level-headed and sedate. *Come on, come on.* But the voice is dissolving, I can't find it. Wander further, deep in the ocean, fish without names that don't fit the rules. Maybe I'll stay here forever. Fuck the Meatworld.

Till Roz pulls me back.

"Junior says hi, hang in there."

Hi, Junior.

"Flip says Zoloft has fewer side effects."

Hi, Flip.

"Junior says Flip should stop pushing drugs on you and D'isMay says everyone should just back off and give you some space. Right on, D'isMay."

"Has anyone heard from—"

"Not yet."

*So what's it like being dead?*

*Depends. Being dead in a vacuum cleaner bag isn't the most fun I've ever had. I don't know why you're so keen on Stephen's dust.*

*What if I sprinkle you on the lupines?*

*It's bound to be an improvement.*

"Why didn't you tell me about this Australian occupation? The executive guy is still threatening to call the cops. Billy says Terry made him talk to reporters. Who's Terry?"

Who's Terry, how to explain Terry? "Ask Junior."

"Lucy says hi from the Baltimore Public Library."

"Lucy? What did she say?"

"Not much. 'Hi from the Baltimore Public Library. There are too many people here and I don't like talking to strangers. But I will.' Who's Lucy?"

Drift. Outside, night now, no rain. Roz comes back from the corner store, gives me my pills and makes me eat those instant burrito things she likes. Yuk. If I go off Prozac, I can buy rice crackers.

"I sent an email about the U.S. senate stuff. Do you want me to write one for you?"

"Sure."

I could ask Roz to dump the vacuum cleaner bag in the garden. But it would be hard to explain. Easier to do it myself. Maybe tomorrow. Or the next day. Whenever I can track again.

*You can be compost.*

*I like that,* says Stephen's lover. *Nature red in tooth and claw. The sex lives of lupines up close and personal. Did you see that bumblebee, what a hunk! You keep your petals off him, I saw him first!*

Okay. I'll even water the lupines. Maybe.

< POSTSCRIPT >

Senate Bill s-1180 was passed in committee on
October 12, 1995. Senator Kassebaum withdrew
the involuntary outpatient commitment  amendment before the vote, acknowledging it
was controversial.

< ABOUT THE AUTHOR >

Persimmon Blackbridge is a writer, performer, sculptor, cleaning lady and member of the notorious lesbian art collective, Kiss & Tell. She is the winner of the VIVA award for visual art (1991) and a Lambda Literary Award (with Kiss & Tell: 1995). Her 1996 novel, *Sunnybrook: A True Story with Lies,* was a finalist for both the Ferro-Grumley Prize and a Lambda Literary Award.

Press Gang Publishers has been producing vital and provocative books by women since 1975. For a complete catalogue, write to Press Gang Publishers, #101 - 225 East 17th Avenue, Vancouver, B.C. V5V 1A6 Canada or visit us online at http://www.pressgang.bc.ca

OTHER BOOKS BY PERSIMMON BLACKBRIDGE

*Sunnybrook: A True Story with Lies*
ISBN 0-88974-068-2 cloth; ISBN 0-88974-060-7 paper

Lavishly illustrated with full-colour images throughout, this is a fast-paced and very funny novel about disability issues. Shortlisted in 1997 for a Lambda Literary Award and the Ferro-Grumley Prize.

*Still Sane* (co-authored with Sheila Gilhooly)
ISBN 0-88974-028-3

Based on a sculptural exhibit, the book combines images and text to portray one woman's resistance to psychiatry's attempts to "cure" her of lesbianism.

*Her Tongue on My Theory: Images, Essays and Fantasies*
(co-authored with Kiss & Tell)
ISBN 0-88974-058-5

A daring collage of explicit lesbian sexual imagery, erotic writing, personal histories and provocative analysis. A Lambda Literary Award winner in 1995.

*Drawing the Line: Lesbian Sexual Politics on the Wall*
(co-authored with Kiss & Tell)
ISBN 0-88974-030-5

40 black-and-white postcards selected from the photographic exhibition which toured internationally, plus viewers' comments on where to "draw the line" on sexually explicit photographs.